SHATTERED VOWS

SHATTERED VOWS

From the Editors
Of *True Story* And
True Confessions

Published by True Renditions, LLC

True Renditions, LLC
105 E. 34th Street, Suite 141
New York, NY 10016

ISBN: 978-1-938877-82-7

Visit us on the web at www.truerenditionsllc.com.

Contents

ON THE BRINK OF DIVORCE
Our boys showed us how to love again

I could hear my nine-year-old twins quarrelling downstairs in the den. Since Paul had moved out, I noticed that they seemed to argue more.

This time it was over who would dominate the remote. When the noise level escalated again, I knew it was time to break the argument up. I finished folding the undershirt I'd started and went downstairs.

"Come on, guys. Enough is enough."

"He started it!" Michael declared.

"'Cause he's been hogging the remote and it's my turn to get it," Matthew whined.

"Uh-uh, I got it first."

"Look, guys. There's enough noise in here to break the sound barrier, not to mention my ears. If you two are incapable of sharing, I'll help out by sending you both to your rooms."

"No! Our show is coming on soon," Michael replied.

"Yeah. We can't miss it," Matthew added.

"So the problem is solved?"

"Yeah," both boys agreed.

I wished it were that easy to solve my own problems. Listening to my twins squabble reminded me of Paul and myself during the last months before our separation and his decision to take a promotion, moving him clear across the state. We seemed to argue about everything. Just like the boys, neither of us wanted to give in. I don't think we ever bothered to listen to ourselves. If we had, maybe we would've talked to one another instead of at one another and things might've turned out differently.

As I continued to fold the laundry, my mind began to wander. One particular morning suddenly came to mind. Paul had an important meeting to attend and had wanted me to wash and iron his blue dress shirt. Despite the fact I'd gotten up with a headache that morning, I forced myself to iron the shirt and hung it on a hanger, leaving it in the bedroom for him to find when he got out of the shower. Getting the kids finished with breakfast and off to school was my next priority. I didn't want them to be late again.

The boys had just gone out the front door to meet the school bus when I heard Paul calling me. I didn't find his tone of voice inviting.

I called up the steps, "What's wrong, Paul?" I caught myself before adding the word now.

"What's right?"

I sighed. This is going to be a fun morning, I thought as I reluctantly went upstairs to find out what his problem was.

Paul was standing in our bedroom, half dressed, holding the shirt I'd just ironed.

"You call this ironed?" he said, dangling the shirt inches from my nose.

"Would you prefer I used the term 'pressed'?"

"Cute, real cute."

I decided to get it over with and asked, "What's wrong with the shirt, Paul?"

"This is what's wrong with it," he said, pointing to a miniscule crease. "And this one and that one."

I thought he was being ridiculous. No one was going to see either crease under his jacket. "If you don't like the way I iron, you have recourse."

"I know. I can do it myself," he said, mimicking my voice.

"Or you can send it out to be laundered. This is America. You have the freedom to choose."

"I'm such a lucky man. I married a comedienne."

"And I married a perfectionist."

"What's wrong with that?"

"With a perfectionist, there's no room for improvement," I said, leaving him standing there as I went into the bathroom, slamming the door behind me.

My head was pounding a rhythm in time with my accelerated heartbeat. Why couldn't the man ever be happy? Why did he constantly have to nitpick? I popped two aspirin into my mouth and chased them down with a glass of water. Staring into the mirror at my bleary eyes, I hoped he'd finish dressing and leave so I could lie down in peace.

It occurred to me that most of our arguments were just as silly and petty as that one. The only ones that turned out to be serious concerned Paul's job. And those were dillies. We'd snip at one another for hours, never accomplishing anything more than being hurtful and mean.

I wondered if Paul might've applied for the new position so that he'd have a valid reason to leave. Perhaps he'd grown just as weary as I over the spats. Since he left, I seemed to have even less patience for the boys. You'd think that with Paul out of the house, all the friction would've gone with him. Then why did I sometimes catch myself snapping at the boys for silly things?

The ringing of the telephone interrupted my thoughts. A few minutes later, I heard Matthew calling, "Mom! Dad is on the phone and he wants to talk to you."

The thought of speaking to Paul made my heart flutter. Why did

I feel a catch in my throat whenever he called? It seemed to happen more and more lately, even when I thought about him. And that quickened step to answer the phone, how do I explain that? Did I truly miss him or had loneliness begun to affect me? Perhaps he was merely a habit I was finding hard to break. If he were back in my life again, would I strive to do things differently? But doesn't it take two to make any relationship work? He'd have to want to change, as well. As I reached for the phone I realized how crazy my thoughts were. It was foolish to even think about this. After all, wasn't he the one who took a new job and moved out? He was probably much happier now that he was on his own.

"Hello, Paul." I hoped he couldn't detect the quickening in my voice.

"Hello, Julie. The boys asked me to talk to you."

"About what?"

"They'd like to go camping for their birthday again."

"They would?"

"I realize that it might be uncomfortable for us with our situation being the way it is, but perhaps we can put our own feelings aside and do this for the kids?"

"But will it be warm enough? It's only May."

"Our last camping trip was around the same time and it was fine. There's no reason to think that it won't be as warm this time."

I had to admit that despite everything that had happened between us, Paul tried to remain close to the boys. No one could fault him for not being a good father. A vision of our last camping trip floated back to my mind. I remember trying to argue against it. My idea of going camping had been to check into a room at a motel. The thought of sleeping on the ground in a tent didn't thrill me much, to say the least. But Paul talked me into it. "Don't disappoint the boys," he'd said. "They really want their mother to join in the fun."

"Fun? You call sleeping on the hard ground and offering oneself as fresh meat to all the insects around fun?"

He laughed. "It won't be that bad. Try it. If you don't like it, we won't do it again. I promise."

The camping trip had turned out to be an oasis of fun in what had been a continuous sea of arguments. Being separated and soon to be divorced, things would be uncomfortable for certain.

"I'm not sure this would work out." Being so close to you, I wanted to say, remembering how that romantic evening under the stars ended.

"We shouldn't disappoint the boys because of our irreconcilable differences. It wouldn't be fair."

His choice of words echoed in my ears. It was obvious he thought there was no way for us to get back together. I wanted to say no and keep our distance, but knew I'd be letting the boys down. I realized that the separation itself, with their dad so far away, was difficult enough for them. To disappoint them by not going would only make matters worse.

Without warning, I heard myself reply, "You're right. The boys shouldn't suffer because of us. Let's go camping." I'd probably regret going, but it was only one weekend out of my life.

"Great! The boys will be so happy."

Paul sounded happy himself, but after what he said before, I was probably just reading something into his reaction.

We were all packed and ready to go when Paul honked. He came into the house to help us carry our stuff. He looked excited and happy, the way he used to look when we were going away together as a family. Our hands brushed as I handed him a bag. A jolt of excitement rushed through me and he seemed to react in the same manner. Had I not heard him tell me we had irreconcilable differences, I would've thought it possible that some old feelings were still alive.

When we arrived at the campsite, we began setting up. I admired Paul's ability to put things together. He didn't even need directions, whereas I was directionally challenged and could read them twenty times over and still not be able to follow them.

As soon as the tent was up, the twins began to clamor about going hiking.

"Come along with us, Julie. It will be fun," Paul said.

"I think I should get dinner prepared," I answered. The thought of encountering snakes and dangerous animals didn't have the same thrill for me.

While Paul and the boys were gone, I found myself thinking again. Being together as a family on this camping trip and seeing Matthew and Michael enjoying their father's company, I kept forgetting that we weren't together anymore.

I was quite glad that when the boys returned with Paul they didn't have any snakes with them. We barbecued franks and hamburgers; afterward the boys had birthday cake.

When it was time for bed, I put my sleeping bag on the other side of the boys. I'd given this a great deal of thought. Even though we were in separate sleeping bags, I just didn't feel comfortable putting it next to Paul's. I had no idea whether or not he felt the same. He didn't comment about it and put his sleeping bag down by the edge of the tent.

Despite all my original fears about going on this camping trip, it had been an enjoyable day. I closed my eyes and waited for sleep. I found myself listening to the quiet breathing of the twins, but hours passed and I was still wide-awake.

Quietly, I slipped out of my sleeping bag and went outside. It was a magnificent starry night. Realizing that I should've taken a blanket or sweater to ward off the slight chill, I wrapped my arms around myself.

"Couldn't sleep, either?" I heard Paul whisper behind me.

I turned to see him wrapped in a blanket. He sat down on an overturned log we were using as a chair.

"Join me before you catch cold."

I sat down right next to him and Paul wrapped the blanket around the both of us.

"I've really enjoyed myself being with you and the kids," he said.

"Me, too," I admitted.

"As I lay in the darkness, I suddenly remembered the night you went into labor."

"Oh, dear, why that day of all times to think about? That was such a horror show," I said, recalling the biggest comedy of errors I'd ever experienced in my life—except it wasn't too funny then.

"I don't know. It just made our relationship unique. I doubt if another couple had a similar experience."

I found it strange that he should bring it up now of all times.

"First I got stuck in traffic on my way home to get you."

"Then when you finally got there you discovered that the elevator was out of order."

"It was the first time I ever regretted living on the sixth floor," Paul said.

"I'll never forget the look of surprise on your face as we began our descent and my overnight case opened and everything spilled out down the steps," I said.

"That wasn't too funny."

"Nor was that walk down."

"I honestly didn't think you were going to make it."

"I know. My contractions were coming fast and furious and I'd get down half a flight before I had to sit another one out."

"I was so afraid you were going to give birth right there on the steps."

"At the rate I was going, it was quite possible, but I made it to the car."

"Only to find that we had a flat tire."

"I really felt sorry for you when you had to run back up the six flights to call a cab," I said.

"Yeah. That was a real bummer. But the biggest kicker was when we finally reached the hospital and the doctor examined you."

"By the look on your face, you were just as shocked as I was when he discovered the second heartbeat."

"I could never understand how the boys were able to fool the doctor by lying on top of one another."

"They were beautiful, though, and certainly worth every bit of trouble."

"That's for sure. Being together as a family made me realize what I'd been missing," he said as he reached for my hand under the blanket. "I really thought the new position was what I wanted with its higher salary and perks. I was wrong. The past few months have been so empty for me."

I turned to face him. My heart was nearly singing in accompaniment to his words.

"They haven't been the best for me, either. If it hadn't been for the boys, it would've been worse."

Paul gently squeezed my hand underneath the blanket. The pressure of his fingers on mine sent shivers of delight right through me. I hadn't felt that wonderful in such a long time. And I wanted that feeling to last beyond the moment.

"I've had a great deal of time to think and must've gone over everything at least a thousand times. If I had done this or if I had done that . . ."

"It wasn't just you, Paul. I was as much to blame."

"If I hadn't put work before you and the kids . . ."

"Perhaps I should've been more understanding and cooperative."

"I guess we both could've been more understanding and bothered to take the time to listen to one another."

"Yes, there had been hardly any communication between us. How could we allow things to snowball as they did?"

Paul dropped my hand and gently caressed my face as he looked into my eyes. I peered back into those beautiful eyes, the same ones I'd often find myself drowning in, as I did now. I heard him whisper, "I don't want to throw our love away."

"It's much too precious to let go."

"Does that mean that you want to try and put all this behind us?" Paul asked, drawing me close.

I smiled and a moment later he covered my mouth with his and tenderly kissed me. I kissed him back hungrily, wanting more and needing it. I couldn't remember the last time I was held in those strong arms of his as we rekindled our love under a sky of twinkling stars.

Driving home the next day as the boys happily chattered away, I wondered how Paul and I would work things out. I knew it was going to take a great deal of compromise, especially when it concerned where we'd live. At that moment, it occurred to me that I really didn't care if the kids and I remained in the house we were living in. What had seemed so important was no longer an issue. I was beginning to believe in my heart that no problem was insurmountable when love was involved. We'd come to the brink and were aware of what was at stake. We would be more careful.

Michael interrupted my thoughts by asking, "Dad, are we home yet?"

I turned to Paul. He was smiling. "Son, it doesn't matter where we are. Whenever all four of us are together, we're home."

THE END

A NEW YEAR'S
TO REMEMBER

"What's your New Year's resolution for the coming year?" Paula asked me.

"I don't really have one," I told my friend.

"You have to have one. It's the tradition," she said, walking over and sitting in the chair next to my desk. "You're going to the party tomorrow night, aren't you?"

I nodded. "Bernard expects me to be there."

The following day was New Year's Eve—the day Mountainview Retirement Center held its annual party. Many of the staff attended, including Paula and I, who worked in the administration office. Cake, ice cream, and punch were always served, but the highlight of the party was when everyone announced their resolution for the coming year. Many of the residents had disabilities that limited what they could do, but that didn't stop them from coming up with creative resolutions that showed they were looking positively ahead to the next year.

I always looked forward to the party, until this year. The formal ending of this year was only a painful reminder of all the mistakes I'd made during the previous twelve months—mistakes that were serious and heartbreaking. I cringed as I mentally listed them: an affair with a married man, breaking up with a nice guy, and not keeping my promise to see my grandfather before he died. Right now I couldn't think of next year; I was still troubled by the mess I'd made this year.

"Sandy, I know the party won't be the same without your grandfather," Paula said, her voice filled with compassion.

"That's why I want to be there for Bernard," I said.

When Gramps moved into the center, he and Bernard became best friends. They were always together. Through my visits to Gramps I got to know and love Bernard. Now, I made daily visits to see Bernard and talk for a few minutes.

"He and your grandfather were quite the pair," she said, crossing her arms across her chest and reminiscing about some of their jokes and antics.

As she talked, it was easy to remember the good times when Gramps was alive—the talks we had, the private jokes we shared, and the stories he told. Listening to Paula talk it felt like only yesterday when I sat at Gramps' side, instead of last spring. If only I'd seen him before he died.

8

"Do you have plans after the party tomorrow night?" she said, changing the subject as though sensing we'd talked long enough about Gramps.

"No. I'll probably watch the New Year's Eve celebrations on television."

"I'm sure you're kicking yourself for breaking up with Trey," she said with a knowing look.

"Every day," I said soundly. Trey was a paramedic I'd dated last spring.

"I know things didn't work out like you planned, but breaking up with him was the kind and honest thing to do."

I nodded. Paula was a supportive friend—I don't know what I would've done without her this year.

"Looks like it's about time to go home," she said, stretching her arms over her head and getting up from the chair.

I followed suit and got up from my desk. "I'll see you tomorrow. I'm going to visit with Bernard before I leave," I said.

Bernard was in his room watching the evening news when I stopped in on my way home.

"What's new in the world?" I asked as I gave him a warm hug. His shaky arm reached up to my shoulder and he returned the hug.

"Same as yesterday, and each day before," he said with a snort, as he clicked the remote control to turn off the television. "Countries fighting, economy troubles, and crime stories. What's new with you? Any new people moving in?"

That was Bernard's most frequent question. Since Gramps died, he didn't have anyone to buddy with, so he was always hoping a man his age would move into the center.

I shook my head. "No new residents today."

"I miss your grandpa," he said through thin lips. "Especially this time of year. I still have his resolution from last year." He pointed to a bulletin board where both his and my grandfather's resolutions were posted.

I'd seen the bulletin board a hundred times, but today seeing Gramps' bold handwriting brought a lump to my throat.

"Each year we wrote down our resolutions before the party so we couldn't steal each other's idea," he said with a chuckle.

"You two did have a lot of little games," I said, giving his hand a squeeze.

"Yeah, I miss that," he said, his eyes getting teary. He shook his head as though clearing his mind of the painful memories, then he looked up at me. "You have big plans for tomorrow night?"

"I'll be at the party here."

"And?" he asked, peering at me through his glasses.

"That's it."

9

He wrinkled up his nose. "Seems like a pretty girl like you would have a date—one of those dates where you go to a fancy place with a band, horns, and balloons. Then at midnight everyone kisses and drinks champagne."

I laughed. "Not this year."

"Whatever happened to that young fella, the one who wore the blue uniform?"

"His name is Trey; he's a paramedic. Remember, I broke up with him."

"That's right, I remember now. You had two boyfriends and had to choose one. But then things didn't work out with the other one, did they?" His face screwed up as he struggled to remember.

"No, they didn't," I replied softly. Bernard never knew what happened with Gene, the other man I had been dating. There was no way I could tell him that Gene and I stopped seeing each other because he wouldn't leave his wife.

"Too bad things didn't work out. I never met the other guy, but Trey seemed nice."

"He was," I said.

"You can't get back together with him, can you?" he asked with a serious frown.

I shook my head. "What did you do today?" I asked, eager to change the topic. Unfortunately, the conversation drifted to another topic I'd just as soon avoid.

"I worked on my resolution. It's on a piece of paper right here in my pocket," he said, patting his shirt. "Have you got yours all figured out?"

"Not yet, but I'll think of something before the party. Maybe something about working harder."

"That doesn't sound like a resolution. That sounds like you're just making-up something. A resolution isn't any good if it doesn't come from the heart," he said, pointing to my heart.

I nodded absently and glanced at my watch. "It's almost time for your dinner," I said, getting up. "Do you want me to push you down to the dining room?"

"Sure," he said as he released the brakes on his wheel chair.

As we wound our way down the halls to the dining room, we talked about what was being served for dinner, the snow, and the center's New Year's decorations. I was relieved to be talking about topics not related to myself, but the relief was short-lived.

"You've only got until tomorrow to figure out your resolution," Bernard said, straining his neck to look into my eyes as I pushed his chair.

"I'll work on it tonight," I said, not meaning a word, but hoping to move on to another subject.

"You need to think of a resolution that will be good for you," he said as I positioned him at his favorite dining room table. "You've had a tough year. Losing your grandfather, and then your boyfriend troubles."

"I'll always feel bad that I didn't get to say good-bye to Gramps," I said with a sigh.

"We all knew his heart was getting worse, but none of us knew he was going to leave us when he did," Bernard said, reaching for my hand and holding it in his. "You were so good to see him every day. He loved your visits so much—just like I do now."

"But if I'd only stopped in for a minute before I left. . . ."

Bernard shook his head firmly and argued, "You saw him at lunch that day; I was there when you came in to see him."

"I told him I'd see him before I went home. I didn't keep my promise; I should have stopped back."

"Should have. Those are words we use when we later realize we didn't do the right thing," he said thoughtfully. "You've got to forget your 'should haves' and remember all the things you did right. Tell me, are Trey and that other boyfriend of yours 'should haves,' too?"

"Yeah. I have a lot of 'should haves' this year," I said, forcing myself to laugh so he wouldn't know how painful the memories were.

I saw other residents coming into the dining room, so it was the perfect opportunity to end the conversation. I was more than ready to leave—I'd opened my soul more than I had intended.

"I'll work on a resolution for you just in case you don't come up with one," Bernard said as I kissed him good-bye.

As I drove home, I passed St. Luke's Hospital and wondered if there would ever be a time when I could drive by it without thinking what a fool I was to have gotten involved with Gene. I knew the day I met him that he wasn't someone I should become involved with, but his charming personality and dark, sexy eyes made me overlook the fact that he was married.

Gene was a radiologist at St. Luke's; he took X-rays of Gramps when he had stomach pains. After Gene took the X-rays, I talked to him about Gramps' symptoms and what the X-rays would show. He took me into his office so we could talk confidentially.

I liked him immediately because he was so kind and patient with my questions. He didn't intimidate me, and his voice was filled with genuine concern. After he'd answered my questions about Gramps, I asked him about the photographs posted on his wall.

"Looks like you have a great family," I said, pointing to a picture where he was at the beach with two children and a woman I assumed was his wife.

He smiled and nodded. "Yes, I do." His face became serious and he shook his head. "It's too bad reality isn't as pretty as pictures. Oh, I'm sorry. I shouldn't be telling you my troubles."

"Why not," I said. "I just told you more than you need to know about my grandfather."

He smiled again. "I guess you're easy to talk to. Right now, I'm heading for a divorce, and it isn't always easy to talk about."

Before I knew it, I was making plans to see him after work to talk. We met for coffee and wound up having dinner. The time flew as we bounced from topic to topic and learned about each other. We touched on Gene's divorce and marriage problems, but that wasn't the focus of our conversation. In fact, I respected Gene because he didn't badmouth his wife or dwell on his marriage troubles. He briefly told me that their marriage had never been strong, and they'd drifted so far apart that it was impossible to maintain a relationship even for the sake of the children. In order to save money, he and his wife were working out the divorce details themselves rather than spending a fortune on attorneys.

As we left the restaurant he asked me to have lunch with him the next day. I hesitated, and then accepted. I told myself we were friends, and there was nothing wrong having lunch with a friend.

I'd just gotten home from my evening with Gene when I got a phone call from Trey, asking me to the movies and dinner that Saturday. I'd met Trey a couple of days before when he came into the administration office about some missing paperwork on a patient the medic unit had taken to the hospital. Paula and I were both eyeing the last doughnut in the bakery bag when he walked through the door. He joined in the teasing duel, and we wound up cutting the donut into three pieces and sharing it, laughing all the time.

He and I were sharing lively conversation by the time I started looking for the information he needed. He had an athletic look to him. But it was clear the way he talked about his work that he wasn't shallow or hung-up on himself. He liked people and genuinely cared for their well-being. That was one of the reasons he was a paramedic.

When he left, he joked that he was having such a good time visiting that he'd like to see me again. I agreed, but never thought he'd call me.

For the next couple of months I juggled my time between Gene and Trey. Since Gene had a wife and family, I usually saw him after work or for lunch. That left the weekends for Trey. Having two boyfriends had always sounded like a dream, but I found it to be a burden. Although neither relationship was serious, I still felt like I was two-timing each of the men. My worries grew as both relationships approached the point where making love would be a natural event—I certainly couldn't go to bed with both of them.

Of the two, Gene seemed the most serious about me. He gave me cards and little gifts, and often talked about the things we would do together when he was divorced. My relationship with Trey felt less serious. While he acted like he cared, and even made friends with Gramps, he seldom talked about future plans that included me. Every day I asked myself which one would I chose if I could only have one, and I couldn't answer.

The decision was made for me one night when Gene brought me back to my apartment after a romantic dinner at an Italian restaurant. The whole evening had been charged with sexual electricity, beginning with his hello kiss when he picked me up. His lips were so warm and soft that I felt the kiss to my toes. I had to tear myself away to go to the restaurant.

At dinner he kept stroking my hand with his fingers, and our eyes would meet and lock for minutes. Heat flooded through my body every time he looked at me. For desert he ordered a large dish of spumoni ice cream for us to share. He'd dip the spoon into the cool ice cream, and then slowly slip the spoon into my mouth while his eyes met mine.

By the time we got back to my apartment, my desire for his kisses and touch was so great that I fell into his eager arms, desperate to be closer to him. His desire was as great as mine, and his hands were pulling off my clothes as we kissed our way down the hall to my bedroom.

Gene's lovemaking left me craving more, and it was agony when he pulled himself away from me to search for his clothes. I wanted him to spend the night and hold me in his arms, but I knew he had to go home to his wife. My stomach ached at the thought of him going home to her, yet that was where he belonged.

Gene's good-bye kiss was deep and long. "I'll be divorced soon," he whispered, running his hand through my hair and sending even more sensations through my body.

Now that I was going to bed with Gene, I had to stop seeing Trey. I couldn't morally go to bed with two men at the same time. Besides, I didn't want anyone to get hurt more than they had to.

That weekend, I told Trey that I'd met someone else. His bright blue eyes clouded as we talked, and I knew he was hurt—more than I had expected. He didn't say much, just that he understood and wished me well.

As much as I loved being with Gene I still missed seeing Trey. He and I shared many common interests, and we had fun visits with Gramps and Bernard. I reassured myself that I'd get over my feelings in time, and that I'd made the right decision to be with Gene. Now that we were going to bed together, Gene and I didn't go out as often. Our dates were usually in my bedroom, making intoxicating love, followed by home-delivered Chinese food or pizza. I wished we could go out more, but Gene's time was limited.   In April Gene went out-of-town to a conference for a week, and then he immediately went on a vacation with his family for spring break. During this time, Gramps began having serious heart problems. There was a brief stay in the hospital and then he came back to Mountainview, but he was put in the nursing wing rather than his regular room. The doctor put him on new medications and he seemed to be on the mend, but he was still weak and not himself. I spent as much time as I could with him.

On the day he died, Paula and I were busy with month-end work, so I could only spend a few minutes with him at lunch. I promised him I'd see him after work when I'd have more time. Shortly after five o'clock, I turned off my computer and was going to see him when Gene called. It was the first time I'd talked to him in weeks, and my heart raced just hearing his voice. He was back in town and wanted to see me. He was waiting for me at a nearby motel we sometimes went to when he didn't have time to go to my place.

I grabbed my coat and ran to my car. I'd missed him so much, and my body ached to be with him. All I could think of as I drove to the motel was his tender touches and kisses that ignited every nerve in my body. As soon as he closed the door to our room we fell into each other's arms. He didn't have much time, but even the short time we were together was wonderful. As I left the motel I thought about stopping at the center to see Gramps, but I figured he'd be asleep. Besides, my hair and make-up were a mess from Gene's eager lovemaking, and I didn't want Gramps to be suspicious or concerned.

I'd just gotten home, still flushed and warm from being with Gene, when I got the call that Gramps had died. I'd missed my chance to see him one last time, and I broke my promise to come back after work—all because I wanted to make love with Gene.

A couple of months after Gramps died I was still depressed. I was also overcome with guilt for not seeing him like I'd promised. I was still seeing Gene, but lately his lovemaking was unfulfilling. I really needed less lovemaking and more verbal communication and moral support from him. Because he was married, I couldn't see him or call him when I needed him most; he could never spend the night with me; his family always took first place. I could tell he felt the difference in our relationship because he visited less frequently and there was a coolness about him. I'm sure my depressed moods and diminished interest in sex were starting to annoy him.

"Things would be different if we had a real relationship," I said to him one night after an evening of lukewarm lovemaking. "How are the divorce plans coming?" He hadn't mentioned the divorce in some time. I didn't want to hound, but I was curious how long until we could be together like we'd planned.

"These things take time," he said, sitting on the edge of the bed and reaching for his clothes.

"You've been working on it for months," I said, struggling to keep the edge off my voice.

He paused before answering and then said, "It will be a while longer."

"A couple of months?" I didn't like the evasiveness of his voice, so I pressed him.

He shrugged. "I don't know. I'll just have to see what happens."

"You are getting a divorce, aren't you?" I asked, pulling the blankets around me and sitting up in bed so I could see his face.

"I'm not so sure anymore. Natalie and I have been getting along better since our vacation," he said as he slipped on his shoe.

His words were a knife cutting through my already aching heart. "What about us?"

"I don't know. Things haven't been the same between us since your grandfather died."

"I'm depressed," I defended. "I'm having trouble coping with Gramps' death, and I want us to be together like a regular couple, not just when you can get away from your family."

"I'm not sure when we can be together like you want. We'll just have to see what happens," he said, getting up from the bed and walking toward the hall door.

I grabbed my robe and followed him into the living room. Hurt, anger, and feelings of betrayal flooded my heart as I told him we didn't have to wait and see what happened—I didn't want to see him again. I didn't want a partial relationship; I wanted a relationship with someone who was committed to me.

The stoplight near my apartment brought my thoughts back to the current moment. I usually thought about my foolish relationship with Gene, and the resulting missed opportunities when I drove home—it was like a daily ritual. I passed a supermarket sign advertising New Year's Eve deli trays and was reminded that I still had to come up with a resolution before the party tomorrow night. I'm sure Bernard would have one for me, but I should at least have something of my own to show that I'd tried. I told myself I'd think about it later after I'd had something for dinner.

The next morning I was busy preparing insurance claims when Bernard rolled into the administration office.

"Service, service," he called in a joking tone from the counter. I got up from my desk and went over to him. "I need a lunch partner today," he said. "Are you available or are you all booked up?"

I laughed. "I'll fit you into my busy calendar," I said. "Do you want to bring your tray down here and eat in the conference room, or do you want me to join you in the dining room?"

"I'll come down here," he said, slowly rolling his chair away from the counter and heading down the hall.

Seeing him reminded me that I still hadn't come up with a resolution. I put the insurance work aside, took out a blank piece of paper, and began writing possible resolutions. None of them sounded right, or even like something I wanted to do. My creative thinking was interrupted by the all too familiar sound of an ambulance siren in the front drive, followed by the sound of running feet as the paramedics raced down the hall.

Since I broke up with Trey, I always had my head down when the paramedics passed. Even when we were dating I never followed them down the hall—until today. Today, I wanted to see if Trey was with them. I sprang from my desk and followed them down the hall until I was close enough to see who was on the ambulance team. It was easy to pick out Trey as he stood towering over a short dark-haired paramedic. I started to go back to the office when Trey turned his head in my direction and our eyes met. Before I could decide what to do, he and the paramedic with him quickly followed a nurse down one of the corridors toward the nursing home wing.

What was I thinking to follow them down the hall? Trey didn't want to see me. Even if he and I were on good terms he couldn't talk to me—he was busy saving a life. Hopefully, he'd think I just happened to be in the hall. But that seemed unlikely. It was all too obvious that I was standing in the hall, staring at him because I couldn't get him out of my mind.

I went back to my desk and worked on the insurance claims. When I heard the medic team leaving, I kept my head down and didn't look up. I was still hard at work when an aide wheeled Bernard into the office. Bernard was balancing a lunch tray on his lap. I'd felt so embarrassed about following Trey that I'd totally forgotten Bernard. And my resolution!

While the aide wheeled Bernard into the empty conference room, I got my salad and diet soda from the staff refrigerator.

"So, did you come up with a resolution last night?" he asked when I took a seat next to him.

"I've got a few in mind," I hedged as I poured dressing on my salad.

"I came up with one for you, too. It has to do with your 'should haves.'"

"Let's hear it," I said, forcing myself to be interested.

He set his fork down and looked into my eyes. "You need to forgive yourself for your mistakes."

Stunned, I could only look at him.

16

"You've been wearing a cloak of guilt ever since your grandfather died, and you won't let it go. Same with those two men you were seeing. I don't know the specifics, but I can tell you're beating yourself up over whatever you did or didn't do."

"I did some stupid things," I admitted.

"But that doesn't mean you have to let your mistakes ruin your life and your attitude. That's even more stupid. Rehashing all those bad decisions won't change a thing. It just makes you miserable. You and your grandfather had a wonderful, loving relationship—don't let thoughts about what you didn't do ruin all those good memories. Same with those boyfriends. What's done is done."

As he talked, I thought about my daily trips by the hospital when I was filled with self-loathing for getting involved with Gene when I knew better. And then there were all the times I saw a medic van and was angry at myself for breaking up with Trey. Not to mention my guilt whenever I thought of Gramps, which was several times a day. Bernard was right; I was rehashing all of the past and letting it cloud my good memories.

"It's a new year tomorrow," he said. "Take all of those old mistakes and throw them away forever. And do the same with the ones you make next year, because you will make a few next year."

"Not like this year," I joked.

"Is my resolution better than yours?" he asked with a sly smile.

I nodded. "I like it." How could I not use it? Bernard's insight was right.

After lunch, Paula and I helped the staff hang streamers and balloons in the recreation room. I felt like Bernard had waved a magic wand over me. I was happier and more hopeful than I had been in ages.

"Got your resolution for tonight?" Paula asked as we hung a Happy New Year sign on the wall.

"Yes, I do. Bernard helped, but I think I've got a good one."

"You're a loving friend to him, just like you were to your grandfather," she said with a warm smile.

I nodded and thanked her for her comment. I remembered my lunch with Bernard and reminded myself that I needed to remember the good things I did for my grandfather. I couldn't let my feelings of guilt diminish the wonderful relationship I had with him. As for Gene, there was no point reminding myself of my mistake. I learned a painful lesson, and I wouldn't make the same mistake again.

By the time the party rolled around I was in a festive mood. The room was filled with residents, staff, family members, and others. When it came time for me to tell my resolution, I took Bernard's hand in mine and said, "I'm going to forgive my mistakes."

My resolution was met with applause and comments like, "That's a good one."

I reached over and gave Bernard and hug. Then I looked up to see Trey standing across the room. He gave a little wave, and I waved back.

"Hey, isn't that Trey over there?" Bernard asked, squinting to see better, and waving one hand while he poked me in the ribs with his elbow. "Go say hello to him."

I couldn't say no to Bernard without causing a scene, so I walked over to where Trey was standing. I noticed he was still in his medic uniform.

"Are you working?" I asked, thinking that was a good way to start the conversation.

"Yes, I'm on call. When I was here earlier today I heard there was a party tonight and thought you might be here. That was you in the hall today, wasn't it?" he asked.

I nodded. "I knew you were working, so I didn't want to bother you," I said, trying to cover for following him down the hall.

"I would've talked to you, but I had my hands full," he explained with a smile. "I liked your resolution. Does it apply to forgiving others for their mistakes?"

"Yes," I answered, puzzled why he asked.

"Then maybe you can forgive me for a mistake I made," he said. "After we broke up, I realized I should've let you know how much I cared for you. I've often thought if I'd made my feelings more clear you wouldn't have found someone else."

"I don't think you did anything that requires forgiveness," I said softly. "Just so you know, I'm not going out with him anymore—we broke up months ago."

His eyes lit up, and his lips curled into a smile. "Does that mean you're free tonight after the party?"

I smiled and nodded.

"I get off work at ten o'clock. I could pick you up and we could try to find a bar that isn't too crowded," he suggested.

"Or we could watch television at my place and have deli food and champagne," I countered, remembering the supermarket near me with the ad for New Year's Eve platters.

"I like your idea better," he said, gently taking my hand in his and giving it a squeeze.

After Trey left, Bernard was all ears about what Trey and I had talked about. "So are you going to one of those parties with the decorations and champagne?" he asked.

"Sort of," I said, thinking I'd get some balloons when I was at the supermarket.

That night, Trey and I toasted our glasses of champagne and welcomed the New Year with a kiss. I'd had a troubling year, but I'd learned the importance of forgiving myself for my mistakes, and not revisiting them over and over. I'm glad I listed to Bernard—his insight and wisdom will change my life forever.

THE END

MY EX VOWED, "I'M GOING TO STEAL YOUR BABIES!"
Will I ever see them again?

Although it was Saturday, I was up early because of a bad dream. The sun was just beginning to stream in through the bedroom window as I quietly slid out of bed.

Out in the kitchen, I tied to shake off the bits and pieces of the dream that had stubbornly clung to the edges of my mind. I poured dry dog food into Boomer's plastic bowl. Then, after he'd eaten, I opened the back door to let him out into the yard. By that time, the kettle on the stove was whistling. I made myself a cup of instant coffee, then I padded to the front door to pick up the morning paper from the porch. I paused a moment to look at the dew sparkling on the grass and to sniff the fragrance of the roses that were tumbling over my neighbor's fence.

It was springtime again—a full year since that other spring day when my whole world had collapsed.

Suddenly, I shivered, not because of the coolness of the early-morning air—not even because of the frightening dream, which had finally begun to fade—but because of the thoughts that had begun crowding into my mind. My memories of the past twelve months were like the scenes in a child's kaleidoscope—turn it one way, and I could see my laughing children tumbling on the grass; turn it again, and the picture shifted. Suddenly, Mark's and Katie's smiles had turned into expressions of fright—their laughter into screams of terror.

In an attempt to block out those memories, I unfolded the paper and glanced at the headlines. They were about the usual things— crime, politics. Then, suddenly, the smaller headline on a story near the bottom of the page fairly leaped out at me: after kidnapping, area mother lives in fear. Then, below that, were the words: Custody Laws Can't Safeguard Her Child.

For a moment, I could hardly breathe. I carried the paper back to the kitchen and sat down at the table. I didn't need to read the story printed below those headlines—I didn't have to. I knew what it would say. I knew all too well the heartbreak, the worry, and the despair that that poor mother was going through.

In my heart, I knew that every woman has her own special nightmare—the worst thing in the world that could possibly happen to her. Ever since I'd become a mother, my fears had always seemed to revolve around Mark and Katie. Almost from the day that they were born, I'd worried that they might get lost or hurt or sick, or even that some deranged person might harm them. But, I'd never expected what had really happened. I'd never expected them to be put in danger because of the actions of their own father.

I pushed away the newspaper, my memories sliding back all the way to that day, ten years before, when Chuck and I had gotten married. I could see it all again—the small-town church filled with our friends and relatives, the altar decorated with flowers from my grandmother's garden. I could feel the stiffness of the white lace gown I was wearing. It was my "something old"—my mother's gown, which had been carefully preserved from her wedding so many years before. It still smelled of the lavender sachets that had been tucked away with it.

And then, I heard my father's voice.

"Francine, honey, are you sure that you want to go through with this? Are you sure that marrying Chuck is what you want?" he asked just as he was about to start down the church aisle with me on his arm. "The two of you are so young—and marriage isn't all honeymooning and holding hands, you know."

"Daddy, we know that," I whispered impatiently.

The organist was beginning to play the first strains of the wedding march. I watched as my younger sister, Stacy—she was my maid of honor—started down the aisle ahead of me in the rose-colored silk gown that Mom had made for her, teetering a little because she was wearing her first pair of high heels. I touched my veil to make sure it was straight. Then, I smiled at my father.

"I'm ready, Daddy," I said.

"It's still not too late to change your mind," he told me.

"We'll be happy," I promised.

And I didn't have a doubt in the world that we would be. When I saw Chuck standing there at the altar waiting for me, I thought that I would burst with joy and love. I wanted to rush to him instead of taking those slow, measured, sedate steps.

If ever there was a bride with a heart full of hope and stars in her eyes, it was me.

Chuck Keating and I had dated all through high school. We hadn't surprised anyone by deciding to get married right after graduation. I knew that our parents felt that we should have waited at least a few years, but when you were eighteen and desperately in love, how could advice like that have seemed reasonable?

Chuck had been hired full-time as a mechanic at the garage where he'd worked after school and on weekends, and I'd planned to keep my job at a local clothing store. We knew we wouldn't have a lot of money, but we figured we'd get by. And we did, for a while. I loved cooking meals for Chuck in the cramped kitchen of our tiny furnished apartment. Sometimes we had friends in for an evening of watching videos, or just talking. Chuck and I would bustle about, serving cold drinks and snacks. We were the only married couple amongst our friends, and I guess we enjoyed the status that it gave us. We enjoyed playing the roles.

I wasn't sure when the glow had begun to wear off. Looking back, I believed it was when I'd first gotten pregnant with Mark. Children had been in our plans, of course, but not so soon. Even though we kept assuring each other how grown-up we were, actually, deep inside, I think we'd both realized that we weren't far past childhood ourselves. The fact was, we weren't ready yet to be parents. Still, when I started having morning sickness and the doctor confirmed my suspicions and told me that I was really going to have a baby, I couldn't help feeling a little thrilled. I'd thought that Chuck would share that slightly scared, slightly giddy, slightly proud feeling with me, but he didn't.

"Francine, how could you let something like this happen?" he asked when I broke the news to him.

Suddenly, all my happiness over the baby seemed to drain away. I felt close to tears.

"I told you that I forgot to take my pill a few times," I reminded him, "and you said that it probably wouldn't matter. You still wanted to make love." I tried to choke back a sob. "I didn't get pregnant all by myself, you know!"

He put his arm around me then. "I'm sorry, honey. I didn't mean to yell at you that way," he whispered, trying to comfort me. "Don't worry. We'll manage."

But it wasn't long afterward that Chuck started needing a night out every once in awhile. Gradually, his nights out became more and more frequent. Before long, he was spending more time with his friends than he was with me.

I kept telling myself that after our baby was born, things would change. I really believed that becoming a father would make Chuck settle down. But, the night when I started having labor pains, Chuck was miles away, at some sporting event. I was hoping and praying that he'd get home in time, but, finally, I knew that I didn't dare wait any longer. I had to call a cab and get to the hospital by myself. Mark was born before Chuck even arrived.

Chuck made all kinds of apologies to me. "I'll really start staying home more, Francine," he vowed as he held my hand. "After all, I've got a son now. It's time for me to start growing up, right?"

Right then, I would have forgiven him anything—believed any promises that he'd made. I wanted our marriage to work so badly that I was willing to push my fears aside and put all my faith in him.

But when Mark and I came home from the hospital, things got worse instead of better. Mark was colicky, and he fussed quite a lot. His crying drove Chuck right up the wall. If our apartment had seemed small before, it seemed to shrink almost by the day after that. Baby clothes and equipment, boxes of disposable diapers—they all took up so much of our meager space. And I was usually too tired from trying to cope with a new baby to bother either with cooking or fixing myself up much. I couldn't really blame Chuck for wanting to get out with his friends. As much as I adored Mark, I sometimes found myself wishing that I could close the door behind me and escape for a few hours of fun, too.

Nights out for Chuck and me together were few and far between. My sister, Stacy, or my mom were willing enough to baby-sit, but even a simple evening of a movie and pizza would have cost money that we simply didn't have.

I had planned on finding a job just as soon as Mark was older, but he wasn't even two years old yet when I learned that I was pregnant again.

I could understand why Chuck wasn't overjoyed. I felt more than a little panicky myself, wondering what we were going to do. The apartment was too small with one child—with two, it would be impossible. Yet, there was no way—at least, none that I could see—that we could move.

Then, a few months before Katie was born, my grandmother died. My mother inherited her house, and, to my delight, she offered it to Chuck and me. She told us that we didn't have to pay her rent. All she asked was that we take care of minor repairs and keep the garden looking nice.

Grandma's little house, with its big, fenced backyard, seemed like a palace to me after the place where we'd been living. We didn't have any furniture of our own, but relatives gave us odds and ends, so we were able to manage.

"I'm going to make curtains for the kitchen windows," I told Chuck on the day we moved in. I was filled with ideas for the house, but while Chuck was as glad as I was to be out of the cramped apartment, he didn't seem to share my interest in fixing things up. I'd hoped that working on the house together would bring us close again, but Chuck's main interest was still hanging out with his buddies.

Not long after I got home from the hospital with Katie, I began to realize that it wasn't only "the boys" that he was out with at night. I began finding all kinds of telltale signs. I still loved Chuck, and I tried convincing myself that I was wrong, that I was imagining things—but, finally, I couldn't ignore the facts any longer.

One night, I made a point of waiting up for Chuck, and when he finally came home, reeking of perfume and alcohol, I tried to remain calm.

"Chuck, let's see a marriage counselor—or maybe the minister at church," I suggested. "We have to talk to somebody—do something to save our marriage."

Chuck sank heavily into the nearest chair and looked at me for a long moment.

"I don't think we have any marriage left to save, Francine," he said finally. "I'm sorry. I really am. I thought I was ready for the responsibility of being a husband and a father—but I guess I'm really not. I don't know what else to say, honey."

He cried, and I cried, but the next day, he moved out.

I couldn't believe that it was happening. Just like that, I was a single parent with the job of raising two small children. Still, if it hadn't been for Mark and Katie, I don't think I could have made it. I think I would have just given up.

I hoped for awhile that Chuck would change his mind and come back to us. When I finally realized that that was never going to happen, I reluctantly filed for divorce. Divorce was something that I'd never really believed in. I'd always felt that marriage was a forever kind of commitment. Because of that, for a long time, I carried around the huge burden of feeling that I was a failure. I'd think that if I'd just cooked better meals, or put on lipstick more often, Chuck might still be with us. But, gradually, I realized that I couldn't spend the rest of my life regretting my ruined marriage. I had to pick up the pieces and go on.

Chuck didn't contest the divorce, and when my final decree was granted, I was also given custody of the children. Chuck had visitation rights, but he rarely used them. For the first time, I was glad that he had been gone so much of the time when the children were babies, because they hardly missed him after the divorce.

The few times when Chuck to did come to see them, he didn't stay long, and he usually had a girl sitting in the car. It was never the same girl twice, either. That didn't bother me, but something else did. I'd been hearing that Chuck had developed a drinking problem, and that he was becoming an alcoholic. Even if I hadn't believed the gossip, I could see for myself that, sometimes when he'd stop in, he'd had a beer or two too many.

Whenever that happened, I wouldn't let him see the children. He never pushed for his rights then or became argumentative.

"Sure, Francine," he'd mumble. "Maybe next time. Tell them that I miss them, okay?"

I'd end up feeling sorry for him as he'd turn to leave. I knew by then that I didn't love Chuck any longer—the romantic feelings that

I'd had for him had all burned themselves to ashes—but I still cared about him. He had been my husband, he was the father of my children, and it seemed to me that he was just throwing his life away. He was still in his twenties, and yet, all too often, he'd begun to remind me of the sad old men that I'd seen sitting in the park.

I tried talking to him about joining Alcoholics Anonymous, but when he was sober, he'd deny that he had a problem.

"I'm not drinking anymore, Francine," he'd insist. "I've quit for good. You don't have to worry about me." He'd sound so sincere that I'd believe him. Then the next time I'd see him, he'd have had been drinking again, and I'd know that he'd been lying to me.

I was careful not to say anything negative about Chuck to the children, but I could tell that they didn't feel close to him—the way that they should feel toward their father. It was my dad they turned to, instead. Dad was always ready to play ball with Mark or to hold Katie on his lap. And, he was always eager to take both of them to the zoo, or to the beach.

We didn't have much contact with Chuck's family beyond Christmas and birthday cards. Still, I was shocked and saddened when I learned that my former father-in-law had died suddenly because of a heart attack.

I attended the funeral. Chuck, I could tell, was taking the loss of his father very hard. We talked a little after the burial.

"I'm so sorry, Chuck," I said to him.

He nodded and looked away for a minute. "You know, Francine, maybe I needed something like this to shake me up and make me take a look at my own life," he told me. "These last few years, Dad and I were like strangers. I hardly ever went back home, and I know how much that must have hurt him. I could have stopped in once in awhile, or I could have suggested that we go fishing together up at the old cabin up by the lake. Do you remember the cabin, Francine?"

I nodded. Chuck and I had gone there sometimes ourselves. It was located in a beautiful area of hills and tall trees.

"But I never did any of those things," Chuck went on, "and now, it's too late."

I waited while Chuck stopped again to try to get hold of his emotions.

"It's made me do a lot of thinking," he said finally. "It's made me realize that I want to spend more time with my own kids—get to really know them. Do you think that Mark and Katie would like that?"

"I'm sure they would," I assured him.

"And about the drinking—that's all over," he promised. "That's not going to be a problem anymore."

On his next regularly scheduled visitation day, Chuck arrived alone, right on time, and offered to take the children on an outing. But Katie cried at the thought of going anywhere with him, and even Mark hung back.

"It's going to take time, Chuck," I tried to explain. "Why don't you play with them here in the yard today? When they get a little more used to you, you can take them somewhere."

The afternoon didn't go too well. Chuck tried, but the children didn't warm up to him in the way that he would have liked. I really felt sorry for him when he left, but I could understand the children's reluctance, too.

The whole scene was repeated several times over the following weeks. Chuck didn't seem to be making any progress with the children at all. They were still wary of him, and they were obviously relieved when he'd finally go.

Then, one day, he seemed awfully excited when he arrived.

"I've got a great idea!" he exclaimed. "I'm going to take the kids up to the lake for the weekend. They'll love being up at the cabin and—"

"Chuck," I interrupted, "they're not ready to be with you for a whole weekend yet."

"I'm tired of waiting," he insisted. "I'm tired of having my own kids scared half to death of me."

He went ahead and told the children about the planned trip, but just as I'd expected, they weren't excited.

"We can fish and go out in the boat—" he began.

"I want to stay here with my mommy," Katie announced flatly.

"Grandpa takes us fishing almost every week," Mark added.

"Aw, the fish around here are nothing like the ones up at the lake," Chuck tried to persuade them.

But both children refused to change their minds.

Finally, Chuck gave up and left, but he returned a few days later. That afternoon, as soon as I spotted him getting out of his car, I could tell that he had stopped off at a bar. I'd been washing the lunch dishes, but I quickly reached for a towel to dry my hands. I wanted to stop him at the front door and head him off before the children, who were playing out back, had a chance to see him in that condition.

When I opened the front door, though, he wasn't standing on the porch. I realized then that he must have guessed that the children would be in the yard and had gone directly there. Sensing trouble, I hurried to the back door.

I heard Katie's frightened shrieks. "Mommy! Mommy!" she cried.

Then, I heard Mark calling out something, but by the time that I'd gotten out the back door, the yard was empty, and the gate was standing open. Frantically, I turned toward the street just in time to see Chuck's car pulling away from the curb.

26

He had the children! I could see Katie's terrified little face pressed to the back window.

"Stop!" I cried out as I raced toward the car. But he just picked up speed. A moment later, the car and my children were out of sight.

I was numb with shock. I couldn't even think of what to do. Finally, I went back inside and, my hands shaking, I called the police.

"My children—they've been kidnapped!" I said frantically the minute someone answered the phone. "Please, please get them back!" I was crying so uncontrollably that I could hardly give my name and address.

It seemed like hours before a police car pulled up out in front. I met the two officers at the door. As calmly as I could, I told them exactly what had happened.

"I don't know my ex-husband's license number," I finished, "but I can tell you the color and make of the car. And I'm almost sure that he's headed for his cabin by Bear Lake."

"You say that this man is the children's father?" one of the officers asked.

I nodded. "We're divorced. We have joint custody of the children. But, he's definitely in violation of the custody agreement. There's no way that he's allowed to come here and just grab the children. I can show you all the original court agreement—"

The other officer stopped me. "Don't bother, ma'am. There's no crime in a parent who has joint custody spending time with his kids."

"But there must be something that you can do!" I cried.

"We can put out a bulletin and maybe stop him on drunk-driving charges, but I'm afraid that's about it," he told me.

The officers left, promising to let me know if Chuck was stopped before he managed to cross the state line. They weren't too hopeful, though, and, by that time, neither was I.

I called my parents and sobbed out my story. They were equally incredulous that the police hadn't believed that anything could be done to get Mark and Katie back.

"I'll pick you up and take you down to the police station," my father offered. "Maybe if you talk to somebody down there, they can help."

But the police detective I finally spoke with told me pretty much the same thing that the police officers had.

"But Chuck kidnapped the children!" I persisted. "Isn't that against the law?"

The detective leaned back in his chair and shook his head. "Technically, it's not considered kidnapping when the person taking a child is the parent."

"Do you mean to tell me that Chuck didn't even commit a crime?" I was shocked.

"At the most, he could be charged with a misdemeanor."

"Isn't there anything that I can do?" I asked.

"You can try a civil suit through the courts," he answered. "I'm sorry, Ms. Keating." The detective shrugged and spread his hands. "I sympathize with you, but what can I say?" He paused a moment, then lowered his voice. "Off the record, if I was in your place, I think I'd find myself a good lawyer, or a private detective who's had some experience in recovering children in cases like this. There are some that I've heard of who have actually tracked kids down, then gone out with the parent and physically recovered them."

"Do you mean that they've kidnapped them back?" I asked.

"It's called 'child recovery,' Ms. Keating. It's something to keep in mind, anyway. But, first of all, why don't you take a trip up to this cabin that your husband was talking about? Maybe he and the kids are there, and you can talk him into handing them over."

Of course, I should go to the cabin, I thought. Why didn't I think of that myself?

As I got ready to leave, I turned to the detective. "If Chuck is there, I could go to the police station there, couldn't I—for help?"

Again, the detective shook his head. "This is a civil problem, remember, not a criminal one."

Everywhere I turned, it seemed as though I was faced with a blank wall. My children's well-being—their very lives—might be in danger, yet people talked of technicalities and state lines and other equally unimportant things. I'd always believed that laws were meant to help people, but, suddenly, I began to wonder.

Dad and I started out immediately for Bear Lake. He drove as fast as he dared. As the road changed from a level highway to one with frequent dips and turns, our speed slowed considerably. We passed the small marker that told us that we were leaving one state and entering another. I wondered how many times I had passed a similar marker and had barely paid any attention. But, suddenly, the fact that my children might have been brought across that invisible dividing line had become extremely important to me.

Finally, in the distance ahead, I glimpsed the glitter of water. I realized then that we were almost at our destination. My heart began to pound as I wondered what would happen once we got there.

When we finally arrived, though, the pounding stopped, and my heart sank.

"Chuck's car isn't there!" I cried.

"Maybe he guessed that we'd come here looking for him, and he parked it somewhere else," Dad suggested.

As soon as the car had come to a stop, I was out and running toward the cabin.

The door was locked. I pulled, pushed, and rattled the knob, but it stayed securely closed. When Dad and I peered through the cobweb-covered, small-paned windows, everything inside seemed dark and silent.

"Mark! Katie!" I called as loudly as I could.

The only answer was the wind in the branches of the trees and the distant hum of a boat's engine.

I called again and again, until I was almost hoarse. "It looks as though Chuck didn't bring them here, after all," I said finally.

We were just starting back toward the car when I noticed a flash of pink hanging from one of the bushes that grew beside the drive. I reached for the dangling scrap of material.

"It's Katie's ribbon," I said. "Dad, they have been here!"

But, even though we carefully searched the entire area surrounding the cabin, we couldn't find another sign of them. We even checked the dock, but the old boat was still moored.

"Chuck could have rented a boat and taken the kids out on the lake somewhere," my father said.

Or, he could be miles away from here by now, I thought desolately. He can take my children so far away that I might never see them again.

We got into the car and drove down to the marina that we had passed when we'd first turned off the main road. Dad gave the man in charge of boat rentals a description of Chuck, and I showed him the photographs of Mark and Katie that I had in my wallet. The man shook his head. He told us that hadn't seen Chuck and the children, let alone rented a boat to them.

Dad tried to reassure me as we headed back toward home. "Maybe Chuck's come to his senses by now, and the kids will be sitting there on the steps waiting for us," he told me.

When we pulled up in front of the house, though, it was as empty as when I'd left. Dad asked if I was sure that I didn't want to go on home with him, but I shook my head.

"I'd better stay here, just in case. Mark's old enough to know our telephone number. If he gets near a phone, maybe he'll try to call," I said.

"Of course, honey. You take care now, Francine." Dad gave me a comforting hug, and then he left.

Days passed, and I still hadn't heard a word about Chuck and the children. Sometimes, I'd get so worried that I was afraid I was losing my mind.

Finally, I decided I had to do something instead of just sitting by the telephone, waiting for it to ring. I started asking around, trying to locate a lawyer in our town who specialized in child recovery. I also went to see Mr. Warner, the lawyer who had handled my divorce, to ask him if he could possibly recommend someone.

"You'd have to go to a bigger city to find someone like that," he informed me, "and the fee would probably be more than you could afford—several thousand dollars, probably."

I sighed. He was right—I didn't have that kind of money.

"There is a man I've heard of, though, out on the West Coast, who sometimes agrees to help parents like you," he said hesitantly. "He works for just a little bit over expenses. You could try contacting him."

"He sounds like the answer to my prayers!" I exclaimed as I took the man's name and address from Mr. Warner.

"Well, not quite. You'd have to locate your children first, and you've told me that you have no idea where your ex-husband's taken them."

"That's right," I agreed. "But couldn't I hire a private detective to track down Chuck?"

"Expenses there can run pretty high, too. Why don't you see what you can do first on your own? Check with all his relatives and friends, and then keep on checking back with them to find out if they've heard anything."

I nodded.

"One more thing," Mr. Warner added. "It might be a good idea for you to contact the man at the head of the legal division of the United States Passport Office."

I gasped. "The Passport Office? Do you think that Chuck might try to take Mark and Katie out of the country?"

"He might. But if you furnish the Passport Office with your children's names, dates of birth, and descriptions, they'll file a notice with your children's names, and you'll be notified if an application is made for them. If that happens, you'll have fifteen days to furnish a restraining order on the Passport Office. So, if you do that, you'll have some protection, at least—some chance of keeping them in this country."

"Do many parents do that—go to another country, I mean?" I asked.

He nodded. "Quite a number of them. Sometimes, the officials in the foreign country will cooperate with the parent who has custody, and sometimes, they won't. Besides, it will be much simpler to find your children and to get them back if they aren't taken out of the United States," he said.

Mr. Warner gave me the address of the office and after thanking him for all his help, I went right home to write the letter. I talked with my former in-laws, too, but they said that they hadn't heard a thing from Chuck since he'd left with the children.

Thinking about how high the expenses for getting Mark and Katie back could mount, I decided that one of the other things I had to do immediately was to get a job. My former boss at the clothing store was willing to hire me back, and although the pay wasn't much, I decided to take the job—at least temporarily. I also signed up for night-school classes to brush up on the computer skills that I'd acquired in high school, in case the offer of a better job came along.

Keeping so busy didn't leave me much time or energy for worrying. Still, a day didn't go by that I didn't think of my children. I couldn't help wondering how they were, and if Chuck was taking proper care of them or not. I hoped they weren't crying themselves to sleep at night, missing me—the way that I was missing them.

Four months passed, and I was no closer to finding my children than I had been in the beginning. It was autumn, and school was already in session. That year, my son was supposed to have been in the second grade. I wondered if Chuck had enrolled him.

One evening, my sister called to tell me that she had a new boyfriend. He sounded really nice, but the important thing that she'd wanted to tell me was that he'd told her that there was an opening in his office for an entry-level assistant. Stacy was happy with her job at a large electronics firm, but she told me that she'd thought that I might be interested in the job.

"I certainly would be," I told her. "What kind of a company is it?"

"It's a collection agency," Stacy answered. "I don't know what the salary is, but it would be more than you're getting at the store."

I went down the next day and applied for the job. To my surprise, I got it. I started working there two weeks later.

Stacy's boyfriend, Duane Phillips, introduced me to everyone. Most of the people were friendly, and I liked them right away. One of the biggest advantages to the position, I soon found, wasn't the pleasant working conditions, or even the increase in pay. It was the chance I had to learn firsthand about some of the investigative techniques that the company used to find missing people.

I kept my eyes and ears open constantly, trying to pick up any ideas that I could use in tracking Chuck. One of the things I learned was that people were often traced through their occupations. Since the only job that I was sure Chuck had held was in a garage, I didn't know if that would help me much. I also discovered how important persistence was, and that paying attention to the tiniest clue could sometimes end a search successfully.

One of the men in the office, Garrett Rizzoli, seemed to go out of his way to be friendly and helpful to me. I asked him so many questions that, one day, he commented on my curiosity.

"Are you thinking of opening your own collection agency someday, Francine?" he teased.

"No," I answered honestly. "But there is someone I want very much to find." I found myself telling him about Chuck and about my children.

"Let's have lunch together," he said when I finished. "Maybe I can come up with some ideas that may help."

We went to a little coffee shop around the corner from the office. As we slid into a booth, I noticed several women at nearby tables glancing over toward Garrett. I didn't really blame them. He was really good looking, but not in a flashy way. There was something about him that exuded quiet confidence. He seemed like he could handle almost any situation well.

We ordered and then we started to talk. That lunch hour flew by.

Garrett didn't come up with any magic way for me to locate Chuck, but he did mention several possibilities that I hadn't considered. One of his ideas was that I should check with the elementary school where Mark had attended kindergarten and first grade. I could find out if a transfer of his school records had been requested, and if so, where the records had been sent.

I called the school as soon as we got back to the office, but the secretary in charge of records told me that Mark's file was still there. I asked her please to notify me right away if such a request did come in.

I felt a little discouraged as I turned away from the phone. Then I looked up and saw Garrett in front of my desk. He smiled at me.

"It's just the beginning, Francine," he murmured encouragingly. "We're going to find your children."

During the weeks ahead, some of Garrett's confidence began to rub off on me. Even Christmas, which could have been a very bleak time, wasn't so hard to face. Garrett and I had begun to see a lot of each other by then. We spent Christmas Eve with his large, friendly family, and we had Christmas Day dinner at Mom and Dad's. Seeing Christmas trees and presents did bring some tears to my eyes, but I kept reminding myself that one day, Mark and Katie would be with me again.

My parents had really liked Garrett, and the more I'd got to know him, the better I liked him, too.

On New Year's Eve, we went to dinner at a very special restaurant, and as we drove back to my house afterward, Garrett glanced over at me.

"It's going to be a happy new year for you, Francine," he said with certainty.

"You knew what I was thinking, didn't you?" I asked.

He nodded. "I've really got a good feeling about this year ahead—a feeling that—"

"Garrett," I interrupted, "have you learned something new about

32

Chuck? Something that you haven't told me?"

"No. But, somehow, I just know that we're getting closer," he told me.

"Oh, I hope so!" I whispered fervently, closing my eyes.

That night when he kissed me, he took my face in his hands. "There's something that I've been wanting to ask you, Francine, but I'm going to wait until we have your life straightened out—until we have you children back where they belong. Then—well, then I hope that we can plan our life together."

I realized at that moment that I had fallen deeply in love with Garrett. It had happened so quietly and so naturally. There had been none of the fireworks and intensity, the urgency to grab a happiness now—the way that there had been for me as a teenager with Chuck. Instead, it was a much more satisfying, more enduring kind of feeling. And, knowing the type of person that Garrett was, and after watching him with his own nieces and nephews, I was sure that someday he'd make a good father—not only for Mark and Katie, but also, for any children that we might have.

Still, just as Garrett had said, before we could begin to plan our future, we had to find Chuck—had to bring Mark and Katie home to me. And, in spite of Garrett's confidence, I lived with the constant fear—fear that made me wonder if that was ever going to happen.

Then, one day, Garrett casually dropped something on my desk. I'd thought that it was some routine form that he wanted me to file. But when I'd picked up the paper and glanced at it, my heart had begun to race. It was the copy of a credit application to buy a used car, and the purchaser's name was Charles F. Keating! The birthdate that was listed was Chuck's, too! I looked at the address and saw that Chuck was living in a small city in a nearby state.

I could never remember how I'd finished doing my work that day. All I could think of was that soon, I might see my beloved children again.

"What do we do now?" I asked Garrett that evening.

"Maybe it's time to talk to an expert," he suggested. He asked me if I still had the name and the telephone number of the man my lawyer had told me about—the man who helped parents to recover their children.

I nodded, and Garrett handed me the telephone.

The man's name, Mr. Warner had warned me, was an alias that he used to protect his identity, so that I wouldn't actually even know who he really was. It seemed as though I was stepping into a whole new world of intrigue, but if it meant having Mark and Katie with me again, I was willing to walk through fire.

I dialed the telephone number that I had been given. Then, I waited.

After several rings, the telephone was picked up and man's voice answered.

"Hello?" he said.

"Hello," I began hesitantly. "Is this Samuel Eldard?"

"Yes," he answered.

I took a deep breath, and Garrett reached over and gripped my hand.

"My name is Francine Keating," I explained, "and I have two children who have been missing since last spring."

The man who called himself Samuel Eldard asked me several questions. He also explained that if he did become involved in recovering my children, I would have to agree to accompany him on what he referred to as the "grab."

By the time I hung up, it had been agreed that since Garrett and I weren't absolutely positive that Mark and Katie were still with Chuck, we would go first to the city where he was living and assess the situation. If we were able to get a glimpse of the children, or to learn, somehow, that they were there, I'd been instructed to call Mr. Eldard again.

Just before we had ended our conversation, Samuel Eldard had asked me a question that I'd considered rather strange.

"What color hair do you have?" he wanted to know.

After I'd described my appearance, he had advice for me.

"Go out and buy yourself a wig," he ordered. "We don't want your former husband recognizing you and possibly getting out of town, so be careful."

I bought the wig the following day, and the next weekend, Garrett and I drove to the city where Chuck had been living. The address turned out to be in a bad neighborhood.

Besides the wig, I was wearing a hat and dark glasses. We drove slowly past Chuck's address but except for a parked car—not the same one that Chuck had been driving when he'd taken the children—there wasn't much to see. Still, just knowing that Mark and Katie were probably right there in that shabby little house caused filled me with anxiety—and hope.

"We're in luck," Garrett said suddenly. He'd just spotted a for sale sign on the house that was located almost directly across from Chuck's.

We got out of the car and knocked on the door. When the owner answered, we pretended to be prospective buyers.

The man and his wife were happy to show us around, but the whole time that they were pointing out special features, Garrett and I were keeping one eye on the home across the street. Garrett kept stalling, asking a lot of questions.

"I've noticed that you don't have any children," he said finally. "We have a seven-year-old boy back home ourselves. The first thing that he'll ask is if there are many kids his age around here."

"Oh, sure," the woman assured us. "In fact, there are a couple of kids right across the street, aren't there?" She turned to her husband.

"Yeah, I think so," he agreed. "Of course, my wife and I both work during the day, so we don't see much of the neighbors."

Garrett nodded and thanked them for showing us their home. "We'll talk it over," he told them. "Maybe we'll even stop back and have another look."

Back in the car, he was just starting the motor, when, suddenly, I reached over and gripped his arm. The door of the house had just opened, and the man who had stepped out was Chuck. He got into his car and drove off. Garrett and I looked at each other. Did we dare go over there on some pretense? Finally, Garrett decided to chance it.

I stayed in the car, slumped down in the seat with the hat pulled down over my eyes, while he went up to the door. He knocked several times before the door was opened by a woman. I couldn't hear what Garrett was saying, but I saw him gesturing toward the home with the for sale sign, and I guessed that he was again playing the part of a prospective buyer seeking more information about the neighborhood. The woman shrugged. Then she turned away from Garrett for a moment to yell something over her shoulder.

A few minutes later, Garrett was back in the car, and we were driving away. I was anxious to find out if he'd discovered anything, but I was almost afraid to ask.

He waited until we were on the main road before he turned to me jubilantly. "I saw Katie, Francine! Your little girl's there! And I heard a boy's voice from one of the other rooms."

"Are you sure that it was Katie?" I asked hesitantly, almost afraid to hope.

"No question. She looks exactly like her pictures. The woman called her some other name, though, when she turned around to yell at her."

All at once, it was too much for me—the tension of the past few days, seeing the place where Chuck was living, and then, hearing news of my precious children for the first time in so many months. I cried as though I'd never stop. Garrett pulled off the road and put his arms around me.

"It's almost over," he whispered. "It's almost over."

But, now that we were so close to getting the children back, I was terrified that something might happen. Maybe Chuck would suddenly decide to move, and we'd have to start tracking him down all over again. Or, maybe Samuel Eldard would back out—he hadn't actually promised to help me, after all.

I called Samuel Eldard as soon as we got back home that evening. He questioned me at length about the area and about Chuck's house. Did we know if the children were ever allowed outside? How far was Chuck's house from the main highway?

Not sure that I was answering everything correctly, I finally handed the phone to Garrett. He spoke to Mr. Eldard for several minutes, then he gave me the receiver again.

"I'll tell you what, Ms. Keating," Mr. Eldard said. "I'm working with a man in Los Angeles right now who's trying to recover his son, but as soon as I'm finished with that job, I'll see what I can do for you. In the meantime, mail me a couple of good, clear color photographs of your children, all right?"

It was almost another month before I heard from Mr. Eldard again. During that month, I'd celebrated my birthday. Under the circumstances, I would have just forgotten about it, but Garrett had insisted that I have a cake. His present to me was a diamond bracelet, along with something that brought me both smiles and tears—a wiggly, affectionate puppy.

"The puppy's really more for Katie and Mark," Garrett explained. "He'll be sort of a welcome-home present waiting here for them."

A few minutes later, as I blew out the candles on my cake, my one wish was that before too much longer, Garrett, Mark, Katie and I— and the puppy—would be together as a family.

Finally, the night arrived when Garrett and I drove to the airport to meet Samuel Eldard's plane.

I watched anxiously as the passengers disembarked, wondering which of the men was Mr. Eldard. He had a photograph of me—one that had been taken with Katie—but I had no idea what he looked like.

A few minutes later, a man walked up to where Garrett and I were waiting.

"Ms. Keating?" He held out his hand. "I'm Samuel Eldard."

I shook his hand. There was something that I liked about him instantly. Maybe it was his friendly smile, or his intent eyes that seemed to miss no detail. Anyway, for the first time in weeks, I relaxed a little and felt that maybe everything would turn out all right, after all.

On our way back to my house, though, curiosity got the best of me. I couldn't help asking him why he'd ever gotten started doing that kind of work.

"I've got a boy of my own—somewhere," he explained. "After my divorce, I was awarded custody, but on one of her visiting days, my wife took Jimmy and ran. She's been running ever since. I tried going through the courts to get him back. I found out soon enough that it didn't work. Then, I hired private detectives. The last I heard, she'd taken Jimmy out of the country. Since then, the trail's been stone-cold. I still haven't given up, though. I figured that while I was waiting, I might as well help other people." He paused. "Besides, it keeps me from going out of my mind."

The next evening, Samuel, Garrett, and I were riding in a rented van toward Chuck's house. I was, once again, wearing my wig and hat.

Samuel was driving. He parked a few miles from Chuck's house.

"You two might as well try to get some sleep," he suggested.

I was far too excited to sleep, though.

At the first light of morning, we drove to Chuck's street. By then, Samuel had attached a special decal to the side panel of the van. To any casual observer, Samuel, wearing a work uniform complete with a belt of dangling tools, was a worker driving a company van. He pulled up near Chuck's home and Garrett and I crouched out of sight. Samuel pretended to be doing some work on the street.

As the morning wore on, the waiting became almost unbearable. Hour after hour passed. My legs developed an ache because of the cramped position I was in. We could hear the occasional clank of Samuel's tools, along with his cheerful whistling. We were waiting for the whistling to stop—a prearranged signal that would mean Samuel that had spotted my children alone outside the house, and that we would have, as he'd put it, "a clear shot at them."

At noon, Samuel got back into the van to eat some of the lunch that I'd packed before leaving home.

"What if Katie and Mark don't come out at all today?" I asked nervously.

"Then this road is going to have a lot more work done on it," Samuel answered as he took another bite of his sandwich.

"Or, what if just one of the children comes out?" I persisted.

"Then we wait for another day," he told me.

Samuel went back to his work, whistling again.

About an hour later, the whistling stopped abruptly. Hardly daring to breathe, I reached out for Garrett's hand. Then, according to the plan of action that Samuel had outlined for us, Garrett moved up to the driver's seat and started the engine, while I quickly let myself out the rear of the van.

A moment later, Samuel was thrusting a struggling Mark into the van, and I was pushing Katie through the door, too.

"It's Mommy," I kept telling her. "It's Mommy, honey."

Both children were frightened and crying, but there was no time then to comfort them. With Garrett still at the wheel, we were driving as quickly as we could away from the house. Once we felt that we were a safe enough distance away, he pulled the van over to a gas station. Samuel jumped out long enough to peel off the decal that had been attached to the side panel of the van. At the same time, I pushed back my hood and slipped off my wig.

"It is you," Mark said in amazement.

Katie just whimpered softly and nuzzled against my neck.

Then I was crying—tears of happiness running down my face.

Soon, we parked the van and all of us got out. Then, we climbed into another rented car and headed for home.

When we finally crossed the line into our own state, all five of us sent up a loud cheer. It had been an agonizing nightmare, but my children were at last safely back home.

During the last few miles home, Mark and Katie and I started singing, and, pretty soon, Garrett and Samuel joined in.

The children and I would be getting out at our house. Then, Garrett was going to drive Samuel to the airport, where he would try to get a seat on the next flight home.

Before I got out of the car, Samuel turned to me. "You know, I have helped in many recoveries. Each time, when the job was finished, I've felt good—felt that the right parent finally had the kids. But, I have to tell you, I've never before felt quite as good as I do right now."

I leaned over and kissed him on his cheek. "Good-bye," I said softly, "and good luck in finding your own son. We'll remember you in our prayers."

"You do that," he answered.

Then I went up the walk to our house, a child on each side of me. We would have a few hours alone to get reacquainted before Garrett would join us for dinner.

The puppy proved to be an instant hit. I had held off naming him, and within five minutes, Mark and Katie had decided to name him Boomer.

They ran off to explore their rooms, and laughed when they discovered that most of their clothes had become too small.

Garrett, when he arrived, was wise enough not to push for a close relationship with the children too soon. Even still, it didn't take many days before they started to warm up to him. By the time Garrett and I were married a few months later, they loved him almost as much as I did. At last, we were the close, happy, complete family that I'd wished for that day when I'd blown out my birthday candles.

Of course, there were still problems. The experience that the children had been through during those months when they were away had left scars. They both had nightmares. And, both refused to go to sleep without a light on in the room. Katie was wetting the bed—something she hadn't done since she was a baby.

Garrett and I didn't press them for details of the life that they'd had while they were living with Chuck, but bits and pieces came out sometimes in their conversations—the almost-constant moving from place to place, the hiding, the threats, the strange women, the fear that they'd felt, especially when Chuck had been drinking. Mark had missed out on many months of school, and that made him feel sad.

I hoped that, gradually, with our loving care, most of their bad memories could be erased. I was sorry that we'd had to put them through that final, frightening ordeal to get them back the way we had, but I'd honestly felt that I hadn't had any other choice.

What I did regret was that I had been forced to become involved in cloak-and-dagger tactics—forced me to take the law into my own hands. I was just thankful I that I had been fortunate enough to meet and fall in love with a man like Garrett, and to have him beside me every step of the way.

Suddenly, I looked again at the newspaper photograph of the frightened mother whose little girl had been kidnapped by her ex-husband, and my heart went out to her.

How many of us are there? I thought. How many heartsick parents? How many emotionally scarred children? I was afraid that the answer would be staggering.

Just then, I glanced up from the paper to see Katie padding down the hall toward me, rubbing her eyes.

"Mommy," she said as she crawled up onto my lap, "I looked in your bed, and I couldn't find you."

"You weren't frightened, were you?" I asked.

"Well," she said sleepily, "at first, I was scared that maybe somebody had thrown you in a car and taken you away. But, when I woke up Garrett and asked him, he told me that you were probably just out here making pancakes."

I blinked away the tears that had suddenly come to my eyes. Then I hugged my little girl, set her down, and took out the pancake griddle.

We smiled at each other. Maybe someday, the bad memories would be gone for good.

THE END

BRAINWASHED
BY HIS MAMA

Peggy's eyes stared straight into mine as she said, "Kathy, I've got to warn you about something. You know that I dated Dave once and that he's one of the best-looking guys here in Seaford Park High School. But I have to level with you. Dave's a brainwashed Mama's boy!"

"Oh, come on, Peggy," I said, knowing what she said was sour grapes. "Dave's a great guy! We've dated enough for me to know that he's not a brainwashed mama's boy."

Peggy rolled her eyes. "Don't forget that I warned you. I was at his house for his birthday. His mother made sure I knew about her tight bond with her son. She laid it on thick, telling me how she'd held Dave day and night while he was teething, then when he had the flu, again when he had colds. On and on, she sounded like the only mother in the world that took care of her 'teenage baby boy' Dave, plus her other doting kids, Charlene and Jennifer. They've all been trained to believe their mother is a wonder woman. She told me her kids would never be far from her to pay her back for all she's done for them."

"You're kidding," I said, wondering if I should be careful. I'd watch for signs of Dave being brainwashed—but I was almost sure that Peggy was exaggerating out of jealousy. I'd heard she was crazy about Dave and he'd dumped her. Her words were sour grapes. So I smiled and said, "Thanks for the clues, Peggy. I'll watch out for them and let you know."

Of course, I had nothing to tell her. Dave told me he was crazy about me and his steady phone calls and attentiveness showed it. I felt such a warm glow when he held me close that I knew it was love. And nothing would keep us apart—ever.

Time flew and Peggy and I drifted apart. She started to go out with a guy who was good in English. So he helped her in that class. In fact, Peggy and Tim got married right after high school graduation. By then, Dave and I were talking about getting married, too, as soon as we could get jobs and afford rings.

I have to admit this. Dave's mother was demanding. Sometimes when we wanted to go to a certain movie, she convinced him that one she recommended would be better. "The critics raved about it being one of the best," his mother insisted, her sharp tone persuading Dave.

"No use going to a mediocre movie when we can see a better one," he said.

40

"I heard that the one we first chose was good," I said, but I saw his determined face. And I sensed he wouldn't go against his mother.

He never admitted his mom influenced him. But I sensed he wouldn't buck her opinion. But it made no difference what movie we saw. I wanted to be with Dave. That counted most to me.

In the dark theater, Dave reached for my hand and held it tightly, kissing the back of my hand every once in a while. Then he'd lean closer to me and whisper that he could hardly wait to marry me—I whispered the same to him.

As Dave's mother's pressures on where we went and what we did intensified, we hoped that the surprise baby boy, Joey, that Dave's parents had, would replace Dave in his mother's possessiveness. But it seemed to only add to her need to hang on to all her children. Joey was a beautiful baby, and I was happy for the family. They'd been blessed, or so I'd thought then.

Then the last shoe dropped. I was heartbroken when my parents announced that my father was being transferred by his job. We'd move a month after I graduated from high school! I couldn't imagine being separated from Dave.

When I told him the news, Dave grabbed me close, kissed me hard, and didn't let go for the longest time. "I can't let you go, Kathy. We'll get married as soon as possible."

My parents frowned on my staying behind, alone in a little apartment. "You'll end up living together, Kathy," Dad said. "It's better if you get married because one look at you two and anyone could tell you're going to get married, anyway."

Mom nodded and smiled. I guess she was glad to move to a new place. Both my parents were adventurous. They'd often said they wanted to live elsewhere someday when I was grown. Now was their chance.

My parents packed their belongings, and I packed my bags and rode the bus to New Townsend. I'd assured my parents that the rest of my things were packed and at my friend Carly's house. She'd send them to me, or Dave could take them when he drove to join me in New Townsend, where we'd be married in a small ceremony by a Justice of the Peace.

I used my baby-sitting and part-time grocery store job savings to pay my way. I also had graduation gift cash. I could afford to rent a hotel room for a couple of nights until I found a room with kitchen privileges in one of the converted mansions in the city. I'd received good grades in high school. I was confident I'd be hired quickly as a secretary.

And I was. I started as a secretary at an insurance company two days after I'd moved to my tiny room with a hot plate and sink plus a bath I shared with another tenant.

Dave came to New Townsend to find a factory job two weeks later. He'd been delayed. His parents wanted him to find a hometown job. His mother had cried and begged him to stay at home.

Dave sighed. "It was hard to see her sob, Kathy. She's been the best mom a guy could want. I promised that after our wedding at City Hall here, we'd visit them often."

"Often?" I gasped. "We'll work all week and drive back and forth often to appease your mom? Parents need to grow up just as much as kids need to grow up, Dave."

Dave's arms came around me and he gazed at me with his shimmering eyes. "Honey, I love you more than anything. It won't hurt us to give Mom attention until she gets used to us being a couple. Her demands will fade out. You'll see. Someday, we'll have time for only each other."

"Honey, if that's the case, get me out of this plan," I said. "I got myself a nice job in a modern office. I like my furnished place. I don't need to be your wife. Go home and be a good mama's boy!"

He stared at me, frowning, and I knew how right Peggy had been. But I didn't tell Dave what she'd said. I'd denied it too long to start believing it aloud now. It was my mistake and my secret. I knew one thing—I refused to become my mother-in-law's puppet. And I told Dave.

"You won't have to be a puppet of any kind, Kathy." He shook his head and I started to think he was changing.

"Are you sure, Dave?"

"We'll be on our own when we're married. I'll visit Mom once in a while and you can stay here on that weekend. You can go to the mall, shop, and relax then."

I smiled, relieved, and hugged Dave. I felt new trust in our future. I was glad that Dave's dad hadn't tried to run our lives. He was okay.

Dave and I had our blood tests, applied for a wedding license, and made the date to be married by the local justice of the peace. We had a quiet wedding dinner together after leaving the office.

That night we slept in the furnished apartment Dave had found and I moved my things there the following day.

Being married was like playing house. We got up early each weekday and went to work. Whoever got home first started our supper. We ate, cleaned the kitchen, took a walk, and came back to watch a TV program or two. Then we went to bed, clung to each other as if we might wake up from a dream, and then made passionate love in our own romantic world.

"No couple loves each other like we do, Kathy," Dave whispered, his breath warm on my ear. And I whispered back the same sweet love words.

I felt dismay when we had to go back to Seaford Park for Jennifer's wedding. The reception was a huge party at the country club. Dave was the best man at the wedding. His mother and father visited with the crowd, mingling like celebrities.

I was given no special place to sit during the reception and Dave was busy fulfilling his best man duties. So I sat alone, waiting for time to fly, so we could leave.

One of Dave's aunts later came to sit by me on her way to the restroom. "I can't stay long. The gang's waiting and our table's crowded. Otherwise I'd have you come and sit with us, Kathy. Just hang on with patience. Dave's mother hangs onto her kids with hooked tentacles. Most women take good care of their babies. So why does she think she's the Queen Mama on earth? Don't let her run your lives, Kathy. Tell Dave his favorite aunt said that, okay?"

"Okay," I said, smiling at her as she walked away.

By the end of the long, boring evening while I sat alone except for a few of my old friends—who reminded me that Peggy had warned me—I was ready to spit nails. Why had I been excluded from the family table? I'd learned my lesson. I'd ask questions before agreeing to anything like this again.

But each time after that when I reminded Dave of his mother's claws on us he said, "Someday we'll be free, Kathy—even if we're old and gray-haired."

That was a grim thought—to spend my young adult life in bondage.

After we were back in New Townsend, life was wonderful again. Dave and I realized our love was more precious than anything. He said he'd try to appease his mother from her pressures about us visiting more often than we could afford.

But before he could do anything about that, Dave was given the chance to get training for a better job at the plant. He was sent to a nearby state to a factory for the instruction. I'd have to stay alone. So I'd make the best of it.

I went to the library for books to read. I baked muffins and put them in the freezer. I'd surprise Dave with his favorite blueberry muffins when he got home.

On Saturday afternoon of the first weekend Dave was gone, I needed to go out for a while to relax at the nearest mall. I'd eat lunch at a fast-food place and read the small magazine I kept in my purse.

When I got back to our red apartment building, Dave's parents were standing by the front door. They glared at me as though I'd been at an adulterous tryst somewhere.

"Where were you all day?" his mother said in an accusing voice.

His usually friendly father shook his head. "You young people can't sit still for a minute. Too much trouble staying home in case your husband calls?" he said.

"I work all week and have a right to go to the mall. Who else would shop for us?" I felt confidence in my rights despite their frowns.

"We left Joey with Jennifer so we could come without him. We wanted to surprise you because you're alone this weekend but no, you had to be gone!" his mother added. "Now it's too late to take you out for lunch and we're getting back on the road in a few minutes."

"If you'd planned to drive here and back in one day, why didn't you call me? I'd have shopped tomorrow," I said, trying to sound patient despite their accusatory attitude.

His parents shrugged. "Oh, well," my mother-in-law said. "We tried. Well, we've got to run!"

I watched them hurry down the walk toward the parking lot. I sighed with relief that I wouldn't have to listen to more accusations about my running around. On the other hand, it was nice they'd come and hoped to pleasantly surprise me. So I called as they were opening the car doors, "Thanks for coming!"

We drove to visit Dave's family two weeks after he returned from his training session. His mother squealed with delight and hugged him. His father vigorously shook his hand as though Dave had come from the battlefront overseas.

I made the best of it. I didn't have to stay there long. I'd called some of my high school friends to meet for coffee and pie at a diner.

The minute my friends and I gathered in the booth, Diana said, "I heard something about you."

"Whatever did you hear all the way from New Townsend?" I chuckled.

"I work at the flower shop and Dave's mother was in there, telling my boss that you're a restless young woman. They got a sitter for Joey and drove to New Townsend to surprise you. And you weren't even home, even though your husband was away at a training school. She sounded so upset with you."

"What?" I gasped. "I was shopping and I dared to stop for lunch and read my book while eating. Wow! Big sin!"

"I'd be upset with her," Laura said as Diana nodded.

Finally, we changed the subject and talked about fun things for a while.

When I got back to my in-laws', I told Dave about the gossip his mother had spread at the flower shop and his eyes widened. "I'm going to tell her what you heard," he said.

Then I worried that Diana would lose her job or get into trouble for telling me. So I asked Dave not to say what I heard or who said it, but that it was gossip about me being restless.

Dave's mother shrieked. "I didn't say that!" But her face reddened and I saw guilt in her vivid eyes. Dave glanced my way and I sensed he'd also sensed her guilt but he kept silent. True to form, he was still Mama's brainwashed puppet.

After that we didn't drive to our hometown as often as in the past. Dave said we still had to honor his parents. "Someday we'll have time only for each other, honey," he said.

I shook my head. "If only I'd known this sooner I'd have said no when we exchanged wedding vows. I would've said 'No way!' and run!"

"Come on! You wouldn't have done that." He pulled me into his arms and smothered me with kisses until we stopped fussing about anything and just melted into our own little world.

That lovemaking could've been when I got pregnant with Ria. As soon as the doctor said our baby was on the way, we shopped for a crib, high chair, and other baby needs. Joy sang in my soul. Being pregnant was the happiest I'd ever been!

We had our baby girl late one December night when the snow was falling in huge, fluffy flakes. The snow again fell in fluffy flakes right after Ria's second birthday. It layered the ground in a white blanket as we packed the car to go home for Christmas. I'd agreed to go because my parents had mentioned the possibility of being in town, too, if they could drive from their new home in the time they had to spend on the road. In the end, they had to cancel the trip. But Dave, Ria, and I kept our plans to travel, anyway.

Just before Christmas, Ria, Dave, and I rode along the snowy highway heading toward Seaford Park, over three hours away. Dave's parents expected us to be there even though they wouldn't be alone. Their daughters and their husbands would be there.

As we rode, my thoughts settled on little Joey. I cringed, thinking about my four-year-old brother-in-law. I'd heard from Diana that Joey was whispered about as a spoiled brat. He'd never been told, "No." Whatever he did was fine with them.

Joey was their idol, so to speak. During past visits, I'd needed to guard our Ria from being harmed if Joey had a tantrum if he wanted what Ria held. The last time we'd visited, Joey had grabbed Ria's cookie after eating his.

Dave reprimanded his little brother. The entire household at the family reunion had shouted at Dave for being "mean" to Joey. "He's just a little boy!" they had complained.

"Joey's a nice little boy, I know," Dave had said. "But he's not nice when he takes what isn't his. He can't go through life taking what's not his. I was told 'no' when I was a little kid."

"That's because your crabby kindergarten teacher sent a note home and said she would expel you from school if you didn't sit still. We had to say no to your peppy ways and insist that you listen to your teacher—even if we thought she carried things too far."

"So that's why you insisted I listen to her every day. I remember that!" Dave had replied.

"Now we don't need to be so strict. Joey's our baby, Dave!" his mother had crooned, cuddling her youngest.

My thoughts faded as we rode and "Silent Night" sounded on the car radio while softly falling snow whitened the countryside and the evergreens flanking the highway.

Ahead of us was a small, black car that suddenly swerved and careened into the opposite side of the road and into the ditch, creating a huge snow spray.

"Dave! Oh, let's hope no one got hurt!"

By the time we braked along the road and Dave headed for the car, the driver was getting out, his expression dazed.

"I'll take you to the hospital. You should be checked," Dave called.

The man shook his head and said, "I'm stunned. Must've fallen asleep at the wheel. It's a good thing I'm alone and didn't get hurt. Could you drive me to the nearest town?"

The nearest town was a half-hour back. The man wanted to pay us, but we felt relieved he wasn't injured. The night before we'd heard the Christmas Eve sermon that it was more blessed to give than to receive.

Dave and I agreed we didn't mind the "detour" we had taken. Ria had looked shy when the man got into the backseat, but soon they both looked relaxed.

We were delayed reaching Seaford Park after taking the man to the local police department. We smelled baked ham as we entered the back door to Dave's parents' kitchen. His mother's expected "Merry Christmas" was silenced with a frown.

Instead, she snapped, "You're late! So you missed out on most of the food. We thought we'd finish it up since you didn't think it was important to let us know if you were coming here or not!"

We had no cell phone and there were no roadside phones along the long forest-flanked stretch of highway we had traveled. We'd thought that Dave's parents would be concerned about our lateness and we'd hoped they hadn't worried. Instead, we'd been reprimanded!

Charlene, Jennifer, and their husbands glared at us, too. Their silence revealed that we had been discussed with disdain before our arrival.

Wow! Merry Christmas to you, too! I thought as my stomach squeezed.

Dave, in his usual, tolerant way about his parents' demands on him and their leniency toward his little brother, stayed silent. Instead he smiled and greeted everyone before explaining that we'd helped a man in a car accident.

46

Silence hung in the air like thick fog. Then, after long moments, one of my brothers-in-law said, "Sure, sure, car accident helper. What else can you think of for an excuse?"

Everyone laughed. I tightened my lips and stared at Dave's face, waiting for him to defend himself. But he shrugged and said nothing.

"It's a good thing we were on that lonely highway to help that man!" I said.

Everyone laughed. "Sure!" Fred said until Charlene poked him in the side and I got the idea she thought her husband's heckling had gone too far.

When Dave changed the subject and said we were going to look for a restaurant because we were hungry, his mother agreed to open some canned spaghetti for us. "Everyone was so hungry and so the small ham's gone already. I didn't want leftovers. So I made sure I didn't make a lot of everything. I plan to bake frozen pizzas for supper. And I've got ice cream in the freezer to go with the ton of cookies I baked."

My head ached from stress and hunger. So the spaghetti plus the leftover cole slaw tasted good. Before we finished the cookies for dessert, though, Dave's sister Jennifer announced that we were all going to go to visit friends of their family that evening. They lived on the next street. "We promised to go and look at their tree. They'll have coffee and fruitcake for us."

"I promised Ria we'd watch the video she got for Christmas," I gently replied.

"Oh, she can see that anytime!" Jennifer snapped.

I gave Dave a pleading look that told him to help me explain it was important that we keep our promise to our daughter. The video only took a half-hour or so. We'd stay behind and view it. The others could go on to visit the other family.

But Dave said we'd go with them to make a holiday visit. "They're nice people," he said. "And we were late today—so we'll make up for it by going with you tonight."

Feeling defeated and refusing to let them ruin the day, I excused myself and took Ria to the bedroom. I told her Christmas stories until her eyes closed for her nap. She listened to every word with such shining joy in her eyes that I felt the day had been rescued for the two of us.

I stayed in the bedroom and rested next to my child. I recalled that for four years I'd gone along with Dave and did everything his parents' way. He'd convinced me that they were not as young as they had been and we had plenty of time to do our own thing later on, anyway. He always said we wouldn't get to visit his family when we had more kids and it was too hard to pack everything and travel.

I had understood and agreed. But now I was convinced I'd been too submissive to keep the peace. I asked myself if it was fair that our plans and Ria's video viewing that everyone could enjoy for a half-hour had to be cancelled to conform to the others' plans. Ria and I'd watch it after the others had left that evening.

I must have fallen asleep, because I woke up and Ria was gone. I sat up and heard my daughter's sharp outcry, then silence. I raced to the next room to see Joey hitting Ria with a metal toy truck.

"Stop that!" I screamed, pulling him away from Ria, who sobbed as her right cheek dripped with blood.

Dave had rushed into the room, too, and found me standing over Joey. The boy glared at me because I'd yelled at him for attacking Ria.

"What do you think you're doing, Joey?" Dave shouted.

The rest of the family came rushing into the room, defending Joey. "Don't be so hard on him! He's just a little boy!"

No one cared that our child had been injured. Shivers crawled over me and I sensed future conflicts. I had seen Joey clenching his teeth and jealousy glint in his eyes as he was hitting Ria as I rushed up to them.

Dave and I held and comforted sobbing Ria. I'd expected Dave's family to hover over Ria to find out why she was bleeding. Most people would feel concern over an injured child they encountered on a playground or anywhere. But it became apparent that Joey's freedom to do as he pleased was stronger than Dave's family's concern over their granddaughter and niece.

Dave and I tended Ria's scratched cheek and she whimpered that the antiseptic stung. But she quieted as I cuddled her close and assured her I would stay with her.

I asked Dave to spend time in the bedroom with us. We could salvage the day's peace if we were together to recuperate from the conflict. But Dave refused.

"I can't just ignore everyone!" he said. "You and Ria rest. I'll visit for the three of us, okay?"

I didn't reply. I was too exhausted from the day's emotional upheavals. Ria and I rested on the bed while everyone else chattered and laughed in the kitchen. I felt utterly alone in the world with our Ria. I missed my parents, who were four states away. I felt abandoned by Dave.

On what should've been a festive visit, Ria and I had needed refuge in the chilly bedroom. As Dave talked and laughed with his family, I felt defeated. He seemed unable to shelter us from his mother's demanding plans. Weren't we enough to visit with? Why were plans made to go to another family's house? Why couldn't they visit them at a different time?

I pulled a blanket over Ria and myself. She soon fell asleep. I remembered his mother's unkind gossip about me because I'd been shopping when she had surprised me in New Townsend that Saturday. My patience broke and melted away like ice cubes in the summer sun.

Suddenly, I could no longer take Dave's mother's brainwashing of him any longer. I had to escape. I couldn't stay here where the very air seemed filled with hostility to me. I was an outsider, even an intruder, in my mother-in-law's mind. Dave's father had been friendlier, but now even he seemed like her puppet.

The house silenced after everyone left. While Ria and I viewed her video, I felt so tense that I might not relax or even sleep if I didn't get away.

When the video ended, I packed our things, then left a note on the kitchen table: Ria and I are driving back to New Townsend, Dave. You can get a ride home. I merely signed my name and walked away, holding Ria's hand.

During the drive back to New Townsend along the highways flanked by holiday lighted homes, the car radio sent forth carols. As "Silent Night," filled the car and Ria slept in her car seat in the back, I hummed along, feeling peace I'd not felt for a long time.

Back in New Townsend I felt continued peace and knew I could no longer take another day as part of Dave's family. I was so glad I still worked part-time at the office. I would find another part-time job if need be. I was glad to have my trustworthy sitter. I looked in the last newspaper we had in the house, found some apartment rental ads, and hoped to find one I could afford. If I divorced Dave, he'd be paying child support. I knew he'd do that without protest. But a stipulation I'd insist on if I decided on the divorce would be that Ria would not be left alone with his parents. I couldn't trust them to protect Ria from Joey's apparent jealousy of his little niece.

I found an inexpensive apartment where I got a discount for being willing to accept the rent payments of tenants. The managers, Artie and Sandy Humphrey, said it would be a help to them. I felt my self-esteem rise when they said they had checked me out and had reason to believe I was trustworthy.

The divorce went through easily. Dave had protested and begged me to stay with him. He held me close and I felt his warm tears mix with mine, but he couldn't promise to put his mother in second place. "She held me day and night so often when I was sick as a boy. She said she'd have died rather than putting me down alone in a bed. I owe Mom allegiance, Kathy. Please don't be jealous of her."

"Jealous?" I shrieked with surprise. "Jealous? She hates me. She claimed you at birth and she won't let go until she's in the grave. I'm too young to wait. I won't wait for anyone to die so I can have a happy marriage, Dave! I'm willing to work and raise our Ria alone."

After many similar talks, it boiled down to a choice between putting his mother first in his life or me, his wife. His demanding mother came first.

The divorce came through and Ria and I stayed close. But I promised I'd never put a ball and chain on her. I'd guide and love her. I'd take her to church and have her attend Sunday school. She would learn the values I'd learned from those sources and from my parents.

Ria visited her daddy and he was good to her. He kept his promise not to take her to his parents' home without his supervision. Joey often got in trouble at school because he disobeyed the teachers. I sighed with relief that Ria received good reports from her teachers.

I dated some of the single men who worked in my office or from other offices in my building. I enjoyed dating but none became serious. I was grateful for the peace in my life. I attended movies with friends, went to cookouts where Ria and I were invited, and enjoyed the suppers I hosted to reciprocate. I also took classes to enhance my job skills as Ria grew old enough to stay alone one evening a week. My daughter's life and mine were ordinary but happy.

Ria and I realized we liked to sing, so we both joined our church choir. Ria liked to sing so much I provided a good voice teacher for her. Ria did her best in school and wanted to become a music teacher or a singer.

Suddenly, she stopped getting invitations to go places on weekends with her father. Ria sighed. "I don't think Daddy feels well, Mom. He's got a poor appetite and seems so tired all the time."

"He's probably working hard and could be under pressure from his family, Ria. He's probably getting a needed rest. He'll call you soon, I'm sure," I said and Ria agreed.

Then I got the news from a nurse at a local hospital that Dave was a patient there. "Your ex-husband asked me to phone you. He hopes you'll visit him here." I agreed to visit as soon as possible.

Ria and I drove to the hospital the following evening. Shock reeled in me when I saw Dave's pale face and sunken cheeks. We were shocked and heartsick to learn he had been diagnosed with terminal cancer of the stomach.

"When were your parents here last, Dave?" I asked, noticing how forlorn he looked.

During the pause before he answered, recollections of my former love for him flowed back into my soul with renewed caring. Compassion filled my eyes with tears as regret over our wasted years raked over my emotions like claws. We'd missed out on so much together!

In faint words between long pauses, Dave said his parents had visited. "But Mom couldn't take seeing me like this. She had to leave.

She said it broke her heart. She said she'd try to come again soon."

"I'm glad you asked the nurse to call me, Dave," I whispered, leaning over him, kissing his cool cheek.

Ria leaned over then and kissed his cheek, too. With tears glistening in her eyes so much like her father's she said, "I love you, Daddy, and always will!"

Ria had told me several times that she knew her father loved her but was unable to be a live-in father like her friends' dads.

Ria and I stayed until the end of visiting hours and promised to visit again soon. On our way out of the hospital, Ria asked for a status report because she was his daughter and still a family member. She was told that his doctor had noted in the record that Dave had from two to four weeks to live.

Ria and I visited Dave every evening. She and I wept before and after visiting him. But at his bedside, we tried to sound upbeat with our love and concern for him.

Then one evening, Dave whispered as he gazed at me with loving eyes. "I wasn't there for you but you're here for me. Thanks. I love you, Kathy. I love you, Ria."

Ria told her father she loved him and urged me to take my turn to visit alone as she sat back.

So I leaned over Dave and whispered, "I love you, Dave. I've always loved you."

I opened my mouth to say, You told me we'd spend our older years together but needed to give our young years to your mother. Now look where you are!

Instead, I silenced those words and whispered, "You and I were special together. Dave, when we fell in love we had a beautiful, early married life together. I did love you, my dear Dave." My heart swelled with pity as the surging waves of the old love, revived. I swallowed the lump in my throat as I blinked away tears.

I pressed my lips to his cool cheek and let my kiss cling and soak through his being. It was my fervent blessing on our young love's memories.

Dave died the next morning—and Ria and I went to his funeral in Seaford Park. Charlene came up to me, hugged me hard, and whispered in my ear, "You were the love of Dave's life. I'm so sorry it was ruined. I've changed. Would you visit me sometime? I'm alone now, too. Fred left when he couldn't take Mom's pressures any longer. Did you know that a month ago Joey was killed in a car accident? He was speeding and hit a tree."

I hugged Charlene. "I'm sorry, and I didn't know about Joey. Yes, Ria and I'll visit you."

As my daughter and I walked away, I felt sadness tug at the wasted lives that possessive people like Dave's mother could cause. She'd been rejected as a girl when her father abandoned the family. It could be why she'd become so possessive.

While driving back to New Townsend, I prayed God's healing for Dave's family. I also prayed that Ria and I would have health and happiness in the future.

That was two months ago. In my new life chapter, I realized that lanky, cheerful Dylan, a caring man at my job, has taken more interest in me than ever. And I've felt surges of romantic caring for him, too.

When I told Ria how I felt about Dylan, she smiled. "Daddy would want you to be happy, Mom."

"He'd want your happiness, too, honey."

"I'm happy with my life, Mom. I know you want me to have a good life now and always. We've both learned from our hard times."

Our hard hug punctuated our words.

THE END

HANDYMAN HUNK
He was the special of the day!

M_y feet ached, my head hurt, and the noises from clattering silverware, glass, and dishes aggrivated my already shot nerves. Two tour buses had arrived at the restaurant where I worked right at lunch time, and of all days, we were short one server. So Barbara, Peggy, and I tried to handle our regular crowd and the tourist group. They were a loud, jovial, gabby—and grabby—group.

When the last of the tables were wiped off, I went back to the kitchen. I was taking a break no matter what. Almost all the customers had left, so I made a glass of iced tea and went back out to the dining room. I sat at the back table and put my feet up on the opposite chair. Relief for a busy waitress is resting your feet.

The restaurant was a quaint café with rustic wood walls decorated with an odd assortment of hanging plant baskets. Antique odds and ends sat here and there. It was a nice place to work.

Our only problem was room. When we had a crowd like today, we ran over each other trying to get our orders in and out of the kitchen.

So Bobby, the boss, was tearing out a wall and rearranging our serving station. He was waiting for the lunch crowd to leave so he could get a couple of construction workers in there to work afternoons after we closed.

The door opened and in walked a couple of guys wearing leather tool belts. I thought: Must be the workers. They walked straight to the back where I was sitting.

The one in front was nice-looking with a bright smile. "Bobby around?"

I nodded. "I think he's thanking the cook for doing extra duty today." The guy winked as the two men walked by and pushed the door open to the kitchen.

I glanced at the other guy. He was good-looking, too. He looked my way for a minute but didn't speak or smile. I went back to my tea and enjoyed a few more minutes with my feet up before I finished my duties for the day.

That night I dreamed I was at work. Something disastrous happened and before you knew it, I was in the arms of the construction worker. His arms felt good around me as he whispered his attraction for me and that he would keep me safe. His warm breath sent shivers through my body.

Thankfully it was just a dream. I wasn't ready for anyone in my

53

life. Three months ago, my husband walked out, leaving me for a younger, different woman. I say "different" because she didn't appear to have a brain in her head. Jacob hated when I tried to talk to him about something other than beer, football, or his work. I guess the new girl knew to keep her mouth shut—or she didn't have anything to say. I wanted conversation. I yearned for a companion who sometimes thought of me, my needs, my wishes, my dreams. Jacob sure wasn't it. He was, I found out during our marriage, a pretty boring guy.

The next man, if there was one, would have to be interested in something besides the basics.

By work the next day, I'd completely forgotten the dream until I turned to get a tip from a table and the hunky construction worker was staring straight at me. I felt my face blush as though he could read my mind and see the image I'd dreamed.

I turned away quickly and got busy back in the kitchen. I couldn't help thinking that his eyes and that blue work shirt he had on surely looked good together.

Bobby came out of the back, where supplies were being unloaded, and looked into the dining room. "Oh, good. Mike and Ron are here. I guess they can get started with that other wall today." He winked at me. "You're going to like the new station."

I smiled back. Bobby was the best boss you could work for. He was really understanding about the hardships and hassles that came with the job. No one was ever allowed to pick on us or he'd be onto them in a snap. And he did his best to see to it that we got good tips.

"So Mike and Ron are their names?" I asked.

He nodded. "Mike's quite a joker. Don't fall for any of his stunts. He loves to tease."

"Mike's the taller one?" I asked.

"Yes," he said, and then he clammed up.

"What about Ron?" I asked.

"What about him?" he snapped back. His eyes grew hard. "You stay away from him."

"Why?" I asked.

He didn't answer. He just looked at me as if to say: Don't question me on this.

I finished up early so that I could head downtown to shop. By the time I closed the door, Mike and Ron were hammering away.

My car had been giving me trouble, so I'd put it in the shop. I'd planned on walking to the service garage to get it, then drive out to the superstore to shop.

But when I got to the garage, the mechanics were still working on it.

"Sorry, we've been backed up. You can wait a while and see if we can finish it today."

"I'll come back later. I can shop downtown." So I walked to the downtown stores, picking up some things from the drugstore that I had to have. I hated paying extra when I could've bought them cheaper at the superstore, but by the time I got my car it would be too late to drive out there and back.

I walked with the bags back to the garage.

The head mechanic came out with a sad look on his face. "Donna, I'm sorry. But we're going to have to find a new part. You can't drive it like this."

He saw the look on my face. My tiredness was hard to hide.

"I'll have one of the guys drive you home."

"What about work in the morning?" I asked.

"If you can't find someone, I'll take you myself," he offered.

By the next afternoon I hoped my car troubles were behind me. I told Bobby about my car and that I was going to walk to the garage to get it. Bobby barely heard what I said. He and Mike were studying the blueprints for the new area.

Ron heard me, though. "I'll run you down there," he said.

I remembered what Bobby had said about Ron, but I didn't see how any harm could come from accepting a lift in broad daylight. Besides, my feet were exhausted from all the extra walking I had done the day before. "Okay," I said.

We hopped into his construction truck. He moved papers and a hammer out of my way and tried to brush away some of the dust. It struck me as a sweet gesture.

As we drove, he began to talk a little. When Mike was around, Mike did all the talking. I realized that I had not heard Ron speak. His voice was deep and sexy.

I didn't know what Bobby's objections to him were, but he seemed just fine to me. I trusted Bobby and his judgments on most things, but maybe this was a woman thing that he didn't understand.

"What's wrong with your car?" he asked.

"Bad starter at first. But when they tore into it, something else had to be replaced." I smiled and added, "There's always something else."

He drove me to the garage and said, "I'll wait around. Make sure it's ready."

I went inside where the mechanic assured me that I was ready to roll. I told Ron he could go on.

"Why don't I follow you home? Make sure you get there all right," he said.

"That's not necessary. I'm sure I'll be fine. Thanks for the ride."

I pulled out of the garage and headed down the street to my house. When I checked my rearview mirror, there was Ron's construction truck following me home.

A bit of fear ran through me, all based on what Bobby had said. Was there a problem with the guy?

I was a bit nervous pulling into my driveway, letting him know where I lived. But this was a small town and if you wanted to find someone, you could without a whole lot of trouble.

He pulled to the curb and parked. Then he came up the drive.

"See, I made it," I said. I trembled from nervousness. What was he up to?

He nodded. "Let me take a look at the car. I just want to make sure everything's okay."

I got out and let him in, watching the muscles in his leg as he slid into the front seat. I wanted him to hurry up and leave, but I said, "I'm sure it's fine. They've done work for me before now."

He got out and smiled. "It looks fine to me. But you can't be too careful."

"Thanks again for the ride," I said as I turned toward the front door.

He nodded and walked off.

Tomorrow, I'm having a talk with Bobby, I told myself. What is it with this guy? He seems just fine to me, but Bobby is serious about him. Too bad the good-looking ones always have a terrible flaw.

The next day at work I tried to say something to Bobby, but either he was busy or I was.

The workers came in at the close of lunch and sat down to talk to Bobby. I could feel Ron looking around for me. It made me both nervous and excited.

Other than Bobby's warning, I could see nothing wrong with the guy, and he was really sexy looking. It was hard not to stare.

I finished work and headed home without ever talking to Bobby.

No matter, really, I told myself. It's not like Ron's going to ask me out or anything.

But he did. Late that afternoon I was sitting on the front steps of my porch watching the sun set and sipping coffee. This was my time to relax. It became a retreat for me after Jacob left. I did a lot of sitting and a lot of soul-searching, wondering if the divorce was all my fault—which is what Jacob said—or if the marriage had been a mistake right from the beginning. I think I was so infatuated with Jacob I didn't see the selfishness, the immaturity, the slob in him, all the things I was thankful each day to be rid of.

The little clues I saw I explained away. I made excuses for him. I, in my mind, erased what I didn't want to see, and enhanced, and even created out of nothing, things I did want him to be.

In the end, Jacob was two different people—the person he really was and the person I made him out to be. How many times did he say, "I'm not like that," "I don't like that," and how many times did I say,

"Oh, you're just saying that to get to me?"

He never wanted a nice home to live in. When I started shopping for furniture, he'd say, "We don't need that. We can't afford that." And so year after year passed with us living like paupers. And that was just one of our many differences.

I was shaken out of my daydreaming by a car pulling up out front and stopping.

Ron got out, dressed in clean, neatly pressed jeans, a white shirt with the sleeves rolled up, his hair neat and combed back.

My heart stopped, then began to pound hard.

"You look really busy." He smiled.

I couldn't help but smile back. He sat down beside me.

"What are you up to?" I asked, completely nervous.

"I heard I could get a mean cup of coffee here," he said, looking over into my cup.

"Wait right here," I said. I ran inside and got a tray. I poured him a cup, freshened mine, grabbed a pitcher of milk, the sugar bowl, and a plate of cookies. I carried all of that back out to his surprise.

He said, "I didn't mean for you to go to any trouble. I just wanted a cup of coffee."

"No trouble," I said.

He tasted the coffee and said, "I heard right. A good cup of coffee."

"Where did you hear that?" I asked.

"Oh, you can't keep a thing like that a secret. Serious coffee drinkers like me have a nose for the best coffee."

It was hard not to look into his eyes. There were tiny creases around them. The sun had bleached strands in his hair. Had he been on a beach, you would've thought he was the sexy lifeguard.

My senses were heightened. I wanted to flirt, but Bobby's warning caused me to be more reserved. After all was said and done, that reserve was the best thing that could've happened.

"I take it you're not married," I asked.

He shook his head.

"Ever been?" I asked.

"Yep," he said. "For a while. But it's over." He leaned back. "You?" he asked.

I smiled at him. "You're thinking my husband is going to drive right up and be perfectly happy about me serving coffee to a total stranger."

He laughed. "I resent that. I'm not a total stranger."

"Almost," I said.

"Let's fix that. How about having dinner with me tomorrow night?" His eyes were so intense, the question so seriously asked.

I said, "Yes."

I wanted to talk with Bobby before I went out with Ron. I wanted to know what he meant when he said that I should leave Ron alone. But once again, the next day at work was too busy.

Okay, I told myself, what can happen at a restaurant?

I certainly wasn't going to put myself in a dangerous situation with him on a first date. Ron picked me up at seven o'clock, and we went out for Chinese. We ate and talked. Ron asked me a lot of questions about what I liked.

It seemed we both liked to read thrillers. Jacob never picked up a book in his life. He thought reading was a waste of time. Like getting drunk was a positive use of his time, energy, and money?

We liked antiques. He was refinishing an antique kitchen table to use in his dining room. He already had the chairs. "You should see them sometime," he said.

He wasn't much interested in watching sports. "If I get that still, I fall asleep." He laughed.

By the time we were standing on my front porch, I felt I'd gone out on my first real date with an honest-to-goodness, grown up real man. Everything had been play acting for the real thing.

I thanked Ron for a wonderful evening. He thanked me. Our eyes locked. He seemed a bit hesitant, then kissed me softly on the cheek and said, "Good night."

I mumbled, "Good night," barely able to speak. I went inside feeling like I had gotten off the planet I'd been living on and onto another one—a richer, sharper, more vibrant world where every whisper and breath was magical.

What could Bobby have meant? Oh dear, I hope it's something petty. Please let it be nothing, I thought as I went to sleep.

"You did what?" Bobby exploded. "I told you, Donna. Stay away from him. He's bad news. If you want to go out with someone, I'll fix you up with someone nice."

"I don't want to be fixed up with anyone. We had a nice dinner together. That is all. But I want to know why you don't like him."

Bobby took a deep breath. "He beat his wife, Donna. Only the sorriest of the sorry would ever strike a woman. And if he ever did that to you . . ." He didn't finish the sentence. He just shook his head.

I felt sick. Ron seemed so nice, so gentle, so caring. There was not a hint of that anger in him.

When he and Mike came in, I kept myself busy finishing my duties, then I slipped out the back door, unable to face him.

My planet got tilted back into its ordinary state, only this time the air was thicker than before. Just when I think I've met someone interesting and sweet, I have to find out he has a dark side. While I certainly didn't want to mess up my life and my newfound independence with a loser, there still was something about Ron that I couldn't let go of. Were my senses that wrong that I could get mixed up with a second creep?

The next day I went to Bobby and asked, "How do you know that Ron hit his wife?"

"My wife knows them. During the divorce, his wife said he beat her. He didn't bother to deny it."

"Did she press charges?"

"No. She just said she wanted out. I figure she was afraid he'd really come after her if she made it any worse." He started to leave, then he added, "To be perfectly honest, we thought he was a really nice guy. But when Alice came home and told me that, well, we both lost complete respect for him."

"But you don't know for a fact he did this, right?"

"He didn't deny doing it, Donna."

Late that afternoon I was back on my front porch with my cup of coffee when history repeated itself and Ron pulled up. I had a feeling he would. And I had a feeling we had to get this settled between us.

"Was my company so bad you couldn't stand to see my again?" he asked.

"No," I said. "It's just that someone said something to me about you, and I thought we needed to get something straight." I didn't mention Bobby by name because I didn't want him involved.

"Okay," he said. "Shoot."

"Did you abuse your wife when you were married to her?" I just came right out with it. I guess having gone through my divorce and being on my own had also made me less subtle than I would've been before. I figured there was no need to beat around the bush.

He looked at me for a moment. "What do you think?"

"Personally, I don't see it. But this person said you didn't deny it, either."

He looked down for a moment, rubbed his hands together, and wiped them on his knees.

"I'm going to tell you this because I like you. I enjoyed the other night. You're the first person I've asked out since my divorce. I really didn't think I'd ever be interested in anyone again."

He took a deep breath.

"Okay, here goes. I didn't hit my wife. Not ever, not once. I don't hit women, or anyone else, or anything. She hit me. She'd get angry over my being five minutes late or not pushing the closet door completely shut, and off the handle she'd fly. I never knew what would set her off. She had an uncontrollable temper. When she said she wanted a divorce, frankly I was relieved. I didn't care what she said or to whom. The legal grounds were irreconcilable differences. What

59

she said to people, I didn't care. People who know me know better.

"So, no, I didn't deny it. And no, I never hit her—not even to defend myself. I usually just got away from her and left until she cooled off."

I nodded. "Did she ever get any help? Sounds like she's mentally ill."

"I suggested it. But to tell you the truth, I think she likes throwing those fits."

"Wow," was all I could say. Then I asked, "Was she the jealous type?"

He nodded. "Oh, yeah. If I had my eyes open and a woman walked nearby, she'd claim I was staring at her."

"Where is she now?" I asked.

"I don't know, and I don't care. As long as she leaves me alone."

We sat there in silence a few minutes, then I asked, "Want a cup of coffee?"

Those eyes lit up like Christmas trees.

We made another date, but this time I decided to make him dinner. I'm a believer in the idea that the way to a man's heart is through his stomach.

I reassured Bobby that there wasn't anything to worry about. He'd have to trust me on this.

Ron and I continued to enjoy learning more about each other. The more we found out, the better. Neither of us wanted to risk being burned again.

One day I was having a busy workday. That station had been finished. Ron and Mike had moved on to another job. My time to see him was usually our evening coffee time on my front porch.

I'd taken an order back to the kitchen and was turning to go to the dining room when the swinging door popped open, right into my face.

A young woman wearing big, gold hoop earrings, a short red dress, and stiletto heels jumped right into my face. Her eyes were wide and her expression was full of fury.

"You leave Ron Henry alone." She shook her finger at me. "I'll tear you apart if you go near him." She backed me against the counter. "I know where you live, and you're dead if I ever catch him at your place again."

A knife was lying on the counter. She picked it up and held it in front of me. "Don't think I'm kidding." She glared at me, then threw the knife down just as the cook, Nate, had reached from behind to grab her. She stepped on his foot and was out the door in a flash.

Nate turned to me. "Want me to call someone?"

I shook my head.

"Who was that?" he asked.

"I'm not sure," I said, trying to get my breath. "I have a feeling she's an ex-wife."

"Ex?" he asked. "She didn't act like an ex. She acted like a current wife. You better watch your step."

Nate's words echoed in my ears the rest of the afternoon. She'd acted like a current wife.

You don't suppose, I asked myself, that woman is Ron's wife and they never divorced? No, I won't believe that about him.

But I did believe that was the raging wife. And I wondered just how violent she could get.

Later, as I sat on my porch with my cup of coffee, I thought about what had happened. Nate said I should report it to the police just in case she really came after me. There should be some record. But I had never had any experience with anything like that, and calling the police seemed drastic.

Ron's truck rounded the corner and he pulled into the drive behind my car. He jumped out with a smile on his face and walked to the porch, leaned down, and kissed me on the cheek. Then he sat down.

He looked me in the eyes and said, "I'm beginning to like this routine."

"Beginning to?" I asked, smiling at him.

"You know what I mean." He gave me a serious look. "Where's the coffee?"

I leaned over and dragged a tray I'd set behind the banister. There was a carafe of warm coffee and a plate of cookies on the tray.

"Hmm," he said as he smelled the coffee.

We sat there a few minutes enjoying the peaceful afternoon. I hated to break the soothing silence by speaking, but I did. I knew Ron was not going to like what he was about to hear. "Does your ex-wife have dark hair?"

He glanced over at me. "Why?" he asked.

"I think I met her today. Dark hair, big hoop earrings, short red dress, long, sharp knife."

"What!" he yelled. "Did she threaten you?"

"In a way. She said if she caught us together I'd be dead."

Ron shook his head. "That woman. What can I do? I hoped I'd seen the last of her."

I told him what had happened, about her showing up at the restaurant.

He turned to look at me. "Don't worry. I'll take care of her. But keep your eyes open just in case. To my knowledge she's never hurt anyone, except me, of course. But let's be safe."

I agreed that I would.

"Would you feel better if I stayed here with you until I can do something about her?"

"No, I'll lock up. If I hear anything, I'll call the police. Do you really think she might do something, or was she just raging?"

He shook his head. "I don't know. Let me call around and see if I can find out what she's up to. Frankly, I thought she'd moved away to start a new life. I'm surprised she's here."

The whole idea of someone I didn't know hating me enough to hurt me was hard to take.

The next day at work, Bobby was waiting for me. He said, "I want to see you in my office."

Barbara and Peggy exchanged glances and quickly turned to find some work to do. I guess they thought I was about to get fired.

Bobby closed the door. "Nate told me what happened. You know, I pride myself on running a good place here. I don't want things like that happening. If word gets out there are brawls here, I'll start losing business."

"I know. I had no idea who she was."

"I told you not to get involved with Ron Henry. Didn't I tell you there would be trouble if you started seeing him?"

"Yes, but I thought you were afraid he'd hurt me. You didn't warn me about the wife."

He sat down heavily in his chair and leaned back and took a deep breath. "I don't really care about the business. You know that. The main thing is I don't want you hurt."

"Ron's a nice guy, Bobby. He's very good to me. Everyone makes a mistake. I did. My first husband was a lost cause. Ron's first wife was his mistake. But you're wrong if you think Ron was at fault. She hit him, not the other way around. Surely you can see now which of them has a temper problem."

He nodded. "I suppose. We always liked Ron. It's just so unusual to hear of a woman trying to beat up her husband. It was easy for us to think he was the one." He stood up. "Is there anything I can do? I will keep an eye out for her. Next time, she won't get past the front door."

"Thanks, Bobby."

He waved his arm for me to get out.

Barbara and Peggy were waiting for me to say something. "Everything's fine, girls. I promise."

They didn't say anything, but they didn't believe me, either.

I couldn't understand why life had to get complicated. Here I was beginning to enjoy life again after my terrible years of marriage and divorce, and now I was dealing with something that was way out of my experience.

I guess being on my own had taught me more self-reliance than I'd known when I was married to Jacob. I was brought up to depend on a man, but that hadn't worked so well. Having lived a while now on my own, it bothered me that I was letting Ron take care of this. On my way home from work, I decided I didn't like having something so important, something that could have really bad consequences, being dealt with by someone else.

I turned around and headed toward the police station. I decided I was going to file a complaint or do whatever legal thing I could do. Nate was right. There should be a record.

I had never been inside the police station before. It seemed a pretty loose organization, at least at first. We have a small town where everyone knows everyone, and our crime rate is low. Small burglaries, people running stop signs, that sort of thing was the height of our crime.

I told the person behind the desk that someone had threatened me, and everyone in the room got very serious. The policeman who'd been sitting at his desk got up and came to the counter.

"Come back here," he said.

I sat beside his desk and began to tell him who I was and what had happened. He started nodding his head as if he heard that kind of thing all the time.

What goes on in this town that I never hear of? I wondered.

But he interrupted me. "Mr. Henry has already been in. He told us Mrs. Henry had threatened you. He wants us to keep an eye out for her. Rest assured, we're taking care of this right now."

I breathed a sigh of relief.

"It was good of you to come in."

I left feeling better—better that I had taken the initiative to take care of myself and better that people who were equipped to take care of these kinds of things were doing something about it.

That afternoon I sat on the porch and waited for Ron, but he never came. I was let down. I was so used to his coming that I had grown to like our routine, the comfortable way we sit and talk and share our day with each other. After it grew dark, I picked up the tray I'd prepared and went inside. I took the tray to the kitchen and went back to lock the door.

A car pulled up outside. I closed the door and locked it, then peeked out the window to see who it was.

A familiar figure came up the walk. It was Ron.

With relief I unlocked the door. He looked at me for a moment, then drew me into his arms. He kissed the top of my head and held me for a few moments. Then he said, "It's over. Chrissy has been taken to a hospital for observation and tests. Her parents convinced her that she needed help. I went to see them. And the police did, too. Her parents have known for a long time that she needed help. I think they've finally been able to buckle down and do something."

I relaxed. We stood there wrapped in each other's arms, feeling a closeness that promised a nice future.

Ron asked, "Is it too late for coffee?"

I shook my head. I know we're going to have a better go of things this time than either of us had before.

THE END

SECOND WIFE,
SECOND PLACE

I never knew that I could love a man the way
I loved Dave. He was the prince of my childhood
fairy tales—my knight in shining armor. . . .

When I looked into his eyes, I knew that I'd be lost forever in their passionate depths. But, with the love of my life, came one seemingly insurmountable obstacle—his ex-wife! They had ties that would bind them forever—most importantly, his children. I didn't see how I could possibly ever compete. No matter what I did, I knew that she would always be first in his heart. . . .

Dave wrapped his strong arm around my waist as we walked around the campground. It was beautiful there. It was our mystical, magical place—the place where our love was born. It was as though Nature had blessed our love by giving us such a breathtaking landscape. I sighed as I took in the wonder of it all. The water on the lake glistened like diamonds. The sweet-smelling breeze ruffled my hair. And the sun shone on the mountaintops, highlighting rows of majestic trees.

"Do you think you can handle the graduation tomorrow?" he asked, shattering my sense of calm.

"I can cope with anything you can," I said, forcing a smile.

Dave's oldest daughter, Melanie, was graduating from eighth grade. Since we lived so far away and he didn't see his children as often as he liked, we came to give special attention to his daughter.

"Just don't let Phyllis rattle you. You know how she can get to people."

Sighing, I nodded. From everything Dave and his daughters said, I learned that my husband's first wife could be very trying, indeed. In fact, she seemed to go out of her way to make things unpleasant for him whenever he visited the girls.

Luckily, I'd managed to avoid her as much as possible. In the two years since Dave and I had been married, I'd only seen her a few times and we'd exchanged very few words. So far, that was the way everyone in the family, including me, liked to run things.

We stopped to watch some galloping horses. I took a deep breath of the blossom-scented air. Dave wrapped his fingers around mine.

"Holly, you know I love you," he said.

"Of course I do," I said, brushing my hair out of my eyes.

He looked out over the pasture. "This reminds me of our love hideaway," he said.

Tears came to my eyes as I remembered our wonderful honeymoon. It seemed so far away compared to some of the family problems we'd been having lately.

Dave had built a camper with his own hands. An excellent mechanic and carpenter, he loved to putter in the garage. We'd been going together for six months when he announced that he had a surprise for me.

"Once we get married," he said, "this will be our little love nest away from home. We can take our honeymoon in it."

"Oh, Dave, it's wonderful!" I cried, climbing into the camper. Because we both loved camping, hiking, and nature, that type of honeymoon would be perfect for us.

The camper had a small sink, a stove, an refrigerator, and a small bed. Maybe it would be a little cramped for space, but if we were together, that's all that mattered. We'd spend most of our time outdoors anyway.

Our honeymoon was wonderful, so whenever we got too overburdened with stress in our lives, we'd head out into nature to what we called our love hideaway. Actually, the hideaway was anywhere nestled in nature where we could be alone together.

Breaking the spell, Dave said, "We'd better get ready if we're going to pick up the girls for dinner."

"Okay, hon," I agreed.

I might have sounded calm on the outside, but inside I was a catastrophe waiting to happen.

From the first time we met, there was some kind of jealousy between thirteen-year-old Melanie and me. Alyssa, his ten—year-old daughter, was cute, but she was definitely her mother's child. Melanie was more possessive of her father. I knew they'd both been hurt by the divorce, but I was still frustrated by their behavior.

Dave introduced me to his children about the time he showed me the camper. Realizing he still had some guilt and remorse about the divorce, I wanted to do everything I could to help them feel comfortable with us as a couple.

That first day his children and I met, Alyssa wasn't even at the house. "Mom didn't even tell Alyssa you were coming," Melanie said, "so I'll have you all to myself."

She stared at me, and I saw jealousy in her eyes. "I'm sure we'll have a wonderful time," I said. "We're going to get some fried chicken and take you out into the country for a hike."

"Dad usually takes us out to a restaurant," she insisted.

"We can do that some other time," Dave said. "If you know where Alyssa is, let's go pick her up. I'm sure she'll want to go with us."

As it turned out, we had fun. But I became aware of one thing—Dave was bending over backward to try to give equal attention to his girls. From then on, I usually stepped aside while they were together and let him lavish attention on them. It didn't really matter to me anyway, because I had him most of the time.

I thought things would get better in time. However, as we approached their house now, I suddenly felt a green monster rear up inside me. This was their house, the one Dave and Phyllis had lived in with their children. I hadn't had the experience of having Dave's child yet, and might never have, simply because he wasn't sure he wanted to start another family.

I stayed in the truck while Dave went into the house. I wasn't afraid of Phyllis, but I felt it was for the best if I saw her as little as possible. Melanie ran to the front door and hugged her dad. I felt a lump in my throat.

Oh, don't let me cry, I thought. For some reason, I didn't want to let myself be vulnerable around his children. Maybe I wasn't sure how they would accept me, deep down.

Melanie and Dave walked toward the truck. "Hi, Melanie," I said, forcing a smile. "Is Alyssa coming, too?"

Before she could answer, Alyssa came running out the door dragging a sweater. Melanie jumped into the truck, wedging herself between me and Dave. Alyssa jumped in on that side, too. The four of us just barely fit into the cab of the truck.

"How's your camper?" Melanie asked.

"Just fine," Dave replied. "Someday I might build another one. Gives me something to do and keeps me out of trouble. "

"Someday maybe I'll be a mechanic, too," Alyssa said. "Mom says I'm good with my hands."

"If you fixed a car it would probably blow up," Melanie told her.

"Would not," Alyssa retorted.

Dave pulled into the restaurant. "Look girls, I came all this way to see you and find out how you are doing, not to hear you fight."

Obviously, they were trying so hard to compete in his eyes. I thought it was sweet, and yet sad, somehow. And I was one girl who didn't want to be part of that competition.

After we ordered, Dave turned his full attention to the girls. "So, how were your report cards?" he asked.

"I did all right," Alyssa said. "But Melanie almost flunked history. Her teacher says she might have a hard time in high school."

Melanie glared at her sister. The competition kept up all the way through the meal. Melanie ordered five items on the menu and wasted most of the food. I did well to choke down a hamburger and a few french fries.

During dessert, I tried to find a common ground with the girls. "Melanie, do you like to sew?" I asked.

"No," she answered sullenly.

"I like riding horses," Alyssa interrupted. "Mom says I can get a horse if Daddy will give me the money."

After I choked on my water, my eyes met Dave's. With both of us working, we were still having a hard time making ends meet. That's one of the reasons we went camping instead of staying in a fancy hotel.

Dave snorted. "If you get a horse, you'll have to get a job to earn money to feed it and keep it at a stable."

"Maybe when I'm in high school," she said, disappointed.

Then Melanie dropped the bomb. "Mom says you're rich because you have a camper. She said she might need more money, but all she does is go out at night and leave me to baby-sit. I hate it."

I saw Dave's jaw tighten, but he didn't say anything. Phyllis had gotten to him through the kids again. By the end of the evening, we were frazzled. Dropping the girls at home, we returned to our love nest. Glad to be back at the campground, we snuggled together in bed.

Although Dave kissed me, he was more silent than usual.

"Are you worried about the girls?" I asked. "Melanie sounded upset."

He shook his head. "She exaggerates sometimes, Holly, so I don't believe everything I hear."

"Still, maybe we really ought to check it out—" I began.

Pulling away from me, his eyes glared with anger. "Don't go messing where you don't belong," he snapped.

The words stung me, and I turned away from him. I had learned early in our marriage that when he was in one of his moods, it was better for me to leave him alone.

Had Dave and Phyllis exchanged similar words while they were married? If so, they seemed to use the girls to further their fights. Suddenly, I felt sympathy for Melanie and Alyssa, who seemed wise beyond their years. My tears fell silently until I finally slept.

The next day, with my strength restored, I felt better. Dave and I cooked bacon and eggs outside on the portable stove. Hummingbirds buzzed up to the feeder, drank the nectar, then darted away. They were such curious, wonderful miniature creatures that we enjoyed watching them.

I resolved to try to get close to my new stepdaughters at least to find a few things in common with them.

"What does Melanie like above all else?" I asked Dave.

He laughed. "Boys, video games, and rock music, in that order."

I couldn't help smiling, too. Melanie was becoming a typical teenager, whatever that was. "I want to find something in common with her," I explained.

He hugged me close to him. "I'm sorry I was in a bad mood last night," he said. "Phyllis really knows how to manipulate those kids. Just give the girls a chance—they'll warm up to you in time."

Scrubbing the dishes in the small sink, I let out a long sigh. With the various personalities involved, the weekend held the potential of a bear hunt. But I was searching for something meaningful—a key to a relationship between the girls and me.

The graduation ceremony was long and drawn out. I could see the pride in Dave's eyes for his daughter. Phyllis, seated a few rows in front of us, kept turning around and darting us quick glances. Smiling in spite of myself, I wondered if she was more scared of me than I was of her.

When it was her turn to get her diploma, Melanie walked proudly on stage. She looked beautiful, like a real little lady.

Dave shook his head sadly. "They're growing up so fast, and I hardly get to see them."

After the ceremony, I took pains to avoid Phyllis, but Melanie cornered us and introduced us to some of her friends. They were all giggling about one of the boys in class who had tripped across the stage. When Alyssa ran over to join us, Phyllis glared at me. Was she jealous, too?

Then Melanie said, "Oh, Mom is having a barbecue party for me tonight. All my friends will be there and my aunts and uncles. Please, Daddy, say you'll come, too."

My stomach lurched. Dave looked at me, and I nodded. Going to the party would be rough for me, but it might break the ice between all of us. "Of course, we'll be there, provided Holly is invited, too," he said.

"Of course, she's invited," Alyssa said, giving me a tiny smile.

After they left, Dave put his arm around me and we walked out to the camper. "You don't mind going to the barbecue, do you?" he asked.

"No, I guess not," I said.

I would feel awkward meeting all the ex-relatives, but I supposed it wouldn't kill me for just one night. And, if we were outdoors, I could choose a corner all my own and concentrate on Dave and the girls.

That afternoon, Dave and I took a hike together. The girls had to help their mother get ready for the barbecue. I was glad for the break, and for the time alone with my husband.

Back in the camper, we nestled together and made love. Then, I felt I could get through anything that could possibly happen at the party.

When we got to Phyllis's house, most of the people were already there. Alyssa came running to us.

"Hi, Dad. Holly, I want to show you my new cat."

Laughing, I said, "I'd love to see your cat."

"I'll bring him out."

When she opened the door, a little dog ran out into the yard and jumped onto the guests. "Fluffy, get down!" Melanie yelled.

When Melanie hugged her dad, I longed for some sign of affection from her. To my surprise, she gave me a quick hug, too.

"I'm glad you came, too, Holly," she said.

Dave handed her a gift, and she tore the paper off. Dangling the watch I had picked out, she looked pleased. "It's beautiful. Thank you, Daddy."

"Holly picked it out," he said. "We're proud of you, Melanie. Don't be like your old man and quit high school."

She shrugged, then went back to her friends. Dave meant what he said, I knew, because his one regret in life was that he never got his high school diploma, even though he now had the equivalent and good vocational training.

Alyssa came out carrying a big, fat cat who looked like he was barely putting up with her sudden burst of attention. When he had enough, he jumped out of her arms. "Cinnamon doesn't like to be carried," Alyssa explained.

I laughed, while she added, "Do you like cats or dogs better?"

Uh, oh, that's a loaded question, I thought. "I like both about the same. But, right now, a cat might be better for us since we're both away all day," I said. Then I had a sudden inspiration. "Maybe when you and Melanie come to visit us, we can go hunting for a cat for us."

Alyssa beamed. "Sure, I'd love that."

Phyllis opened the door holding a tray of hamburgers. "Alyssa, don't be bothering the guests. I need you to put these on the grill."

"Oh, Mom, why can't Melanie do it?" Alyssa protested.

"Because it's her party. Now do as I say," Phyllis said firmly.

Alyssa grabbed the tray and headed for the barbecue. "I'll help you," I told her.

"Mom wouldn't like that because you're one of the guests," she said.

I helped her, anyway. After we were done, Dave introduced me to Phyllis's sisters and their husbands.

No one acted like there was anything out of the ordinary about me being there, and I began to relax. Playing with the animals and talking to the kids and relatives seemed to help, too. The only one acting funny was Phyllis, who seemed to be spending most of her time in the house. Part of the way through the evening, I noticed Dave getting moody.

"What's the matter, hon?" I asked.

"I have something to talk over with Phyllis. I'm just waiting for the right time, that's all," he said.

Uh, oh, I thought as he headed into the house. This could lead to trouble.

I couldn't hear what they said until their voices rose in anger. "Be reasonable, Phyllis. With what we're paying you, we can barely support ourselves. We can't even afford a house of our own," Dave said.

"I need it for the girls' clothing. A mother can't possibly support two children on such a meager income," Phyllis replied.

"But you're working, too. What are you doing with all that money?" Dave asked.

"Anyone who could afford a camper has plenty of money. I suppose I'll have to see a lawyer," she threatened.

Fuming, Dave came out the door. I felt like sinking into the ground. If she sued us, we'd be in debt for the next ten years. Phyllis glared at us through the window, while Melanie darted toward the door.

"You both ruined my whole party. I'll never be able to face my friends again. You'll be sorry when I run away," she said.

Dave tried to grab her, but she darted through the door, slamming it behind her. When we tried to say good-bye to Alyssa, she turned away, a sullen look on her face.

"Come on, Holly, let's go," Dave said.

We were quiet as we drove to the campground. If that was the way they fought when they were married, I could see why divorce was the only solution. Dave was moody through the next day and refused to talk about anything. When we got home to our apartment, I felt relieved. I could wash my hair and soak in the tub. In his mood, Dave would probably putter in the garage most of the night. I was glad, in a way, because I desperately needed to sort out my own feelings.

The fact that Dave cut me out whenever he was upset really hurt me. I wondered if Phyllis was really the monster everyone made her out to be. She was a human being, after all, with emotions just like me. And as a new stepmother, I wondered how much of the problem was my business and how much I should ignore.

The next morning at work, I still felt exhausted from all the emotional turmoil of the weekend. Sally, a woman I worked with, wanted to know all about the trip. She knew a lot about stepchildren, having coped with some of her own.

"Let's go sit in the park at lunch," she said. "Then you can tell me all about it."

Sally and I munched on sandwiches as I poured out the story of the weekend.

"Don't let his kids get to you," she said. "They can be more trouble than they're worth. In a few years, they'll be out on their own. Then they'll ignore you, you'll see."

"But they're just warming up to me," I said.

"They'll break your heart, if you let them. It's better to keep a reserve around you," she warned.

She launched into another story about how her husband's children almost broke up their marriage.

After lunch, I felt gloomy for the rest of the day. By five-thirty, I was exhausted. I just felt like going home and falling into bed.

My mother called after dinner. "Is something wrong?" she asked.

Mom was good at telling my mood from my tone of voice. Dave was in the other room, so I felt I could talk freely. I told her everything.

"Honey, things will straighten out in time," she said reassuringly. "Why don't you two come out this weekend? We can have a long talk, and Dave can play golf with your stepfather."

"I'd like that, Mom," I told her.

Dave liked my folks, so there was no problem getting him to go. After they left, Mom and I went out in the garden to transplant seedlings that she nurtured all spring. I guess that's where I got my love of the outdoors. I handed her a marigold plant.

"Holly, do you remember how you felt when I married your stepfather?" Mom asked.

I shrugged. "I didn't like it at first."

"You certainly didn't. You threatened to run away and everything. I couldn't understand your attitude, because you hardly even knew your own father when he died."

Tears came to my eyes. "I know. As a child, I figured he didn't love me at all so he left me."

"Your dad loved you a great deal. When he found out he had cancer, his biggest concern was leaving you when you were only a baby," she told me.

Tears streamed gently down my cheeks. "Oh, Mom. I hated my life for a while when I was a child," I admitted.

"Maybe that's how Dave's children feel." Mom held me as if I was a little girl again. We'd never shared those feelings before.

"I worried about you so much, honey, the way you're worrying about your new stepchildren. Like you, those kids will take time to adjust to the divorce and Dave's marriage to you. Children have a tough time accepting major changes in their lives. It took you three years to accept your stepfather, and then you went into your teenage rebellion."

Those painful teen years were vivid in my memory. Maybe that's why I felt so bad for Melanie. "I know, Mom. I'm sorry if I caused you and Dad a lot of pain," I said.

"Nonsense. You're our only child. When your stepfather adopted you, he felt proud to be your father."

Choking up, I couldn't say anything. The love and gratitude I felt for both of them flooded back to me.

"And all my worry was needless," Mom added, "because you turned out to be a lovely woman with a lot of love to give."

I suddenly realized what she'd been trying to tell me: I had to concentrate on my marriage. My relationship with Dave's children would fall into place, though it would probably take time.

When Dave and Dad came home, Mom fixed a special dinner of steak, baked potatoes, and salad. Since my stepfather had talked to Dave too, our mood was lighter than it had been all week.

During the next week, Dave and I acted like newlyweds— laughing, playing around, and making love. The kids were coming for the weekend, but I didn't worry about it. At work, I tried not to let Sally's negative talk get me down.

Melanie and Alyssa arrived on Saturday morning. At the bus terminal, they seemed shy and unsure of themselves. My heart went out to them. Maybe I could share more of myself. Perhaps telling Melanie about my own teen years could help break the ice between us.

Right away, Alyssa said, "Can we go cat hunting?"

Dave looked at me quizzically.

"We can look for a cat this weekend," I said. "If it's okay with your father."

When he nodded, Alyssa and I smiled with delight. Something was bothering Melanie, though, I could tell.

Dave took us to the animal shelter after the girls settled into the spare room. There were plenty of darling kittens to choose from.

Melanie picked up a kitten. "I want this one," she said. "It's just like one I had when Mom and Daddy were still together."

My heart jumped into my throat. I suddenly saw how destructive jealousy could be. Since Alyssa liked the kitten, too, we decided to adopt him.

"This will be your kitten when you come to visit," I told the girls.

The afternoon went smoothly, with us setting up a place for the kitten to stay. Between playing with the kitten and making dinner, we had a wonderful time.

After dinner, Dave wanted to change the oil in the truck. "I want to help you," Alyssa said.

Melanie turned up her nose. "Not me. Working on cars is messy."

"You can help me bake a cake for tomorrow," I said. "What's your favorite?"

"I like angel food cake because it doesn't make me break out," she said. "Are they hard to make?"

"Didn't you ever help your mother bake?" I asked.

"No, she doesn't like to cook."

As we set about baking the cake, I could hear the bitterness in Melanie's voice when she spoke about her mother or Dave. I knew the divorce had been hard on her, and it reminded me of my own feelings years ago.

I showed her how to separate egg whites from the yolk. After a few tries, she did it almost expertly. "You're doing a fine job. You have a good mind for following instructions," I said.

"I do? I sure hope that helps me get through high school."

"I'm sure you'll do fine," I said encouragingly.

The cake turned out beautifully, and I saw the glow in Melanie's eyes when I took it out to cool.

Alyssa and Dave were playing with the new kitten. "Look at the cake Melanie baked," I said.

"Hey, maybe you can cook, after all," Alyssa said.

When I tucked them in bed later, I sensed Melanie wanted to talk to me. "Has something been bothering you, honey?" I asked.

She looked over to see that Alyssa was already sound asleep. "Mom has a new boyfriend. She said when Daddy married you, he wouldn't care about us anymore. Now she won't either."

I shook my head. "Honey, nothing could stop your dad from loving you. When people remarry, it's because they love each other. But there's room in my heart to love you, too. You and Alyssa are part of your father's life."

Tears sprang to her eyes. So Phyllis had been filling them full of her own bitterness. Melanie hugged me tightly. "I hope you and Daddy have a baby brother for us soon."

"Who knows what time will bring?" I said. Feeling like laughing and crying at the same time, I left the room.

When I told Dave, he was delighted I'd made so much progress. "Your parents were right," he said. "If Phyllis could only see beyond her own hatred, she wouldn't have to fill them so full of bitterness."

Smothering him with kisses, I said, "It's time we forgot her and thought more about us. Melanie ordered a new brother."

"Oh, she did, huh? Well what does my new wife think about that?" he teased.

"I'd say it would be great, if we could swing it financially."

Dave smiled. "Well, I wasn't going to tell you until it was sure, but I may be promoted to foreman in the next few months. If that happens, we'll be able to think about a little one."

I saw such love in his eyes then that all the unhappy times in the last few months melted away.

The weekend ended on a happy note, and we were left with a kitten named Frisky. I could sense that the girls were both sorry to leave. Their sadness tugged at my heart.

"Call when you get there to let us know you're safe," Dave said.

When the bus drove away, they waved. I blinked tears from my eyes. "It's too bad the girls couldn't live closer so we could see them more often," I said.

"Yeah. Maybe I'll take that up with Phyllis," he said.

The phone call from the girls never came. Around ten o'clock, the phone rang and Phyllis's shrill voice almost burst my eardrum.

"You didn't send the girls back to me!" she cried. "What's the big idea? You can't kidnap them, you know, because I'll call the police."

"Calm down, Phyllis. We sent the girls on the afternoon bus. Didn't you meet them at the terminal?" I asked.

"I was a little late, I admit, but the girls were nowhere to be found."

I felt as if my heart stopped. "Oh, Dave! The girls are missing!"

Immediately, he grabbed the phone and started shouting. "Where could they have gone? Did you check the terminal there? Okay, okay. I'll check the bus station here."

After he hung up, Dave started walking toward the door.

"Honey, wait, I want to go with you!" I cried.

For a moment, he seemed to turn on me. "This is family business—" he began, then stopped. "Oh, honey, I didn't mean—"

But his words had cut me deeply. "I thought I was part of your family by this time, Dave. The kids are warming up to me, and they're my stepchildren."

"I didn't mean that. I guess it was a flashback to the old days," he said.

"I know you're hurting," I said. "But don't cut me out because of that. If we don't stick together as a couple, we might as well give up now."

"I'm sorry, Holly." He hugged me. "My relationship with Phyllis was so bad—we never shared anything. I guess I still have to learn how."

He pulled away from me. "I'd rather you stayed here in case they call," he said. "Maybe they just got off at the wrong stop."

For the next hour, I wrung my hands, waiting for some possible word. Had Melanie really taken Alyssa and run away as she'd threatened to do? Scrubbing the kitchen counter, I tried not to think about all of Sally's horrible stories about her own stepkids. Then, when I sat down, Frisky climbed into my lap as if to comfort me. The ringing phone jangled my nerves.

Dave's voice boomed over the line. "I think they found them," he said. "They got off at a station about an hour from here. One of the bus drivers kept an eye on them. I'll be by to get you in a few minutes."

"I'll call Phyllis," I said

We rushed to the station in Locustville. The girls were huddling in a corner. I hugged them warmly. "You almost scared all of us to death," I said. "You should have waited for your mother."

"We didn't want to go back to her," Melanie said.

"Melanie made me run away. I didn't want to do it," Alyssa sobbed.

Rubbing his hands, Dave was stern. "Melanie, why did you do this? You know how worried we all were."

"Like I said before, Mom is always leaving me to baby-sit, and I hate it. I don't want to live with anyone," she insisted.

We loaded them in the truck and drove another hour to meet Phyllis at the halfway point.

She was white as a sheet when she arrived in the restaurant. "Please, don't take my girls away from me," she said. "I couldn't help it if I was late."

Suddenly, my jealousy melted away. That tortured woman surely couldn't be any better than I was as Dave's second wife. I knew it was time to speak to Phyllis like a human being.

"We don't want to take the girls from you," I said. "They need you, too. But Dave would like to see them more often."

"Maybe you'd consider moving back to town," Dave added. "Then we could take care of them on the nights when you go out."

"I'll talk to the social worker," Phyllis said. "Maybe I could get a job there."

The girls smiled. I knew it was time to stand my ground.

"You know, Phyllis, filling these girls with bitterness doesn't do any of us any good."

"I didn't mean to harm them. I guess I've still got a lot of forgiving to do," she admitted.

"So do I," Dave said. "I can see how our fighting only confused and upset the girls. Maybe we ought to hang up our swords."

Since that day, there's a whole new way of thinking in our family. Broken families aren't easy to cope with, as Sally said. But there are a lot of joys, too—happiness that her negative mind fails to see.

A few months after our second honeymoon in our love hideaway, I found out I was expecting a child of our own. Melanie and Alyssa have curiously watched the physical changes in me. I hope they'll be delighted with their new brother or sister.

Phyllis is working on a move back to town, so we can see the children more often. She and the girls seem to have grown more positive now. Best of all, I learned I can be an asset in the girls' lives. And I don't mind that one bit.

THE END

OUR HUSBAND, MATTHEW
"It's a man's duty to have more than one wife,"
Matthew insisted, and I finally agreed. I married
him, not knowing how I really felt until I saw another
one of his "wives" going into his room. . . . .

Ben and I had been married five years and we were contented, if not ecstatically happy. We lived in a small town where the local mill paid Ben a good, steady salary. We had two children: Wesley, four, and Mary Ellen, two. If the gilt had been rubbed off our marriage, it was certainly no wonder: scrimping to pay off the mortgage on our small bungalow, plus the usual woes of everyday living, left little time for romance.

Ben's good-bye kiss each morning had become a hasty peck, and as I look back, I can hardly blame him. The smart-looking secretary he'd married had become a harried housewife and mother who rarely bothered even to curl her hair. As for Ben, it seemed to me he was always too tired for anything but wolfing down his dinner and growling if the children made too much noise. Occasionally, he drank beer with the boys in the evening, but he never spent his weekly check on a big binge the way some husbands did, and he never flirted with girls, although he was boyishly handsome and girls were always attracted to him. I had no real cause for complaint until he lost his job.

It was on a Monday morning when Ben came home and announced that the mill had shut down for an indefinite length of time. He looked stricken—lost! Ever since he had been old enough to work he had been employed at the mill, and he had fully expected to continue there, working himself to better and better jobs. Now, suddenly, he was a man without work—without a future.

He looked helpless, and without his moral and financial support, I felt helpless, too. Neither Ben nor I had ever faced a real crisis, and instead of facing the situation realistically, I tried to hide my panic by ignoring its seriousness.

"This is only temporary," I said cheerfully. "You can find another job to tide us over until the mill calls you back."

Ben sighed hopelessly. "I'll try, but the unemployment situation is the worst this country has ever known."

He did try, at first. Every morning he started out early with a look of grim determination on his face. Every night he came home silent and defeated. After a while he stopped going out at all—he said it was no use. It seemed to me he was giving up too easily, but at first I said nothing.

Gradually our savings melted away until six months later, I drew our last dollar out of the bank to buy food. There was a sick feeling in the pit of my stomach.

"Ben, you've got to do something!" I cried that night.

"What can I do?" he asked helplessly. "There just aren't any jobs. Lord knows I've looked."

"Well, if you can't find a job, suppose you run the house and I'll work!" I exploded. "I always found a job when I wanted one."

Ben's pride was stung and he flew into a rage. We fought long and bitterly, then he stalked out of the house. When he came home he was drunk.

He began to drink regularly, night after night. I stayed at home on those nights, sobbing bitterly, and blaming the economy for wrecking our whole way of life—for destroying our marriage itself.

I guess the climax came on the night Ben didn't come home until dawn. I lay awake all night, worrying for fear something had happened to him, and the more I worried, the angrier I became. By the time he came reeling home, I was fuming with rage. He stood in the doorway swaying drunkenly, his hair tousled, his face smeared with lipstick. My relief at seeing he was safe was smothered by the realization that he had been out with another woman. Again I had that sickening feeling of insecurity. I couldn't depend upon Ben for anything anymore.

"Sonia, don't be mad," he began. "It was only a little party. A guy has to have some fun during these gloomy days."

"Fun!" I shrieked. "You should see your face!"

Ben took out his handkerchief and wiped his face, embarrassed.

"Well, all right, there were some girls at the party. So what?" he said defensively. "All I get at home is nagging, nagging, nagging! Some girls understand that a guy needs a little sympathy and understanding and a few laughs when he's down and out."

I had a mental picture of Ben at a party telling pretty girls self-pityingly what a shrew of a wife he had. It hurt almost more than I could bear. I was seething with resentment and jealousy.

"So you admit you've been unfaithful to me!" I shot at him.

"Aw, honey," he said, "don't make such a big deal of it. I wasn't unfaithful at all. Maybe a little silly, but not unfaithful. I came home after the party, didn't I?"

"You're a little late remembering this is your home," I said bitterly. "We're about to lose this house, and you spend what little money we have on liquor and women! You don't care what happens to your family!"

"Now you listen to me!" Ben said furiously. "I'm not to blame for the economy. I can't help it if I can't find a job. It's a tough world out there—"

"Tough or not, it couldn't be any worse than being married to a lazy good for nothing like you!" I retorted.

The quarrel raged on for hours, but finally Ben put his hands wearily on my shoulders and tried to make peace. "Sonia, let's stop this and go to bed. Tomorrow we'll feel differently. We've both been under a terrible strain, but these hard times will be just a bad memory someday. Have some faith in the future—and in me. I'm sorry about the party. I've never loved anyone but you." He tried to kiss me.

"Don't ever touch me again!" I said angrily.

"Don't you love me at all anymore?" he asked, hurt.

"No! I despise you! You've destroyed everything our marriage stood for. You're a failure all around—as a provider, a father, and a husband!" It was the cruelest thing I could have said and I'd meant it to be. I wanted to hurt him as badly as he'd hurt me.

Ben crumpled up as if he had received a knockout blow. "All right," he said in a beaten tone. "So I'm no good. Maybe you and the kids would be better off without me. I'm leaving right now."

"Good!" I said hotly.

He stalked out of the house, and still furious, I went back to sleep. I expected he'd be home in the morning, but he wasn't. I waited that day and the next.

"Where's Daddy?" Wesley kept asking.

"He's gone away for a little while," I told him.

Another day passed, and I was weak with terror at the thought that Ben might not come back. By then my anger had cooled and I was aghast at the angry words I had flung at him. Fearful and contrite, I began telephoning friends. No one had seen him. By the end of the week, I realized that Ben had meant what he said.

There was no money in the bank! No money in the house. The grocery store refused to extend me more credit and a payment on the mortgage on the house was overdue. Tearfully, I bundled up the children and ran home to Mother.

She listened as I told my story, but she gave me no sympathy. "Ben's probably gone out of town to look for a job," she said. "I always liked Ben—and he's no quitter. You must have hurt him badly during that last quarrel, Sonia. A man needs someone to build him up during a time like this."

"You're always taking his part!' I said hotly. 'You don't know him like I do! He's no good, I tell you. I never want to see him again as long as I live!"

I paced the floor resentfully. "Mother, I'm going back to work. Will you take care of the children?"

"Of course. I'll do all I can to help you, Sonia. You can move over here with me, but you know all of Dad's savings were lost in bad investments. I'm afraid we'll have to go on welfare," she said.

"Mother, I'll find a job! I'd have too much pride to go on welfare," I protested.

"Work is scarce. You'll forget your pride when you and the children are hungry," she said grimly.

She was right. Ben had not exaggerated when he said it was a tough world. Conditions were much worse than I had ever dreamed. I went from office to office looking for work, and it was always the same: No help wanted! I saw with my own eyes the things Ben had told me about: rows of empty stores, relief lines, factories shut down, men begging for jobs with tears in their eyes, banks closed. There was a scared look in everyone's face. There seemed to be no hope anywhere.

During the next month, I knew real desperation. The bank foreclosed the mortgage on the house, and Mother spent her last penny feeding me and the kids. Pride was no longer important to me. We were hungry. I went to ask for welfare.

The welfare office was located in a long, bare hall with wooden floors and glaring lights. The air was sickening with body smells. Hundreds of people were standing in a long lines, and most of them, like me, hung their heads in humiliation. We were the newly poor who had never dreamed we would have to ask for charity. I stood in a long line and filled in some papers, and then I waited until I was called. A woman questioned me a bit sharply. It was almost closing time and I suppose she was tired, but she seemed so smug just because she had a job.

"Where's your husband?" she asked.

"I don't know. He deserted me. I only need a little help until I can find a job as a secretary," I said hoarsely, trying to save a little of my pride.

"We'll see if we can find housework for you," she said. "Secretarial jobs are scarce."

She handed me some food coupons. I shoved them into my pocket and left. Outside, I leaned against the building for a minute, tears filling my eyes. I was more miserable than I'd ever been in my life.

"They sure put you through the third degree, don't they?" a girl next to me remarked with a little nervous laugh.

"I'd rather die than go through that again," I said.

"Oh, you'll get used to it after a while," she said ruefully. "But those women behind the desk sure get me sometimes. They think they're so smart."

"They're just lucky, that's all. I'm a good secretary."

"I wish I could type," the girl remarked wistfully. "I heard a rumor about a secretarial job open. Say, maybe you'd be interested!"

My ears pricked up. "Where's the job?" I asked eagerly.

"Well, my boyfriend said he heard someone say that Perkins Printing was looking for a secretary, but they don't want to advertise because they'd have hundreds of girls storming the place. It seems the president, Matthew Perkins, is an old-fashioned, religious guy who won't hire a girl who drinks or wears makeup, so not just any girl will suit him. He sounds like a big pain, but what the heck—he needs a secretary."

"And I need a job!" I said.

The girl gave me the address. "Well, good luck," she said.

"Thanks—thanks so much," I called after her gratefully.

Later, I was to regret ever laying eyes on that girl, but at the time I felt my spirits rising. There was a ray of hope.

The next morning I dressed with special care. I wore no lipstick and combed my hair plainly. My shabby suit was neatly pressed and my blouse was clean and crisp. I tried to keep from trembling as I approached the office, located on the outskirts of town.

Inside, the office looked very prosperous, with modern furnishings and equipment. Telephones were ringing, and people scurried here and there. Business seemed to be good. Nervously, I entered the main office and spoke to the receptionist.

"I—I'd like to apply for a secretarial position," I stammered.

"Who sent you?" she demanded suspiciously.

"Uh—no one," I explained. "I just heard there was a job open. I have experience—"

"I'm sorry, we don't hire anyone except through recommendation," she interrupted shortly.

"I can give you good references," I offered.

"I'm sorry, but there's no position open here," she told me coldly.

"But could I at least leave my name—in case?" I asked pleadingly.

"We promote entirely from within the organization and there are seldom any vacancies."

My heart sank. "I've got to find a job!" I cried desperately. "I have two children and my husband deserted us!"

"I'm sorry," the woman said again, and her aloofness frustrated me beyond endurance.

"I've got to have a job!" I shouted, pounding my fist on her desk. "And I know there's a job open here! Why won't you give me a chance at it?" As I yelled, I suddenly remembered the stories Ben had told me of men begging, crying, and even fighting at personnel offices. And, there I was, doing the same thing!

Alarmed, the woman pushed a button under her desk, and almost immediately a man with an expensive suit burst out of his office.

"What's going on here?" he asked in a calm, pleasant voice.

"An outsider! Can't get rid of her!" I overheard the receptionist whisper to him.

They were going to throw me out! Suddenly, I felt weak and sick. That was the final humiliation. I buried my face in my hands and sobbed. Then I felt a heavy hand on my shoulder.

"Come to my office," the man's voice commanded me.

I followed him meekly. "Now sit down," he said. "I'm Matthew Perkins. What's the trouble? Can I help you?"

I sat across the desk from him and wiped my eyes. Then I took a good look at him. Matthew Perkins was strikingly handsome, and powerful looking. The power showed in everything—his shoulders, his chin, his strong, well-kept hands. It radiated across the room, even though he sat calmly, speaking gently.

Quickly, my embarrassment showing in every word, I blurted out my story. Matthew's eyes became warm and sympathetic as he listened.

"I know the employment situation is bad," he said, "but why do you need a job so desperately? I see you're wearing a wedding ring."

He drew out the intimate details of my life without seeming to be prying, and suddenly I was telling him all about myself. Matthew was so easy to talk to—so understanding! When I told him about Ben leaving me, he looked shocked.

"How could a man with any sense of responsibility do a thing like that?" he exclaimed, his voice rising with righteous anger. "He should be beaten!" Then he caught himself. "May God forgive me for raising my voice, but it's a husband's sacred duty to take care of his family."

In Matthew Perkins's censure of Ben, I found new excuses for hating my husband.

Matthew is a man who would never desert his family, I thought admiringly. I assumed he was married and had a family, although he hadn't mentioned it. He looked at me sternly for a moment, then he shot out a question.

"Do you believe in God?" he asked.

I gulped. "Why, yes, of course," I answered.

"Can you be trusted with confidential matters?" he continued.

"Yes, sir," I promised.

"Then I can help you. There is a job open here as my secretary. I need a mature woman without attachments who will be completely loyal to me. Would you like to work for me?"

"Oh, yes," I breathed, overjoyed. The salary he quoted seemed like a fortune! And I was working!

In the following months my life revolved entirely around Matthew

Perkins and his business. I arrived early and often worked very late. I hardly saw my children except when they were asleep, and I put thoughts of Ben out of my mind completely. How could Ben compare with Matthew? Matthew, who was so strong and deeply religious and successful. Matthew who never drank—Matthew whom I'd grown to worship.

By the next spring, I knew I was in love with Matthew Perkins, and I sensed he felt the same about me, although he never expressed it in word or action. I could feel his longing for me when his hand touched mine accidentally and see the hunger for me in his eyes, but he never overstepped the boundary between employer and employee. I respected him for that. I was married and so was he, I soon learned.

"My wife, Shirley," he told me sadly one day, "still clings to her old-country way of life. I married her when I was on a mission in Europe. We were both very young then and hardly knew the meaning of love. Shirley was very pretty and I was too blinded by my emotions to realize she was not very bright. I felt sorry for her, too—she was an orphan. I married her and brought her to this country. I gave her everything. Now, she repays me with ingratitude and suspicion! But we have two children and I'm duty bound to my family."

I didn't know what Matthew intended to do about his unhappy marriage, if anything, because he dropped the subject apologetically and began dictating. I knew, though, that there was something I could do about mine: I could divorce Ben on grounds of desertion. Mother protested tearfully when the very next day I went to a lawyer and started proceedings, but I was determined. I wanted to be free.

My lawyer had a hard time finding Ben to sign the necessary papers, but finally he was located in Nevada. He wrote me a pathetic letter:

I can't tell you how sad I felt when those divorce papers came. All this time I've been wandering the country, looking for work and a way back to my self-respect. The best I've been able to find is farm labor now and then. If I could come home now and ask your forgiveness and provide for you as I used to, I'd fight the divorce, because I still love you and I want my kids. But I can't do that. I guess you know what you're doing. I'm no good for you, nor for myself. I can't blame you for not caring about me anymore. I'm signing the papers and hoping you can build a good life for yourself and our children. Don't let them down."

In spite of my bitterness, I wanted to cry. Ben sounded so beaten! I pictured him penniless, homesick, alone. But then I checked my weakness sharply. Ben had failed us. And, besides, I was in love with someone else. Ben would have to build a new life—just as I had. My life now was Matthew, and someday he, too, might be free.

My only unhappiness at that time was the way my fellow workers at the office seemed to feel about me. They all belonged to a religious sect, and called each other "Sister" and "Brother." They never raised their voices in anger or in jest—no one wore makeup or ever mentioned drinking. They were a clannish, closemouthed group who resented my presence.

And there was something else about the group that puzzled me, too. Aside from taking orders from the outside for printing, Matthew published a religious periodical which I was never able to get a copy of. Occasionally, he dictated religious articles for it to me, but a copy of the magazine itself was not to be found anywhere in the office. I wondered, but I asked no questions. Matthew didn't like questions.

It was in connection with one of his religious articles that Matthew showed me a picture of the community where he lived. It looked very prosperous, and when Matthew pointed out his own home, a lovely house surrounded by heavy shrubbery, I sighed with envy.

"What a beautiful house!" I remarked. "Where is it located?"

"Just below Plainview," Matthew said vaguely.

I was amazed. Plainview was an isolated area almost a hundred miles from town. In order to get to the office, Matthew must have driven like fury every day.

"The house doesn't belong to me," Matthew said, interrupting my thoughts. "I own nothing. All material things belong to God. The whole community is organized into a united effort. We have everything we need. Each person has a job to do and is well-fed, and comfortably housed. We do not know the meaning of insecurity."

I was impressed. I still shuddered when I thought of my near starvation and welfare. Security meant everything to me—everything!

"Someday I will take you to the community for a visit," Matthew promised, "but we prefer to remain unknown. People are suspicious of our religion, but this is America, and through the Bill of Rights we claim freedom to worship God as we choose. We are Fundamentalists."

I knew nothing of the Fundamentalist religion, but everything Matthew had told me about the colony sounded all right. Only later did I realize that he was preparing me slowly.

Later, he gave me certain copies of his religious magazine to read, and after I'd read the first issue, I could feel horror creeping over me. The Fundamentalists advocated polygamy! Matthew saw my shocked expression and he called me into his office.

"You look upset," he began, "but I don't think you understand the principles of Fundamentalism. When you do, you will no longer reject the idea of plural wives. It is God's wish that man should multiply and replenish the earth, and one wife can supply only a limited number of children in her lifetime. Therefore it is the duty of a true

Fundamentalist to take more than one wife."

He went on and on, and all the while I listened, my mind protested against everything he said.

"But polygamy is against the law!" I interrupted at one point. "It is wicked."

"Those are man-made laws. We are married in the eyes of the church with the blessing of God," he explained.

"But it's wrong. It can't work!" I insisted.

"Did your single marriage work?" he challenged me. "Do you and your children have security for the rest of your lives? "

As he shot questions at me, I found I had no defense. Ben had walked out on me. Mother was growing too old to take proper care of the children, and I had little time for them as I worked. They were running wild. Even with my salary, we could afford only the bare necessities, and I spent sleepless nights worrying about our future

"Think this over," Matthew said finally.

I couldn't help myself. I had to ask. "Do you have more than one wife?"

He smiled. "No—only Shirley. But I am free to offer marriage in the sanctity of our church to a woman I love if she is converted to Fundamentalism."

I drew in my breath: His words were impersonal, but I knew he meant me. The telephone rang just then and as Matthew answered it. I backed out of the office. I needed time to think.

Matthew let his words sink in for ten days, and we returned to our impersonal employer-employee relationship. Then one Sunday afternoon, he drove me out to see the colony. I followed him all through the community and I couldn't help being terribly impressed. The crops were good, and the warehouse was overloaded with food. The people were had plenty of clothes and were dressed well, if somewhat plainly. They were totally self-sufficient with their own school, industries, and volunteer police and fire departments. Everything and everyone looked peaceful—unworried.

We attended services at the quaint church, and after services, Matthew insisted I go to his house for dinner. I hesitated, wondering how his wife would feel about me, but when Matthew led me into the living room she welcomed me quietly, with no sign of hostility. Their two children were presented to me proudly, and they were fine-looking, well-behaved youngsters. The whole atmosphere was very pleasant.   As Matthew drove me home later, he laughed. "Now, you see, our colony really isn't a slave labor camp, as the outside world sometimes calls it. We all love one another, and everyone's happy."

I was convinced. If Matthew said so, it was true. I was ready to be converted to Fundamentalism. When he dropped me at Mother's, her house looked more shabby than ever by contrast with Matthew's fine home. Furthermore, my two children were fighting—screaming at each other in loud, shrill voices.

They needed discipline badly. Mary Ellen was very mischievous and Wesley was boyishly rough and unmanageable.

Mother glared as, sighing, I threw myself into a chair. "You shouldn't be going out with your boss!" she scolded. "He's too smooth to suit me—driving around in that flashy car in times like these. Ben may not have been all that successful, but he was honest. There's something fishy about that business of Matthew's making so much money in such tough economic times."

I said nothing. Mother just didn't understand, and I was sick of listening to her worry and complain. Every night when I came home exhausted from work, she greeted me with new problems, and bills. I was so tired of all the responsibility, and so eager to cling to someone for strength and support. Security. Comfort. Safety. Oh, how I longed for those things. That night, as I crawled into bed, I thought of the serene life I had glimpsed at Matthew's community and, in my longing for safety, it seemed like paradise to me.

By the time I received word that my divorce decree was final, Matthew's pronouncements on the Fundamentalist gospel seemed to me the very essence of truth. One by one, my doubts and misgivings were stripped away by the forceful logic of his arguments. I was ready to embrace the faith.

When Matthew learned that my divorce had been granted, his eyes glowed, and he smiled.

"Let's celebrate tonight, Sonia. Just the two of us," he said.

We had dinner at a romantic little roadside inn and afterward, Matthew led me out to a secluded spot in the garden. He took my hand in his and spoke softly. "Sonia, my dear, at last I'm free to speak my heart. I love you. Will you be my wife?"

I had known what Matthew would say, and yet at that moment, fear fluttered in my heart. I trembled and turned sharply away, ashamed to speak what was in my mind.

He turned me around to face him. "What is the matter, my dear?"

I hung my head. "One of your wives, you mean," I whispered.

He was not angry. He smiled. "Sonia, my sweet," he said, with loving reproach, "the world is still very much with you. That will change. I have only one other wife and, as matters stand, I love her no longer. But even if I did, don't you think it would be possible for me to love you, too?"

I stared at him.

"I have two children," he said, "and I love each of them equally. Is either of them betrayed because I love the other? Are your children betrayed because you love them both?"

I opened my mouth to speak, but no words came out. I couldn't answer Matthew. I felt ashamed, petty, unable to rise above my small-mindedness. Most of all, I felt unworthy of so fine a man as Matthew.

When I looked up at him, my eyes were full of tears. He drew me to him. "I love you, Sonia," he whispered. "Say you'll be my wife."

Then I was in his arms, crying. "Oh, I love you, too, Matthew. Help me to change," I pleaded. "Stay with me and give me your strength."

"I will be at your side from now on, my dear," he told me.

But I was glad he was not with me later that night when I told Mother what I was about to do.

"I don't like it!" she fumed. "This is the craziest thing I ever heard. Do you mean to tell me you're going to take the children out to this deserted place in the middle of nowhere? What in the world is out there, anyway?"

"It's a beautiful place filled with kind, wonderful people. It's sort of a cooperative community," I told her. "There's no hunger there—no one is poor. It will be fine for the children." I could not tell her more. Matthew had sworn me to secrecy.

She eyed me suspiciously. "I thought that man was married."

I couldn't tell her the truth. She would never understand, even if I were free to tell her. "He is able to marry me," I said, skirting the question.

"I don't like it at all," Mother said again tightly. "There's something you're not telling me."

"Mother," I tried to soothe her, "you'll have to trust me. You know I'd never do anything that would harm the children. I'll be happy and secure for the rest of my life. You will, too. Matthew insists on providing you with a substantial monthly allowance. That's how kind he is."

"I don't want his money!" she exploded. "The only money I've touched all my life was money that was earned honestly!"

That started a fresh argument and we both ended up in tears. The next morning, when I took the children and our bags into Matthew's waiting car, Mother remained in the house, pale and stiff with reproach. I hated to say good-bye to her like that, but it had to be done.

We drove out to the colony, and went directly to the little church. There we were married by the founder of the community, Elder Leonard, in a short, simple ceremony.

The children, bewildered, stared at Elder Leonard in awe. The man had a very imposing presence.

"Is he God?" Wesley hissed to me after the ceremony, in a voice that could be heard throughout the room.

I chuckled, but Elder Leonard and Matthew frowned sternly.

"They will learn to have more respect for the name of the Lord," Matthew said.

"And be not so forward," Elder Leonard added.

I was surprised that they could see no humor in such an innocent remark, but I said nothing.

Before starting on our honeymoon, we left the children with Shirley, who stood with her eyes downcast, silently taking instruction from Matthew. As much as I'd tried to prepare myself, being in the same house with another wife made me uneasy. I could find nothing to say to her, but I told myself firmly that I would get used to the relationship in time.

For one instant, before Matthew and I left the house, Shirley looked up and I saw her eyes. There was no hatred in them—no envy. Yet there was something—what was it? It was hard to name, but it seemed for that brief second that she had the eyes of a beast of burden, numbed, veiled by weariness. Then I caught myself. She was merely not very bright—Matthew had said so—and that explained the animal look I'd seen. Quickly I forgot the whole thing.

Matthew and I spent our honeymoon week in a resort area, and it was the most wonderful week I'd ever known. We stayed at the finest hotel in town, where Matthew was treated like visiting royalty. Everyone felt the force of his personality and assurance, which was well backed up by the large amount of money he carried—and didn't hesitate to spend. Occasionally, I felt strange, enjoying such luxury and high living while our brothers and sister Fundamentalists lived in plain and simple style back at the colony. I wondered occasionally, too, how Matthew justified spending so much money—money that he claimed belonged to the community—to God?

But those fleeting doubts were easily forgotten as I reveled in Matthew's natural princeliness and our heavenly nights of love. Matthew was a master at love—his magnetic spell claimed me completely. I think, when that week was over, I would have died for him eagerly.

"Oh, I wish our honeymoon could have lasted forever!" I sighed as we headed back to the colony.

His voice was gentle and firm. "What is to come will be even better—knowing the joy of submerging yourself in a united effort. We must not think too much of our own pleasures."

When we arrived at the colony, Shirley and the children were lined up on the porch to greet us. Again, there was that funny twinge at my heart when I saw Shirley, but firmly I suppressed it. I was a Fundamentalist, and there was no place in my life for petty rivalries and jealousies. It was strange, but I would have to get used to it. I went out of my way to embrace her as I called her "Sister." She mumbled a greeting and kept her eyes away from me.

Wesley and Mary Ellen were, of course, delirious with joy at seeing me and they made such a tumult that Matthew had to command them to silence. I thought he was being a bit too stern, for they certainly had a right to express their feelings, but I marveled at the way they quickly became silent. Discipline would be good for them, I told myself, and my dismay at Matthew's sternness disappeared after our lunch, when he called all four children to him, his and mine, and sat listening to them report on what they had done while we were away. He was affectionate and warm, and I admired his ability to keep them under control at all times.

Matthew was called to a meeting of the elders that afternoon, and Shirley and I were left to ourselves. She cleared away the lunch dishes and I hurried to her side.

"May I help, Sister?" I asked.

"Enjoy your vacation while you can," she answered tonelessly. "You will be assigned your work tomorrow."

"But this isn't work," I said. "After all, this is my—well—our home."

A flicker of a smile touched her lips, but there was no humor in it and it was gone quickly. "Nothing here is ours," she said in that same toneless voice. "All worldly things belong to God. Each of us has a special job to do. Taking care of this house is my job. You'll learn yours tomorrow, Sister."

I stared at her as she carried the dishes into the kitchen. I could have understood better had there been hostility in her tone. But there was none. It was a toneless recitation of fact, made without pride or resentment. I looked about at the big, comfortable house—was I permitted to take no pride in it? With a twinge, I remembered how proud Ben and I had been of our little home, how we had planted and painted and hammered to make it beautiful.

Well, I scolded myself, that had all been vanity and there would be no more of that. I must learn not to take pride in material things. It was evil.

Matthew came back from his meeting to tell us he was leaving immediately for California on a business trip.

"See Elder Leonard in the morning. He'll instruct you on your duties," he told me.

"But do you have to go so soon?" I protested. "I should think you had a right to take a few days to get back into the swing of things."

He scowled. "You will have to learn not to question what I must do!"

I winced under his harsh tone, so suddenly changed from the soft, affectionate manner of the past week.

In a flash of defiance, I tossed my head. "I'm not used to being spoken to in that way. Remember, Matthew, I am not a child."

He turned to me in surprise. "You'll get used to it," he said, thoughtfully, as if provoking me to see how far my defiance would go. It was strange behavior for a bridegroom.

"I don't think I will," I shot back. "I'm a grown person and I have a right to know the answers to my questions. Like everybody else, I need some respect."

He stared, a brief flicker of anger in his eyes. Then, softly, measuring his words, he responded. "Respect? I think what you need more is a lesson in Fundamentalist humility. And I shall certainly teach you that lesson the moment I get back from this trip. You will have to change, my dear—yes, you will have to change!"

An hour later he summoned the children and Shirley, gravely said good-bye and went off. I felt numb, frightened and alone.

Shirley led me upstairs and showed me my room. It was small and immaculately clean. The bed was a narrow single bed. Shirley's room next door was similar. Across the hall was Matthew's room and I peeked in. It was larger. There were pictures on the wall, a comfortable chair, a desk, and a fireplace. There was a king-sized bed.

Other doors led off the second floor. "Where do the children sleep?" I asked Shirley. She led me up to the attic. Two bunk beds stood near one another, each made up with Army neatness. There were no toys. Every surface gleamed, and with some amusement, I remembered the wild disarray of the children's room at Mother's and in the home I'd shared with Ben.

I went back to my room to unpack and a short time later Shirley served supper. The meal was eaten in almost total silence and when it was over, Shirley cleaned up.

"We go to sleep early here," she said when she'd finished. "Good night."

I took her hint and went almost immediately to bed.

The next morning, I went to Elder Leonard's house. He sat behind a glistening wooden desk, a striking picture in an expensive suit.

"The council of elders has decided you will work in the dairy, Sister," he told me. "Help is needed there."

"Of course," I said. "But you will remember, Brother Leonard, I am an experienced secretary. Isn't there some work of that nature I—"

He cut me short impatiently. "And you will remember, Sister, that the decisions of the council are final. They are made for the good of the community, for the best service to God."

I bowed my head. "Yes," I said meekly.

"The entrance to the dairy is at the end of this street. Report to Brother Ross—he is in charge there."

I nodded and got up to go.

"And, Sister Sonia—I would advise that you get busy sewing some dresses for yourself more like the clothing of our women here. We are plain folk and your dress is full of the vanity of the world."

"Of course, Brother Leonard," I said and went out. I felt a flash of resentment. I remembered the fine cloth and cut of Elder Leonard's suit, certainly not made at the colony. And Matthew, too, wore only the best suits and shirts. But I stifled my resentment when I remembered that Matthew and the other elders often went into the outside world on business affairs—it was important for them to look their best.

At the dairy, Brother Ross turned me over to Sister Faith, one of his four wives. She showed me how to milk the cows and run the cream separator. She spoke only when necessary, or when spoken to.

At the end of the day, my hands ached and my back felt broken. There were a lot of cows to be milked and the cream separator was operated by hand.

During the day, I learned that only a part of the dairy products was used at the colony—the larger portion was loaded into a truck and driven to the city by Ross, who guarded the keys to the truck as if they were jewels.

But as hard as the work was, it helped pass the long days while Matthew was away. I needed him to reassure me—to give me strength. I still felt lonely and uneasy.

For one thing, it was hard to find companionship. The women just didn't seem to know how to talk or be friends. They knew their jobs and nothing else. I would begin a conversation, only to meet a blank wall of embarrassment and silence. After a week I stopped trying. Like everyone else I remained silent most of the time.

It was alarming, though, to see the same thing happening to my children. At the school they were taught silence and obedience from morning until night. They looked puzzled, a bit frightened, and there was reproach in their eyes as they marched in and out of the house, like trained marionettes. I longed for some of their old exuberance— the shouting and yelling, the wild laughter and naughty tears.

"I want to go home," my son said to me one day.

"But, darling," I protested, "you are home, and you'll like it here once you get used to it. Tell me what's bothering you."

But instead, he studied me, then clamped his mouth shut and walked away. With a leaden feeling at my heart I realized that my son did not trust me. I ran after him, begging him to tell me what was wrong, but again, I was met by silence. Was his silence the same, I wondered, as Shirley's and the others—the silence of distrust, of fear? I was too stricken with terror at the question to even attempt answering it.

Ten days later as I was leaving the dairy after work I saw Matthew's car drive through the village. He was home! Bursting with impatience, I ran toward the house to greet him. How I longed for his comforting arms—how I needed his soothing words to heal my doubts!

Matthew was sitting in his chair, all the children clustered about him, as I came into the living room, breathless with excitement. Shirley clattered in the dining room, preparing supper. Matthew greeted me with a grave smile.

"And how have you been, my dear?" he asked kindly. It was the same tone he had been using with the children. In the presence of the others' calm, my excitement faded away. I controlled myself, stifling the glow that had been in my face.

And then the thought struck me—had my face become as veiled as the others? Weren't we all hiding our feelings? I felt like an actress on a stage. I greeted him quietly, as if he had been gone only an hour, and that seemed to satisfy him. He turned immediately back to the children and continued his questioning of their behavior.

And in that way, kinglike, lord of the manor, he reigned during supper and the rest of the evening. He did the talking and asked the questions. We, Shirley and I and the children, spoke respectfully, and only when spoken to. Secretly, I longed for night to come, when we would be alone together, husband and wife, and I could pour out all my troubled thoughts.

Matthew ordered the children up to bed, read his Bible awhile, and then went up to his room. Shirley and I soon went to our rooms, too. Carefully, I combed my hair, put on my nightgown and wrapper, and waited. Should I go in to him, or was it proper to wait for his summons?

A few minutes later, I heard a knocking on the door—but it was not on my door. Matthew's voice rumbled in the hall and Shirley answered meekly.

Heart pounding, I opened my door a crack and peeked out. I saw Matthew and Shirley go into Matthew's room then his door shut and there was silence.

The bitter taste of gall was in my mouth as I threw myself across my narrow bed. Jealousy, loneliness, hatred, and rejection burned inside me and I doubled up with the pain of it. I had a vague feeling that nothing was real—that it was all an impossible nightmare. But the feeling didn't last, and as the tears coursed down my cheeks, I knew all too well how real it was. I crawled between the sheets like a wounded animal, crying myself finally to sleep.

I awoke to find Matthew shaking my shoulder. It was morning.

"It is time to go to church, my dear," he said.

Involuntarily, I cringed under his hand. His eyes narrowed and he studied me.

"All right," he said, "what's wrong?"

92

"I don't know," I said. "I mean—nothing is wrong." I was on the edge of tears.

"You are jealous," he said. "You can't hide things from me. You are jealous, isn't that so?"

I sat up in bed, covering my face with my hands. "Yes," I said. "I can't help it. I can't get used to this. I was raised in a different kind of world."

His voice was soft. "Is there anything else?" he asked.

It all came out then. "Yes," I said, "lots of things. You said we were all brothers and sisters—but it seems to me, we're divided into bosses and slaves. Why all this harsh, unquestioning obedience? Nobody seems free to speak his mind. And why do you teach the children nothing about the outside world? They are growing up ignorant—how can ignorant people persuade the rest of the world that our faith is right? Why all this secrecy? If we are not ashamed of what we do, why are we afraid to let the rest of the world know about it?"

The questions flooded out in a hot tide, surprising even me. I hadn't put them into words before, not even to myself. I looked up at Matthew, at his eyes glittering angrily. He turned away sharply and went to look out the window in silence.

"Aren't you going to answer?" I asked timidly.

"I will answer," he said, "in good time. This is part of that lesson in humility I promised to teach you. Now you will get dressed promptly and go downstairs."

It was an order. He turned and went out.

Dully, I dressed and joined the others for breakfast. Then the whole family started down the street to the church. Shirley and I, our heads hanging meekly, walked in front. Behind us, all our children marched in twos, and behind them came Matthew in his finest black suit, like a driver herding his sheep. He alone held his head high, and nodded to the other men and elders who were herding their own flocks in the same direction. And each flock was like ours—the women meek, the children subdued, and behind them, the man of the house, proud and rigid with dignity. Only the men had any identity, we women and the children, too, were like cattle and no one could tell us apart.

At church, Elder Leonard delivered the invocation and then, as if by prearrangement, he asked Matthew to speak the sermon.

With no hesitation, Matthew's rich voice rang from the pulpit, speaking about the foolish vanity of the world, measuring it against the simple life of the colony. His tone was angry and scornful. He turned to glare directly at me and for the rest of his sermon his eyes remained on me. It was soon apparent he was speaking to me, and everyone in the church turned to stare coldly. I cringed.

"And yet there are those among us," he thundered, "who are still filled with the vanity of the world, who lack humility, who are filled with self-pride. The saintly quality of obedience is to them a sign of weakness. They have such little understanding of our faith and its absolute truth that they long for the lies of the outside world—lies which pass as knowledge! Our silent, glowing faith they call ignorance. Nor are they beyond covetousness, for they are jealous of their sisters—they covet the joy of the flesh as a miser covets his filthy gold!"

My face burned and I wished I could sink through the floor. That public shaming was worse than a hundred beatings. I could feel every eye on me as if they were daggers. I could feel them scorning, pitying, mocking, laughing.

Matthew's voice softened. "And yet," he went on, "we must not cast them from us, for the world is still much with them. We must take them to our hearts and show them the truth by our example of humility and love. They deserve our pity and our help—but only if they show true remorse."

And then he leaned forward, his eyes burning into me. "Who has sinned7" he whispered and his whisper was like a rush of wind that rustled through the church.

"Who has sinned?" the whole congregation whispered, looking at me.

Desperately, I looked up. For a brief flash, I caught a glimpse of Shirley and I saw a brightness in her face I had not caught before. Her eyes were eager and they seemed to be trying to tell me something. What? What was she trying to say?

"Who has sinned?" Matthew thundered.

"Who has sinned?" the congregation roared.

Oh, anything to make the punishment cease! Anything! I shot to my feet. My voice caught in my throat and for a moment I could not make myself speak. Then, hoarsely, it came out like a frog's croak

"I have sinned!" I yelled. A long sigh of relief welled up from the congregation and at last they were silent. I felt dizzy.

I sank to the hard bench, catching a glimpse of Shirley's face. There was disappointment on it, a flash of contempt—and then, only pity. I looked away. I saw Wesley's face, white with shock, and Mary Ellen staring at me, her dear little face stricken with fear. The dizziness swept over me and a cold sweat came out on my face, then I fainted.

I came to under a tree outside the church. My head was in Shirley's lap and she was massaging my arms and cheeks.

"Lie still," she said, "and don't speak. You'll be all right in a minute."

Gratefully, I lay there, almost wishing I would faint again. Lord, how I dreaded having to face the others. But, of course, there was no escape, and in a short time I struggled to my feet.

"Thank you for your help, Sister," I told Shirley.

"It's all right," she said stiffly.

Suddenly a group of men poured out from the church and began running in all directions. Women and children, herded by their men, rushed out and up the street. Matthew came out with the children and ran up to us.

"Quickly," he ordered, "back to the house. A prowler has been sighted in the vicinity."

He rushed us all back to the house, and shoved us inside with a warning to stay put. Then he grabbed a club near the door and ran off to join the other men

"What happened?" I asked Shirley.

She was at the window, peering intently out. "They've seen someone prowling around. Whenever that happens, they get all the women and children in the house and try to catch the prowler."

"But why?" I asked. "Why do we have to stay here?"

"Don't you understand," she asked tonelessly, "that what we are doing here is illegal? If the facts get known, the police will break up the colony."

"How did they know about the prowler?" I whispered. "Everyone was in church."

"Not everyone," she said. "There are always men on duty as guards outside the village."

"Will they catch him, do you think?" I asked.

"You and I," she said, "are not supposed to think."

Matthew came back in a few hours, dusty and disgruntled. It was obvious the prowler hadn't been caught. In a bad temper, Matthew paced up and down the living room, barking at the children, though they were silent as mice.

Shirley's good Sunday dinner cheered him up, however, and he went briskly out to a meeting of the elders. He returned after nightfall, rubbing his hands.   "I will leave on another business trip tomorrow," he said, "just for a few days." He gave me a sharp look and ordered everyone up to bed.

As I opened the door to my room, his hand was on my arm. I froze.

"Come with me," he ordered and he led me into his room. I sat stiffly on a chair, looking at the floor.

"There, there, now," he said, "you must understand what I did today was for your own good. You had to learn humility and that was the best way to teach it to you. You will be a better person because of your confession today."

Humility? I wondered. I felt dead and shamed. Did one teach humility the way one taught a horse—by breaking a person's spirit? But I said nothing—I, too, had learned silence.

"Come, come, speak up!" he demanded impatiently. "Did you not learn a great deal today? Are you not closer to God?"

"Yes," I said simply. It was the easiest thing to say. From then on I would say only easy things, and I would speak as seldom as possible. I had learned—oh, how I had learned!

Smiling, Matthew put his hands on my shoulders. "I forgive you," he said. He drew me to my feet and pulled me close. "Now," he said softly, his voice changing thrillingly, "let us celebrate our love."

I cringed. "Please. Not now. It's hard for me—I"

The vibrant voice struck hard steel. "Perhaps, you have not yet learned the full lesson of obedience!" I stiffened at the suggestion of menace, feeling his fingers hard on my arm.

Cowering, I said no more, and he took his will of me. There was no love in him, not even any desire. It was his way of punishing me, his way of expressing his unchallengeable mastery. My body and mind dead of feeling, I submitted.

Later, as he lay sleeping contentedly, I crawled out of his bed, clutched my dress around me, and stole to my room. I sat alone in the darkness, whispering to myself.

"Why can't I cry? I hate him. I hate him! Oh, why can't I cry?"

My door creaked, and I looked up nervously. Shirley came in the room silently, closing the door behind her. The pale moonlight from my window touched her face. And oh, the pity in it! So much pity! A dry sob tore at my throat.

She came and stood by my chair and took my head in her hands and pressed me close against her. "Cry," she said, "it will make it better."

But the sob was still dry. "How can you be sorry for me?" I wanted to know. "How can you care about me at all? He was all yours until I came."

"I am not jealous. Where there is no love, there can be no jealousy. Cry," she said gently.

And then clinging to her, I cried at last. I cried until I could cry no more. Then she led me to bed and patted my forehead with her cool hands until I fell asleep.

The next day Matthew left for his business trip, and that evening, after the children were in bed, Shirley and I settled down for a long overdue talk. "You tried to tell me something in church yesterday," I said. "What was it?"

"For a moment," she answered, "I hoped you would defy them, that you would show the spirit no one has dared show before. But you did not."

"I was frightened," I said. "I've never been so scared. I don't know why—all those people staring."

"Yes," she told me sadly, "they count on that. That's the way they break you down, bit by bit. I don't know why I expected you to behave any differently than I did—than any of us did."

"Why did they do it? Why are they here? Why do all the women submit?" I asked.

She smiled. "That's a strange question, coming from you. Tell me, why are you here?"

I searched my own reasons. "Matthew fascinated me," I said. "But even more than that, I wanted security. I wanted to be safe. The world had given me a real scare."

She shrugged. "And so with all the others," she said. "They want to hide. They want a safe place where they will be fed and given something to do. And who can blame people for wanting those things? You can imagine what Matthew and his fine words meant to me when I first met him in my country. I was alone and half starved. My family had been wiped out by floods. To me, he seemed like God and the colony he talked about sounded like heaven. Yes, I, too, wanted security."

"The security of a prison," I whispered. "The security of blindness, of ignorance. We are secure in the way beasts of burden are secure."

"Of course," she said. "You know that now and it did not take you long because you are a woman of spirit and you have known the world. But, I and some of the others took a long time understanding that. I am not an educated woman, but I know one thing—for one moment of real freedom, I would throw all this false security to the dogs!"

She bit her lips, trying to control her feelings. Then she went on. "Once I rebelled—and bit by bit, they broke me down the way they broke you down yesterday. More than that, they whipped me—for the good of my soul, Matthew said."

"They won't keep me!" I exploded. "I'll run away!"

She smiled bitterly. "The guards around the village are there not only to keep strangers out, but to keep us in. Alone, you might sneak past them—but what about your children? With them, it would be next to impossible. And even should you succeed, they would find you before you had gone far."

"Prisoners!" I exclaimed, "all of us!"

"It is not that simple," Shirley explained. "Many are willing prisoners. They like it this way. They like to be told what to do. Some are simply stupid. Others know nothing else and are grimly convinced this way of life is the only truth."

"But what's the reason behind all this?" I wanted to know.

"The reason?" She shrugged. "I thought about that for a long time. But, do you not see the reason all around you, in the fine clothes Matthew and the other men wear? In their many business trips and in the money they throw around? God's money, indeed! How easy to get rich and powerful, by having many people willing to work for only bed and board! Would not any man be a little king with a harem of hardworking wives? Would he not try to persuade them that his right to rule over them was a natural right, given to him by God? In fact, he would even believe that himself."

"Is there no escape?" I sighed. "Isn't there anything we can do?"

She shrugged. "Perhaps you will think of something. You are still new here. I would risk death in the desert for myself, but there are my children to think of. For now, all I can do is to wait. Now and then, prowlers, curiosity-seekers get past our guards. Perhaps one of them will see what goes on and report it to the police. I think yesterday's prowler got away, although I don't know how or why he would have braved possible death to come here."

We sat in moody silence awhile. "I hate Matthew," I said simply.

"So do I!' she said. "Don't you wonder why, after ten years of one wife, he should suddenly seek another? Do you not wonder why, of all the men, he has so few wives? I'll tell you why: In his position, as the chief man for outside contact, he does much traveling. He can have all the women he wants, without burdening himself by marrying them. He has women wherever he goes—I have known that for a long time. But lately, the elders have been pressuring him to increase his number of wives for the good of the colony. You are part of the answer to that pressure. I have no doubt that he will soon bring home other wives."

"I will find a way for us," I told her. "I don't know how yet, but I will find some way. We will be free, Shirley."

She embraced me, her eyes brimming with tears. "We are commanded to call each other Sister, but I feel I have, indeed, found a real sister."

From then my every waking minute was devoted to trying to find an escape. But I could think of nothing. I could not risk taking my children past the guards. The only cars and trucks belonged to the elders and the managers of the colony's small industries and the keys were closely guarded. It looked hopeless.

Toward the end of the week Matthew came home—with his third wife. Her name was Angelina and she was a soft little doe of a woman with big scared eyes that never left Matthew. She watched him as a dog watched its master. When his voice rose, she flinched. When his voice was soft, she flushed with delight and love. My heart bled for her.

"Poor Angelina," Matthew crooned, "her mother died after her father, a drunken and irresponsible man, left her."

Angelina gazed adoringly up at her benefactor. I didn't have to listen to the rest of the story—I knew it already. I wanted to shout to

Angelina to run, to scream at her that Matthew was a liar but instead, I stood meekly, just as Shirley did all through the ceremony at the church. Matthew did not take a honeymoon that time. His presence was needed, for the prowler of the previous week had not been caught and the men suspected he was still around.

Ever since my "confession" at the church, Wesley had avoided me as if I were contaminated. When I touched him he cringed, and his eyes glowed constantly with fear and puzzlement. I worried terribly about him, but I did not know how to reach him.

Tears of relief sprang to my eyes when he came to me after supper three days after Matthew had come home and asked me to put him to bed. I hugged him.

"Why of course, darling—but isn't it early yet?"

"I don't feel too good," Wesley mumbled.

I felt his head. It was not warm.

"Please, Mommy," my son begged. "I want to go to bed now."

I led him upstairs, and as soon as we reached the attic bedroom, he closed the door and stood with his ear pressed against it, listening stealthily.

"What in the world?" I began.

Wesley whirled to me and put his finger to his lips. I thought he was playing some kind of game so I smiled and also put my finger to my lips. I didn't care if he wanted to play cops and robbers at the time, or that such games were forbidden at the colony. I was grateful that he'd included me. He beckoned to me, his face eager with mystery.

"Can you keep a secret, Mommy?"

"Of course," I whispered.

"Cross your heart and hope to die?" His voice was urgent—almost desperate.

Biting my lip, I went through the motions, wishing he would not play the game with such terrible urgency. Then he put his lips close to my ear.

"You go to work an hour early tomorrow. It's important," he said.

I started. What in the world ran through the boy's mind? He shook his head impatiently and repeated his instructions.

"But what does it mean, Wesley? I don't understand."

"I can't tell you what it means," he whispered. "But you promised. You crossed your heart. Just do like I said."

"Are you all right, Wesley?" I asked worriedly.

"I'm all right, Mommy. You've got to do like I told you," he insisted frantically.

I soothed him. "All right, dear."

"Promise?" he persisted.

"I promise." He relaxed then, and allowed me to put him to bed.

99

I thought about it all night, but I could make no sense out of it. Finally, I decided it was simply a child's secret game, and rolled over to go to sleep. Wesley would forget about it by morning.

But long before dawn I awakened to find Wesley by my bedside, shaking my shoulder. Before I could cry out, his finger was on my lips.

"It's time, Mommy," he whispered hoarsely. His eyes burned frantically and his face was pale and pinched. It was clear he hadn't let himself sleep all night, so he'd be awake to get me out of bed.

"Now, Wesley, this is silly," I protested.

He looked as if he might cry. I forced myself out of bed and got dressed. The house was still. Wesley watched until I left my room and then he tiptoed upstairs.

Feeling foolish and troubled I went down to the kitchen to put up some coffee on.

Matthew came downstairs, stared at the clock, then at his watch, and then at me.

"I heard you down here," he said, "and I thought it was time to get up. But it's so early."

Past him, on the stairs, I caught a glimpse of Wesley's pajamas. "Ross wanted me to get to the dairy an hour early this morning," I said. "There's something he wanted done."

Matthew shrugged, rubbed his eyes, then turned to go back upstairs. Wesley's pajamas had disappeared. I stared after Matthew. Now I had to go!

Sighing, I went to the dairy, and stepped inside the big barn door.

"Sonia!" a voice whispered near me. I whirled, a startled cry rising to my lips. Then a man stepped out of the shadows.

"Whatever you do, don't cry out!' My cry was cut off, and I staggered back, staring at the man. White flour dust covered him from head to foot. A dusty cap was on his head. A week's stubble of beard, crusted with dirt and flour, was on his face. And the eyes—the haggard, fierce eyes that burned out at me!

"Ben!" I gasped.

Ben took a step toward me and reached out his hand yearningly. Then he stopped himself, and with a sudden, furious gesture, he swept his cap off his head and slammed it against the ground.

"In God's name, Sonia!" His voice was low and agonized. "What have you done with yourself and our children?"

I covered my face with my arms and rocked in grief and yearning.

"Have you gone crazy?" his voice hissed. "If I'd thought you'd taken a sane step toward real happiness for yourself and the kids I never would have come. But this! This crazy house! Do you believe in this stuff? Are you happy here? What in the world have you done?"

100

I cringed. "I'm miserable," I sobbed. "I didn't know it would be like this. I wanted safety. I wanted to be protected. I didn't think—I couldn't think. Oh, Ben, forgive me! Save me!"

I sank to the floor and lay there sobbing until Ben's hands on my shoulders drew me up. I held onto him, sobbing.

"All right," he said gently. "Now get a grip on yourself. There are things to be done."

"How did you know? How did you get here?" I asked.

"Your mother wrote me. She was worried and she suspected something was wrong. From what she wrote, I got worried and came down to see for myself. I borrowed an old car and drove it out to the turnoff. It's hidden under bushes out there now. The rest of the way I came on foot and I almost died out there the first day. What a place! I didn't know it would be like that. Luckily I saw the guards before they saw me, although I know one of them suspected something. I figured any place worth guarding was worth sneaking up on, so I laid low and finally worked my way in. I've been here about a week now."

"But where have you been staying? They've been hunting for you. They must have picked up your trail somewhere."

"I know," he said. "I've got a little nest built out in the flour sacks in the granary. They prowled all over it the other day without seeing me. I got out all right though, and looked around—and I can tell you I've seen all I want to see and heard all I want to hear."

I hung my head. "You'll never know what it's really like," I said.

"I think I do know," Ben said. "I've seen how this whole place works and I've got enough to hang these people."

My heart withered with shame.

"I got hold of Wesley and put my life in his hands," Ben went on. "He's been smuggling food out to me every night. What a kid! He's the salt of the earth, that boy of mine."

"He never told me." I shook my head wonderingly.

"He's a brave boy." Ben glowed. Then he got grim. "I'm leaving here today and I'm coming back with an army of cops to break this thing up. It'll be rough on you, Sonia, but I don't know any other way."

"I don't care about that," I told him, "but I'm worried about you. They've doubled the guard. You'll never get out."

"Just leave that to me," he said. "When your boss drives his milk truck into the city today, I'll be on it."

I heard the creaking of the dairy gate and my hand flew to my throat. "He's coming now. Oh, hide!"

Ben darted to the back door and peered out. "Damn my soul to hell, I still love you!" he whispered between clenched teeth. And then he slipped out the door and I stood fighting the sobs.

Ross marched into the barn from the front and looked at me with smiling surprise. "You are an eager worker, Sister Sonia."

"Thank you, Brother Ross," I mumbled. He marched past me and threw the back door open and stretched in the sunlight. In horror, I gazed at the floor: Ben's flour-dusted cap was still lying where he had thrown it. Ross was almost standing right on top of it.

"Well, to work!" Ross sang and he marched off to begin loading his truck. Swiftly, I swept up the cap and thrust it under my dress, stuffing it into my bodice.

I worked that day in a dream. I did not dare even look at Ross or go near the truck. I kept my eyes rigidly on the work I was doing, afraid my face would betray me, or that I'd catch a glimpse of Ben sneaking into the truck and cry out despite myself.

When, just before lunch, Ross drove off in the big truck, loaded high with milk containers and boxes of butter and eggs, I fell to my knees in one of the stalls and prayed. I had not seen Ben and I could not imagine how he could have made it to the truck unobserved.

That afternoon, the whole colony was thrown into an uproar. Someone discovered Ben's hiding place in the flour sacks. All work was stopped, and the women and children were sent home. Squads of men roamed the village, combing every possible nook and cranny that could serve as another hiding place. I glanced at their grim, angry faces as I hurried home. "Please, God, let Ben be on that truck!" I whispered. But I doubted it.

It was almost dark when I got home. Matthew was out with the men. The rest of the family were huddled in the living room. I went to the window and peered out. A tiny hand stole into mine, and I looked down into Wesley's eyes. They were afraid, but there was pride in them, too. I pressed his hand and his responding squeeze was the answer.

Matthew came in dusty and growling for his supper an hour later. He was in an evil temper. Shirley went silently to the kitchen to get supper ready. I sent the children up to wash and turned to follow them.

"Sonia!" Matthew barked, his voice taut with surprise. I froze, turned slowly to him and saw him staring in amazement at my feet. I looked down, my heart turning to lead.

Matthew walked toward me, his eyes fixed on the cap. He picked it up and then his eyes darted back and forth from me to the cap. The blood ran out of his face, leaving it starkly pale.

"Upstairs," he commanded quietly.

I climbed the stairs, Matthew one step behind me all the way. His hand was hard on my shoulder as he led me into his room. He shut the door and turned the key. Then he turned to me.

"Where is he?" he demanded, low.

I shook my head. I was afraid, but I was determined not to answer.

"Are you crazy, woman? Do you realize what a spy in our midst can do to us?"

I still said nothing.

He stepped toward me and gripped me by the shoulders. Then he shook me until I flapped like a rag. Splotchy patches of angry red appeared on his face as he shouted.

"Who is this man? What is he to you? In God's name, speak up!" he thundered.

And suddenly I knew him. Suddenly I was afraid no longer. I felt a swell of triumph, of victory. That all-powerful, fearful monarch of a man had suddenly laid bare his heart. I looked into his eyes, then, and I knew the truth.

"You're jealous, Matthew!" I said.

"Who is this man?" he shouted again and then, suddenly, he shut his mouth so sharply I heard the click of his teeth. He drew in his breath, hissing. "Your husband! That man!"

"Jealous," I said with contempt. "You permit your wives no jealousy, no covetousness—but you are worse than any. You are an ordinary man, after all. I could pity you if I thought that with all your evil you at least practiced what you preached. But you don't, Matthew. You have a greedy soul—greed for power, for money, for women. I have no pity for you."

He whirled to his closet and took a thick black leather strap from a nail behind the door. His face contorted with rage. He reached for me, the strap raised. "Tell me where he is!" he roared.

I shook my head.

The strap fell across my shoulders like a tongue of fire. "Where are you hiding him?"

I closed my eyes and waited.

The strap licked its hot tongue across my arms.   "You're hiding an enemy!" he cried. "You'll break up the colony!"

Again the strap snapped and I shuddered under it.

"I'll whip you within an inch of your life if you don't tell!" he threatened.

"Go ahead and whip," I gasped. "I need a whipping, but not from you. You can't scare me anymore."

He howled, then, a long animal howl of rage and frustration. He threw me to the floor and lifted the strap and brought it down. I covered my head and commanded myself not to cry out. The strap came down again and again and again and my body was racked by its fire. My back felt as if it were being torn to shreds. Dimly, I heard a pounding on the door and Shirley's voice crying out.

"Stop! Matthew, stop!" she screamed. I heard, too, the whimpering of children outside the door.

And then through it all, I heard a louder yelling from outside the house.

"Matthew! Matthew!" the voices called.

He stopped, and stood shaking for a moment. Then he went to the window and threw it open. "What is it?" he called down.

Elder Leonard's voice, edged with fear and panic, came up from the street. "Our people in town have just driven out. The prowler got back to town a few hours ago. The police are on their way! Hurry, we've got to get away!"

Matthew nodded dumbly and shut the window. He stared at me, and then, as in a daze, he staggered to the closet and took out a wooden padlocked box. He seized a suitcase and began throwing clothes into it.

Groaning, I raised myself on my elbow, and struggled to my knees. Then I crawled to the bed and leaned weakly against it watching Matthew. Fear had gone from me.

"Making your escape, Matthew? Saving your filthy loot?" I spat at him. "The money you and the elders made out of slave labor!"

He didn't answer. He picked up his bags and the box, and naked fear showing in his face he unlocked the door and clattered down the stairs. Shirley darted into the room then and came to me, holding me in her arms. Angelina stole in fearfully, her face pale and tense, and stood at the doorway staring after Matthew as if she'd seen a ghost. The children massed at the doorway, whimpering, staring, a chorus of frightened eyes. Wesley crept in and took my hand.

And then we heard the roar of many motors. It began as a low rumble distant, and then grew louder until the vibrations shook the house. The roar of motors seemed almost upon us and then brakes squealed and we heard the shouting of many men. From the window, we saw a crowd of police spilling out of masses of trucks and cars.

In a few moments, Ben came pounding up the steps to sweep Wesley and Mary Ellen into his arms. He looked at me over Wesley's shaking shoulders.

"You're going to have to face it just like all the others," he said. "There was no other way."

"I'm ready," I said.

And then Ben saw the welts on my arms and legs. With a cry, he ran to me and took me into his arms. "I'll kill that man!" he groaned.

I put my finger on his lips. "Hush," I said. "He'll get what's coming to him."

We were herded into trucks and carried back to town and put into jail. All during the next few days we passed, a dreary and shamed parade, past the judge. Within a week, though, the women and children were released and social service agencies were alerted to find

104

places and jobs for them. Most of the men were given jail sentences for bigamy. For Matthew and the elders, who had attempted to escape but had fallen right into the hands of the police, there were additional charges of embezzlement, violating labor laws, and conspiracy. A considerable sum of money had been found in Matthew's box and with the men who had attempted to escape. It was all turned over to a fund to help the women and children readjust themselves to normal life.

Ben stayed in town and found a job finally. We could not have survived without him, for there was certainly no place that would hire me, after all the publicity. My marriage to Matthew was annulled, for it had never had any legal standing.

It was a year and a half later that Ben told me that he'd forgiven me.

"We've made mistakes, both of us. The world gave us both a good scare and we both went off, terrified. I don't know that one's to blame any more than the other. I guess I wasn't much of a man."

"You're all the man I could ever hope to know," I told him fervently.

"Do you think we could start all over again?" he asked.

"No," I said. "Nobody starts all over again. But we can go on from here, knowing what we know, and maybe we can make it a lot better than it ever was."

We married again the following week. We don't have a lot of money and I guess we never will, but our home and our marriage are priceless to us, and we guard them as our dearest treasures. I've learned at last that security is not counted in money or jobs. Only in love and trust and faith is there real security.

THE END

WHY I DIDN'T
DIVORCE HIM

Could any husband ever face a wife with a more difficult situation: And could any other wife handle it in any differently than I did?

Lucille Parker's baby was a girl. I watched the nurse bathe it and wrap it in my woolen shawl, for there hadn't been any clothes made for it.

The baby was small and red and wrinkled. Its little hands were so tiny and it cried pitifully. That was the first time I had ever seen a newborn baby. I did not like children. I had never wanted any myself, nor did I go often to visit people who had children.

As I stood there watching the nurse take care of the little thing, I couldn't exactly hate it—it was so small, so helpless. Its cry was so pitiful. My feelings at the moment were strangely mixed, a blend of pity and curiosity and bewilderment. And back of it all was the awful truth about that had so suddenly descended upon our household. For now I knew the truth: It was Gerard's child!

It all came to me in a flash. The meaning of everything that had happened during the last few months. Since that night Gerard asked me for a divorce, and I thought he was surely out of his head.

The idea had seemed ridiculous. Gerard Montgomery and I had been married for many years. We were respectable, quiet and law abiding. We went to church regularly, paid our taxes, and contributed to the community charity fund every Christmas. That we should get a divorce, for no reason at all, would be pure insanity.

What was the matter with Gerard, anyway? I thought he might be ill, and begged him to see a doctor. But he wouldn't pay any attention to me.

Grant his ridiculous request to get a divorce? Of course not. I thought too much of Gerard to let any silly whim spoil his life. He had probably been reading too much about divorces in the newspapers. Scandalous what they printed about them! I should think people would be too much ashamed to have it printed for the public to read about.

Well, anyway, I was not going to let such a crazy idea worry me. Gerard just didn't know what he was talking about. And I told him so.

"I'll provide for you, Isabella," he said thoughtfully. "You can have the house and enough money to keep you. You could go to visit your cousins that you've always been wanting to see. You could run around and have some pleasure."

Have some pleasure! As if it weren't my pleasure to stay at home and look after Gerard! As if I weren't satisfied to go right on as I had been doing all those years: Washing his clothes and mending them and cooking the things he liked to eat. I liked putting out the garden and tending it. I liked to watch for the pinks and marigolds to bloom along the fence and train the morning glory vines that climbed over it. Why, I could have cried at the thought, even, of leaving things.

Of course, Gerard had said that I might have the place, but what would it mean without having Gerard along with it? Even though he wasn't much of a hand to talk, it was company to have him home evenings, reading his paper, with his shoes off and his collar unfastened.

Gerard wasn't so handsome, either; but he suited me. He dressed simply, and he wasn't a striking man. But I always felt proud of him on Sundays when we went to church. He'd wear his good black suit, and I'd wear my best dress and the hat he liked.

"Why, Gerard, what would people say?" I cried in alarm. I thought of his crazy proposal He just looked at me, a little dazed and I repeated the words: "What would people say?"

But I went right on, assuring him. "Of course you don't want a divorce. You're just not feeling well. Everything is going to be all right."

I knew I had to smooth out things for Gerard, just as I had always done. When anything disturbing arose at the grocery store in which he owned a half interest, it was up to me to straighten it out. I half suspected now he had got into a dispute of some kind, and didn't want to tell me about it So I didn't question him. I just tried to soothe him.

I went out of my way to have things nice for Gerard then. I baked his favorite cherry pie and whole wheat bread, and made a roast. I made love with him, feeling that was a wife's privilege and obligation at times.

But, somehow, Gerard never quieted down the way he should have done. He seemed nervous, upset, and irritable. I did my best to ignore it. I went right on being the kind of wife I felt I ought to be to him.

Then, one day he came home in the middle of the morning, which was so unusual that I sensed something was wrong immediately. He opened the screen door so violently that it frightened me.

"Isabella, I want to know who is boss around here!" he demanded, in such a loud voice that I was afraid the neighbors would hear him.

"Why, you are, Gerard, of course," I said calmly. I knew that was the best way to handle him when he was excited. That was no time to argue with him.

107

"Then things are going to be as I say from now on. You've had your way ever since I married you, and now it's going to be my turn."

"Why, yes, Gerard," I agreed meekly.

He talked fast and excitedly. His face was pale and he was shaking. Then he went ahead and told me.

"I know a girl who is sick, and without a home. She hasn't any folks, has no money, and no place to go. I'm going to bring her here."

"All right," I agreed weakly. If that was all that was the matter with him, I guessed I could put up with it. But it did seem a silly thing to do. Why didn't he let the authorities look after her, as they did the other charity cases? It surely didn't mean anything to us.

I never had liked being around sick people, but since Gerard had been acting so strangely, I would let him have his way and bring her there. She probably would be well soon and go on her way.

I got the spare bedroom ready. I wondered who she was and what was the matter with her. But I didn't ask any questions. Gerard seemed so excited and didn't offer me any particulars. Anyway, I would find out about her when she got there. After all, would be a nice turn for me to take in a sick, homeless girl. The church people would notice my generosity. My gesture wouldn't go unnoticed in our community. I got out clean linen, and raised the windows to let things air. I even put some flowers in a vase. Sick folks liked flowers.

It was dark when Gerard brought Lucille Parker home with him. He also brought a nurse. The doctor followed shortly.

I didn't have to ask questions then. I knew there was going to be a baby.

There wasn't anything I could do but keep out of the way. The nurse took complete charge of things. I went into the kitchen and sat down, and tried to figure out what kind of a simpleton I was to allow strangers to walk into my house and take complete command of it.

I decided I'd have a talk with Gerard and find out the reason for all those outlandish happenings. Why had he insisted on bringing that girl to my house? Why should we care for a woman we had never seen before? And why should she come to my house to have her baby? Likely as not, she wasn't even married.

A wave of utter horror swept over me. The idea of Gerard and me harboring that kind of woman! What would people say? Just why had she been brazen enough to come into a respectable home and flaunt her sin? Why hadn't she gone off and hidden herself from decent people? All kinds of thoughts flashed through my mind, but I couldn't find the answer to any of them. So I just waited for Gerard to come home and explain things to me.

It was late when he came from town. He wasn't often obliged to work at night but I didn't think anything about that. I was too much engrossed with my own questions.

"Gerard, why did you bring that girl here?" I demanded at once.

He looked a sickly white under the harsh light.

"How is she?" he asked.

"How should I know? And why on earth did you bring her here? Who is she, anyway? Where's the man who is responsible for her? Why doesn't he come forth like a man and take care of her?"

Gerard stood there and didn't answer me—just looked at me. But he looked like a broken old man, ready to fall to the floor. I had never seen him look like that. I could hardly believe it was Gerard, and yet I still didn't understand.

Then we heard a cry from the room where the patient was with the doctor and nurse. It was an awful cry of agonizing pain. Then, after a minute, we heard the thin, feeble cry of a newborn baby.

Gerard never saw me then. It was as though he was looking straight through me. He seemed like a person possessed. The veins on his forehead stood out like cords, and his hands were clenched at his sides.

Suddenly, I knew! He didn't have to tell me—nobody had to tell me. I knew the reason for everything—why he had wanted a divorce, why he had been upset and worried, why he had asserted himself that day, and why he had brought that woman into our house. He was the father of Lucille Parks's child. He had come forth like a man and was taking care of her!

The first thing that came into my mind was: What will people say?

I thought about it all night. I turned and twisted on my bed and thought about the awful predicament I was in and tried to figure a way out of it. But I could see only the facts. The woman was there in my house. I had to let her stay, for she could not be moved, and she had nowhere to go, anyhow.

"Her father was old man Parker. He died last summer. She hasn't any folks, nor any money. I could have given her money, but she didn't know where to go. And I didn't know where to send her."

"So you brought her here!" I finished for him with sarcasm.

Gerard nodded miserably.

"Well, what about me?" I cried, unable to control my anger. But Gerard answered as calmly and coldly as if he had no feelings at all.

"I asked you for a divorce. I'd have married her and made things right. But you wouldn't let me."

"So you're going. to blame me!" I cried hotly. "You're going to say I'm responsible for this disgraceful thing, and you're bringing it under my very nose to torment me. Me, your lawful, wedded wife!"

Gerard threw out his hands despairingly. "Calm yourself, Isabella. I have nothing to say. You can see the facts for yourself. Since I have been obliged to bring Lucille here, in order to take care of her, and face my responsibility in the only way I am able, go ahead and do whatever you please about the matter. But I must see that Lucille and her baby are taken care of."

And all that night I kept thinking: What will people say?

Since I was obliged to make the best of the situation, I decided to make up my own story. I felt sure Lucille was a stranger in the community and I would say that she was a distant relative—a sort of third cousin I hadn't seen for a long time. It would sound all right. I could just see the ladies at the sewing club getting a big thrill out of the affair. They would probably come over to call later. They would have a shower or something, and bring baby things. Well, the poor little baby needed them. There wasn't a thing in the house to put on it.

I decided I had better go to town the first thing in the morning, buy some material, and make some things for it. With the neighbors and the church women coming in, it wouldn't look well to find it wrapped in a discarded sheet and covered up with my old blanket.

With that thought in mind, I fell asleep and awoke to find the sun up and the birds singing. At first, I didn't remember anything except that it was morning and time to get up.

Then, an of a sudden, I remembered everything: the awful situation that had settled on my household. Gerard and I, married these so many years, peaceful and settled, and now—Lucille and her child.

But I couldn't lie there and worry about it. I had to get up and start the day. Gerard was already up and gone. He often went to the store early to sweep up.

I went into the kitchen and put on the coffeepot. Presently, the nurse came in and wanted to heat some water.

"Good morning," she said.

"Good morning," I answered. I thought I might just as well be nice to her—she was only hired to stay. She hadn't any thing to do with the affair.

"I want to ask you to help me," I said to her, "about getting some things for the baby. You see, I don't know what is needed, and if you'll just help me a little with everything—"

"I'll be glad to do so, Mrs. Montgomery. I'll make out a list of things."

I made a trip to town, and completed my purchases of soft fabric, and bottles, and a high chair, and a baby seat. I was almost home before anyone asked me any questions.

Then old Mrs. Hayden stopped me, and asked what in the world the matter was at our house. She had seen the doctor stop there during the time I was gone to town. I just smiled and tried to look mysterious.

"You'll have to come over after a few days and see for yourself," I told her. "We have the cutest little girl baby you ever did see! It was born last night." I smiled brightly. "Yes, a distant cousin of mine came to stay with us for a time. I told her she was more than welcome to come into my house. I told her I'd do the best I could for her."

"Just like you, Isabella," Mrs. Hayden told me, patting my arm. "You're just kindness and goodness all the way through. I'll surely stop in to meet your cousin as soon as she is able to see folks. And, bless the baby! Why, it'll do you and Gerard good to have a baby in the house."

I felt almost happy by the time I got home. When Gerard came for lunch I was sewing in the dining room, and had things so scattered around that I set his meal on the kitchen table.

By evening, I had a soft little nightgown finished for the baby to sleep in. I watched the nurse put it on her. I wanted to hold the baby, but I didn't ask to. I had never had held a baby in my life.

I hadn't been in the room where Lucille was, and I didn't intend to go until it was necessary. And I never spoke a word to Gerard Montgomery all that day.

But as the days passed, the tightness of the atmosphere seemed to ease somewhat. Gerard and I went on as if nothing had happened. But we did not discuss the matter of the stranger beneath our roof. I even went in now and then with fresh flowers for Lucille's room, so the nurse wouldn't think I acted too strangely. But I never spoke a word to the girl.

I made the baby's clothes. The nurse helped me and made suggestions. I also made a pretty blanket and pillow for the baby's crib.

Once, when nobody saw me, I picked up the baby and held her a bit. My, but she was little! She was as light as a feather and she smelled sweet, like soap and talcum powder. I felt strange, holding that little thing—different from any way I had ever felt in my life. I knew that I would miss the baby when Lucille was able to be up and take it away with her.

But it seemed that Gerard had different plans about the matter. After the nurse left, and Lucille was able to walk about and take care of the baby herself, Gerard made his wishes plain.

"Isabella, I shall expect you and Lucille to live together in this house like two friendly women. I mean to provide for both of you. It is my duty to take care of this child, and I am not one to shirk my responsibilities. Now you two can divide the housework, or to make any arrangements you like between you, but I shall demand one thing: peace. I will stand for no bickering or quarreling between you two."

He struck the table with his fist, and I knew he meant exactly what he had said. Strange too, for Gerard had always left things up to me to handle in my own way. Now he had suddenly stepped into authority about his own household.

I looked across the table at Lucille. It was the first time I had really had a good look at her. She couldn't have been more than twenty, and her skin was pale. Her eyes were big and frightened. She kept biting her lips and twisting her hands nervously, and looking at Gerard as if she were terribly afraid of something, and looking to him for protection.

It wasn't hard for me to understand why my husband had been attracted to one so young and pretty as Lucille. I guess she had welcomed his friendliness too, since she was alone in the world.

Still that did not excuse their conduct, nor make it any easier to live the rest of my life facing the daily reminder of their sin.

I still hoped that I could manage the situation as I wished, and have her leave soon. But I was mistaken.

"I told you she was going to stay here," Gerard said with new strength in his voice, when I had brought up the subject again.

"Then I go!" I announced bitterly. "It's more than human nature can stand to be forced to go on living under the same roof with your mistress. Me, your respectable, wedded wife."

Gerard merely shrugged his shoulders and turned away. I knew what he was thinking. He didn't need to add to the insult by telling me. If I left as I threatened, it would give him the right to sue for his freedom. Then he could marry Lucille. That was what he wanted. That was what they were both waiting for. Well, I'd show them! I'd stay as long as they waited. I'd stay the rest of my life—or theirs. They couldn't outwait me. I'd show them!

Time passed. How I hated Gerard and that woman! I rarely spoke to either of them. I went ahead with the housework, and Lucille stayed in her room most of the time taking care of the baby. She only came out at meal times, or when Gerard was at home.

I tried to figure out just how the two of them felt toward each other. Did Gerard love Lucille? I had never put much stock in the word "love." I'd always considered such things foolish and sentimental. Surely Gerard was too old now to fall in love with that girl. I can't say he loved me, now or ever, or that I loved him. We never discussed the subject of love since neither of us believed in it. But how could Gerard Montgomery make such a fool out of himself over a girl? Perhaps it had only been a sudden fancy that left him as astonished as I was over the affair. Anyway, I never did ask him and he never told me.

But, did Lucille love Gerard? Again, I wondered. She would be the type of person to believe in love. Or she, too, might have been amazed over the whole thing. She had been young and friendless and alone. Gerard had gone to her place on business, and found her lonely and discouraged. He had been kind to her.

The rest of the story was that he was standing by her because he was the kind of a man who would not run away from his obligations. I should have felt proud of Gerard because of that—but I didn't. I tried to make myself believe they were playing a game behind my back; that they were waiting for me to give up and walk out. Although I was sure that they were not having any secret relations, I kept my eye an them with suspicion in my mind. What they had done once could easily be repeated. Whatever their plans were, I must be smart enough to guess ahead of them.

I knew Lucille hated me as much as I hated her. A wall of antagonism seemed to rise up between us. I knew it was true that she had no place else to go, and was not able to work and care for her baby, but this did not make me feel any kinder toward her.

Lucille would retire early to her room early in the evenings and I'd hear her singing to the baby. Gerard spent the time as he used to do, reading, with his shoes off and his collar open.

I'd sit and sew and think over the thing from every angle and hate them both. Sometimes I'd feel that my hate was big enough to slay us all. I knew it was strong enough to build into a mighty resistance, to protect me and keep them from driving me out of my own house so that their sin might be legalized.

But the baby—I found myself growing more fond of her day by day. She had grown plump and rosy and her little chubby bands would cling to my fingers. She would smile at me and I could hardly keep my hands off her. Lucille seemed afraid to let me touch her. If she saw me bending over her crib, she would snatch Daisy up and take her to her room.

"What are you going to name her?" I asked her once.

She shook her head. "I don't know."

"She ought to have a name. Don't you know any name you would like to call her?"

She shook her head again.

"What was your mother's name?" I asked.

"Daisy," she said softly.

"That's a pretty name. Why don't you call the baby Daisy?"

"All right."

After that, I called her Daisy and she soon got to know her name. I couldn't believe a baby could learn so quickly. She would laugh and coo at me, and hold out her hands for me to take her up.

"Please let me hold her a little while," I asked, when Lucille hurried to take the baby from me. "I won't hurt her."

She looked at me but didn't say anything then turned and walked away. But little Daisy was in my arms. At last, I had won out in that. I carried her over to the rocking chair by the window and held her until she went to sleep. I studied her face and thought I could see a resemblance to Gerard. If I had had a baby, it might have looked like little Daisy. Then I thought of a plan: If Lucille would only leave and give the baby to me, everything would be all right.

I asked her very soon.

"If I give you enough money to go away someplace, where no one knows you, and you could find work, would you leave the baby with me?"

She looked at me wide-eyed, and did not understand.

"I'd be good to her. We would raise her like our own child. We would send her to school and make a good woman of her."

Lucille grabbed the baby out of my arms, "She's mine!" she cried. Her face had a look of savage fear which I had never seen on any woman's face before. She took the baby into her room and did not come out again until Gerard was at home.

But I wouldn't give up. I wanted that baby, and I meant to have her. I would think of some plan to get her. If I could only get Gerard interested, and he would tell Lucille to go, she would have to leave. That was my only chance, but how was I to accomplish it? Gerard paid little attention to the baby. Daisy was usually asleep when he was home. I didn't have the courage to tell him that I actually loved that baby so much that I wanted her for my own.

I was still trying to figure out some plan to gain my desire when Fate seemed to step right in and deal a new hand in our affairs.

Gerard died.

They brought him home from the store unconscious. He had suffered a heart attack and fallen while talking to a customer. The doctor arrived at once. I hurried to bring hot water and ice packs, hardly thinking of what had happened. The doctor worked diligently, and I kept feeling hopeful that Gerard would recover. But late that night, the end came.

I had seen Lucille as I hurried about doing the doctor's errands. There was a look of fear on her face. Later, when it was all over, I saw her crouching by the window with her face buried in her hands, sobbing.

I sat stiff and straight through the funeral. The services were held at the church, and the auditorium was full. Many beautiful floral offerings testified as to Gerard's friends in the community. The casket was gray velvet, and stood just in front of the pulpit. The minister, in a long black coat, looked down upon the flower covered box.

"Here lie the remains of a man who will be long missed and mourned," he said in his deep, grave tones. I glanced sidewise at Lucille who sat next to me. We were in the front pew. The undertaker had asked, "You will want your cousin to sit with you and walk with you?"

"Yes, of course," I had said.

Lucille sobbed all through the service. Bitter, racking sobs that shook her slender form. People might have thought she was his widow, instead of me.

I didn't cry. There weren't any tears to be shed. My eyes burned like balls of fire. My heart burned too, at the injustice I was obliged to bear, sitting there and listening to the things the minister said of "our dear, departed brother, faithful Gerard Montgomery." He told about the years of steadfast reliability in church and community, his high standards, his fine ideals, his noble character. I wanted to shout the rest of it—the ugly truth that was naked and indecent before the world. How he had made the awful mistake and then sought to retrieve it by bringing his mistress to live under the same roof with his honorable, wedded wife, damning her days, embittering her to desperation, trying to drive her out so that he could marry this harlot who now sat weeping beside his lifeless body.

When he made the remark, "He opened his door to the poor and homeless," I started up and glanced around. Could they possibly know the truth? But, of course, he was referring to the story I, myself, had told about Lucille being my distant relative, who was alone and without friends.

It came to me then, as I sat there, that now Gerard was dead, Lucille could go. There would be no need of her waiting longer. She would never get to marry Gerard now. And he could no longer force me to allow her to stay under my roof. Finally, it was the time when patient waiting had won.

After the burial, we went back home. Some of the neighbors went with us. While we sat in the front room Lucille, went to her room and I could hear her moving about there. I sensed that she was packing her things to go. She knew that she would not be welcome now. I was glad, for I would not have to tell her to go.

Finally the women left, and I went to Lucille's door, which was partly open. She had everything packed, and was shutting up the box that held her things. The baby was on the bed. She had been put to sleep by the neighbor girl who kept her while we went to the funeral. She was just beginning to wake up, and began to whimper. I went over to the bed and started to pick her up.

Lucille took little Daisy out of my arms and wrapped her in a blanket. Then she took the baby and the box containing her things and went out of the room. Not a word did she say to me. She didn't even say good-bye. She just went through the door and shut it behind her.

I went into the kitchen and put on the kettle. I thought I would make a cup of tea. How still the house was! It was growing late. The fall days were shorter, and night came early. How strange it was going to be without Gerard. How lonely! Strange without Lucille, too, and little Daisy.

I began to wonder where Lucille would go. I knew she had no money, no folks, and no friends. Where could she go? Where did girls like that go, and what happened to them? My heart beat furiously. I was suddenly afraid for her.

As long as Gerard lived, he would have taken care of her and her baby. It was still his child, even though he was dead. It was my place to go on doing the things he would have wanted done.

Lucille and Gerard had sinned, but who was I to say how they should be punished? We can't always help some of the things we do any more than we can understand the reason for things other people do. Little Daisy was Gerard's child and I couldn't let her suffer.

I ran out of the house, and looked up and down the street. It was deserted and dark enough now for the street lights to be on. It was growing colder, too. A crisp autumn tinge was in the air. Where were Lucille and little Daisy?

Then I happened to think of the cemetery. It wasn't far. Two blocks over, and down at the end of the street. I ran almost all the way. I felt sure Lucille would be there. Gerard was the only friend she had. She wouldn't know anywhere else to go.

There she was! Kneeling beside Gerard's new-made grave and crying bitterly. The baby in her blanket, lay on top of the flowers on the grave, waving her little hands.

"Get up, Lucille, and come home," I said. Maybe I spoke too sternly, but she sat up and looked at me. Her face was wet with tears, and her mouth distorted from crying. I put my arm around her and lifted her to her feet. Then I picked up the baby and held her in my other arm.

"I'm your friend, Lucille, though you didn't know it. I didn't know it, either, until right now. Gerard would want us to go on peaceably together and take care of the child. Will you let me be your friend?"

She put her arms around me and cried harder than ever. She clung to me and sobbed and sobbed. For the first time, I felt toward her as if I had been her mother. I knew then I wanted to take care of her and protect her as Gerard had done.

We went home, and began to live like friendly women. I didn't feel mean any longer when I told people she was a distant relative who was going to stay with me, now that I was alone.

Our little house is warm and friendly, and filled with kind feelings toward each other. There are a kitten and a puppy to romp with little Daisy, who throws kisses with both hands, and says happily, "I love Mama—and I love Aunt Isabella."

THE END

HEARTBREAKING HOTEL

My great, new career in the hotel hospitality industry—and great, new, very hospitable coworker—seemed like can't-miss opportunities for me. Until the unthinkable happened...

When I was much younger, I had quite a temper. As I matured, I learned how to keep my "monster" in its box. That was how I looked at it, anyway—as if there was this creature inside of me who kept trying to escape. I guess my mind just conjured up a picture of a box that was neatly wrapped on the outside with several layers of attractive paper and lots and lots of ribbons and bows. No one knew what was inside that box until it was opened. Only, in the case of my box, my intention was to see that that box was never opened.

Sometimes, when life got extremely stressful, I would find the ribbons beginning to loosen, or layers of paper beginning to tear. But thankfully, my monster never got out, and I was able to mend whatever damage was done—restore the outside of the package to new.

I know that's quite an involved analogy, but it was pretty much basis for my sanity. At least I thought it was. I really felt certain I had the monster locked in that box forever.

I'd thought it'd passed the test of durability when my marriage failed. Though the ribbons and paper had been wearing thin for several years, when the marriage finally ended, the binds that held it together proved able to endure. And that hadn't been easy.

I'd decided to go out and recapture the romance in my marriage. Recapture isn't exactly the right word, since it implies there had been romance once. In truth, there had been little of that. Our relationship had started in college as friendship and grew from there. He treated me with respect, which was something that hadn't been the case with a lot of the other young men I'd dated on campus.

We also seemed to have so much in common. Not the least of which was that we both were interested in the hospitality industry and shared the same goals of one day managing a five-star resort or luxury hotel. Marriage fit nicely into that goal, as we both got our first jobs working for a nice hotel in New Jersey.

We were both so busy with our jobs that my getting pregnant with Melody had come as a big surprise. We used to joke that we wondered how it happened, but we were still pleased with the prospect of becoming parents—even if the difficulty of that pregnancy forced me to cut down on my hours at work.

I wasn't even disappointed when Jimmy got the promotion to manager that I'd been vying for. I was ready for my new job as mother, though I still helped fill in behind the desk from time to time when the hotel was short-handed.

Then Jimmy announced he had been offered the chance to manage an even bigger hotel in Boston. It was like moving one prong higher toward the goal we'd once shared. I didn't begrudge him wanting to make the move, despite the fact that moving would be much more difficult since Melody had started school. Not to mention my being eight months pregnant with Hunter at the time.

Jimmy suggested I stay in Jersey until after our son was born. He said it would give him more time to get settled in his job, and that it would be easier for me to remain close to friends and family when the baby arrived.

So that's what I did. But I didn't join Jimmy immediately after Hunter was born. It seemed far better to let Melody finish her first year of school before I made the move.

By the time I finally did make the move, Jimmy had pretty much settled into a routine that didn't include much time for a wife and children. He was focusing all his attention on his career. Or so I thought.

My first suspicions that there might have been another woman started on his birthday when I'd shown up at the hotel with the kids, hoping to surprise him with a special dinner I'd already pre-planned with the hotel chef. The night manager looked at me sympathetically when she told me Jimmy had already left for the day.

I'd taken it in stride, having the special dinner packaged to go, then took it home with me, half-expecting to find Jimmy there when I got there. But he wasn't. He didn't get home until late that night, saying he'd had several important business meetings. I felt a mixture of anger and fear as I told him about the dinner I'd planned. At least he said he was sorry he'd missed it, suggesting I not try to surprise him in the future.

"I have much more responsibility at this hotel," he explained. "That has to be my priority, so I suggest you run anything by me before you plan it from now on."

I'd stood in front of our mirror later that night dressed in the sexy negligee I'd purchased as part of the grand finale I'd planned for his celebration. We hadn't had sex since I'd moved there with the kids, and I'd thought this would be the one night when he wouldn't be too busy. But I'd also been wrong. He was still working in his den and I was asleep by the time he came to bed.

We moved three more times during the next several years. Each time Jimmy said he was moving into a better position. Each time was like the last; he'd move first while I'd remain where we were while the kids finished their school term.

Each time I'd wonder why being apart didn't seem to bother him as much as it bothered me. Then I tried to tell myself it was just that he really was too busy settling into a new job. But, eventually, I had to face the truth: He wasn't happy in our marriage.

He admitted it only after I'd walked in on him with another man. It was then that he also admitted homosexuality had been a constant struggle for him.

I admit to having a difficult time feeling sorry for Jimmy as he told his story, but in the end I did agree to let him be the one to tell the kids when he felt ready. I guess I really didn't want to be the one to tell them. I just wanted to forget.

Jimmy gave no argument when I decided to move back to Jersey with the kids. And I agreed to let them visit him as often as he wanted.

Jersey was where I had family. It was also the one place where I hoped no one knew our dark secret. My ultimate humiliation. Maybe that seems dramatic, but that was how I felt.

Melody and Hunter didn't seem surprised about the divorce. I guess they saw it coming. In reality, I guess I should've, too. Jimmy and I hadn't had much of a relationship in a very long time. They didn't react as well to the move, though.

"Not again!" Melody had fumed. "That will make five moves in ten years. At the rate we're going, who knows where I'll finally be going to school my senior year?"

"Melody, I promise you this will be the last move. New Jersey is our home. It's where we have family. We're moving back for good."

Hunter was no less happy about moving, only less verbal. It was something that worried me about him. He was so introverted. And kept so much to himself. I had always hoped his father. . . .

I had to stop myself from finishing that thought many times after that. To be honest, I wasn't certain what I wanted from Jimmy when it came to our children.

I'd eventually got a job working in one of the city hotels, though not as a manager. It had been a long time since I'd worked in the industry. Still, I was certain it would only be a matter of time until I worked up to a higher position.

The next few years passed quickly for us as we settled into our new lives. Melody did graduate and started attending college in the city. I was selfishly glad she'd chosen a school close to home. Our relationship hadn't been as close as I'd have liked it to be since the divorce, and I was hoping there was still time to bridge the gap.

It was just the opposite with Hunter. We grew closer after the divorce, though I often wished he had more male influence in his life.

However, if Jimmy was an example of what men were like, I wondered if he might be better off as things were.

I'm not talking about Jimmy's homosexuality. Jimmy acted like he was not only divorced from me, but also the kids. Though he had open visitation rights he hadn't once taken advantage of them. He hadn't even come to visit for his daughter's graduation. As near as I knew, he only sent her a card and a check. And in spite of my agreement to send the kids to visit him anytime he wanted, he never invited them.

I knew the hotel's manager was retiring soon and had hoped to apply for the position. I knew it was a big jump, but I went after the job with all I had. I'd even been taking some refresher courses.

Apparently the company appreciated my efforts, because I got the job. Although I knew nearly everyone who worked at the hotel, my first order of business was to get to know them even better.

"I want to know what we've been doing right," I said. "As well as what we've been doing wrong. But don't just tell me what's wrong. Tell me how you think we can fix it."

I didn't just give lip service to what our employees suggested. I looked into the feasibility of each valid suggestion. At the same time I had a concern of my own. Internal theft. It may be a joke to many people, hotel guests taking home towels or other items as souvenirs, but they only took some of what disappeared from a hotel each day.

I knew I had to forget whether I liked someone or not, I had to consider how well they were doing their job. And our hotel security guard was not. I knew he had more important things to tend to; but if he was overlooking the small stuff, was he really handling the big stuff?

I wasn't happy with my answer. Bruce Forrester had been with the hotel for many years. In fact, he'd been the first and only person they'd ever hired for security. He'd gotten comfortable with his job. Too comfortable. He knew just when he could sneak away for a nap in one of the unoccupied rooms.

After speaking with Bruce he decided an early retirement, complete with a gold watch and dinner for two in our restaurant, was far better than the alternative.

That left hiring a replacement. With the approval of headquarters, I didn't openly advertise the position. Instead, I started my own search for candidates in the security industry. Once I narrowed the slate, I contacted several people to see if they'd be interested in interviewing for the job.

I was pleased when the man at the top of my list said he was. Tom Sheridan was a well-respected security consultant. The question was whether or not he was interested in leaving consulting to work for someone else.

My offer seemed to have come at just the right time.

"I've been giving thought to simplifying my life," he said.

"I don't know if I'd call this job simple."

He smiled. "I did work for fifteen companies in eleven different cities last year. I did anything from evaluating and recommending upgraded security systems to training their entire security staff. In one case, I even rewrote their security manual.

"I was home a total of six weeks last year," he continued. "And quite frankly, I'm tired."

I knew by my research Mr. Sheridan had been doing consulting work for the past six years. Before that he'd worked for a private security company. What was most impressive was that his experience had started while he was in the Navy and that his references from there ranked high. However, I learned much of the details about his work during that time were classified.

The people I talked to had many fine things to say about him. All in all, I knew I couldn't find a better person for the job. In fact, he was overqualified. Yet, as much as I wanted to hire him, I couldn't help wondering why he was even interested. He may have said he was tired of traveling; from what I'd learned about him, I suspected he could have the pick of many jobs, including returning to the military.

So it came as a bit of a surprise to me when he said he was interested, and seemed eager, to give hotel security a try. Even at the salary I was able to offer him, which I knew was probably minuscule compared to what he could earn elsewhere.

I told him as much and he smiled. "Like I said, I've been thinking of simplifying my life."

"Then it looks like you're hired," I replied. "I just hope the job isn't so simple that you'll be bored."

Tom Sheridan approached the job as though he were hired as a consultant. After his first week he arrived at my office with a lengthy written report.

"What's this?" I asked, raising my eyebrows when I saw the thick report.

"An assessment of your current security and my recommended improvements."

I leafed through it, perusing the headings. One jumped out immediately. I raised my eyes to his. "You want to hire how many people?"

"Two full time and one part time," he replied. "A hotel this size needs coverage twenty-four seven."

"What we need is a bigger budget," I noted, doubtful I'd be able to get approval for such a big expense. "It's not like we hold big conventions at the hotel. Most of the time things are pretty calm.

And we're not one of the airport hotels, so it's not likely we can use proximity to a high-risk area as a reason."

"I think if you look further in my report to Appendix D you'll see I took the liberty of writing a sample budget proposal which details our needs and the reasons for those needs. That should be sufficient to get you the extra appropriations."

I glanced at the proposal, impressed by what I saw. It seemed the man left no stone unturned; I knew I'd hired the right person. It turned out headquarters was equally impressed.

"You better hang on to this Sheridan guy," Peggy from the main office said when she called to tell me the budget increase had been approved, effective the next fiscal year. "He's impressed the boss and if I were a betting person, I'd say his wheels are already turning about how he can put the man to use for the benefit of the entire chain."

"I knew I should've kept him a secret." I groaned, knowing I could've turned in the proposal without the report attached and taken credit for it myself. But I didn't work like that. I'd sent a cover letter with the entire package, making note that my new hire was already worth more than he was being paid.

"Hey, look at it this way: It's a feather in your cap that you found him," Peggy said.

"Yes, but I want to keep him."

"That good?" I didn't like the way she said that.

"He's one of the best in the business," I clarified.

"Is he good looking, too?"

"That has nothing to do with it."

"So he is." Peggy sounded pleased. I knew she was probably smiling into the phone. She and I went way back. She'd worked for the same chain as my ex-husband before getting the job at corporate headquarters for the one I now worked for. She even remembered me and had been delighted to give me a reference when I returned to the work force.

"It might be time for you to get back on the horse."

"I'm not interested," I replied.

"Methinks she doest protest too much."

"Peggy, please, enough clichés."

"That wasn't a cliché, it was a quote."

"Whatever. Just don't get any ideas about a man and me. I'm not interested."

"You haven't gone Jimmy, have you?"

"Peggy!"

She was laughing. "Only checking to see if you still have a sense of humor."

"Not about that," I snapped. "Even from you."

"I'm sorry, kiddo," she said, and I knew she meant it. Peggy liked to tease and would hound you to death if she thought it was good for you, but she didn't have a vicious bone in her body. "But don't you think you need to get beyond what Jimmy did and start to have a life?"

"I have a very good life."

"How old are the kids now, Tanya? Last I heard, Melody started college. Hunter won't be that far behind."

"He's got three more years."

"Take it from me—I raised three sons—from now on in, you aren't going to be seeing much of him."

If that were only true. Unfortunately, Hunter wasn't exactly showing enthusiasm for much of anything.

I ended our call and tried to put Peggy's suggestion out of my mind. But it wasn't easy. It seemed everywhere I went that day, I kept running into Tom Sheridan. I even saw him later that evening when Hunter stopped by and the two of us went to the hotel restaurant for dinner. Tom entered shortly after we were seated.

It was a busy night and it seemed silly to tie up two tables when Hunter and I had been seated at a table for four.

"Do you mind if I ask Mr. Sheridan to join us?" I asked Hunter.

"He's the new security guy, right?"

"Yes, he's in charge of our hotel security."

Hunter shrugged. "Sure, ask him to sit with us." Though he was trying to look nonchalant, I could tell by the way his eyes lit up that Hunter was very interested in what our new employee did.

I was happy Tom accepted our invitation, but only because it was the most enthused I'd seen my son in a long time.

We were about to leave when I remembered to tell Tom corporate headquarters had approved the budget he had requested.

"Then I can start looking for the extra people right away."

"Actually, I usually do the hiring."

I could tell he wasn't pleased by that prospect. "I found you, didn't I?" I continued, and he finally smiled.

"Why don't we work together on it? I actually have a few ideas and can run them by you tomorrow."

What he wanted to run by me was to suggest we hire Hunter as his part-time person. I wasn't certain I liked the idea, no matter how enthused I knew Hunter would be. He did nothing but talk about Tom Sheridan and hotel security when we got home the previous evening.

"I can tell he's an intelligent kid. He asked all the right questions and he seemed very interested."

"One, he's too young to work security. Two, it reeks of nepotism."

"In answer to one, I wouldn't have him disarming any bombs his first week on the job. Two, it's only a part-time position with very meager pay, so who cares if it's nepotism?"

"If he's not going to be disarming bombs, what will you have him do?"

"Mostly helping sort old video surveillance tapes and help set up a filing system for new tapes," Tom explained. "Did you realize your past security chief just threw them all in a big box in his closet?"

I frowned, nodding. "That's one of the reasons why he's our past security chief."

Tom finally convinced me to let Hunter take on the job if he wanted to. I had very little doubt about what my son's answer was going to be.

"When do I start?" he asked anxiously. "I'm available tonight."

"Only weekends until school's out," I said, although it was difficult to stick to that decision when Hunter kept showing up on school nights insisting he had nothing else to do. I decided to stop worrying about it as long as he was within the legal time limits he could work and his grades didn't drop.

In fact, I was pleased when it seemed Hunter's grades were improving significantly after he started the job. I found out why when I walked in on him and Tom one night and realized the two of them were hunched over one of my son's textbooks.

I made a point of thanking Tom when Hunter wasn't around. "I appreciate you helping my son with his schoolwork," I said. "I guess it's safe to say from the improvement in his grades that you've been doing it quite often."

Tom shrugged as though it were a trivial thing he was doing. I knew he had no idea just how much it meant to me.

"Would the two of you like to join me for dinner tonight?" he asked, surprising me. "But not here, okay? Hunter's been telling me about the restaurants here."

"If it's Friday, Wildwood is the place to go," I said. "You'll be in for a real treat, and I don't mean just the food." On Friday nights, Wildwood had a bit of a carnival atmosphere—not just the food, but also the colorful people. We all ended up enjoying ourselves.

The next day a young man came into the hotel looking for Tom. I knew Tom had feelers out for some more security people, but I didn't know he was expecting anyone that day. Since we had agreed to conduct interviews together, I escorted him to Tom's office.

"We already hired one person, but I know we still need two more security people," I explained as we approached the office. "You do look very young to be experienced."

The young man took no offense. "Not that young, ma'am. I've been in the Navy for the past six years."

"Oh, my, now I do feel old."

"Don't, ma'am," the young man continued politely. "I enlisted while I was still in high school and went in right after I graduated."

It turned out the young man's visit was a total surprise to Tom, who looked at me with a puzzled expression.

"I heard through the grapevine that you may need a good security person," the young man explained. "I'm good, so I'm applying."

The young man, whose name we learned was Roy Smith, got straight to the point with no nonsense. It reminded me very much of Tom's interview. Perhaps that was why he seemed to take the young man seriously, treating him with respect.

"I'll tell you this much, young man," Tom said as he shook Roy's hand. "If your references check out, you've got the job."

"Thank you, sir."

"And you can dispense with the sir," Tom said with a wink. "It makes me feel like I'm back in the Navy. Since you're out, too, you may as well get used to civilian life again."

"Yes, sir, Mr. Sheridan."

Tom shook his head and smiled, watching as the young man finally left his office. "That kid reminds me of someone."

"Maybe if you look in the mirror you'd remember who," I teased.

"You saw similarities?"

I smiled. "In actions and behavior," I said. "But now that you mention it, I imagine you didn't look much different twenty years ago."

"Twenty years ago I was a wild one. A year in juvenile detention and an agreement to go into the service and I was on the road to getting my life straightened out. Of course, it didn't happen overnight. In fact, it took a whole lot of nights. Long, lonely nights."

"But look at you now."

"I often wonder what that judge in Jacksonville would think if he saw me now."

"Probably he would say he knew good material when he saw it." I glanced toward the door. "Just like you do. Young Mr. Smith impressed you, didn't he?"

Tom nodded, but he looked like his mind had already moved onto something else. I left him to return to his work.

Weeks later, I realized I'd never expected it to become such a family affair when I hired Tom Sheridan. It was like a chain reaction. For one thing, he was definitely good for my son—the role model I'd always wanted him to have.

And because Tom hired Roy Smith, I started seeing much more of my daughter. She had arrived at the hotel one day, saying it was a surprise visit to me, but I suspected she had something else on her mind. She'd been hearing her brother talk about Tom Sheridan and his new friend Roy Smith for weeks, and now her curiosity had to be appeased.

After their first introduction, I knew there were going to be more visits from Melody. I saw the look in her eyes when she met Roy, and the return look in his. I wasn't sure I liked it, but then, I knew there was little I could say or do about it. Melody was an adult and so was Roy. I just didn't want things to happen too fast between them.

I said as much to Tom, who assured me that the more he was getting to know Roy, the more he respected the young man. "I don't think you have to worry," he said. "He seems to be a decent kid. He won't take advantage of your daughter."

I couldn't help but smile. "Tom, maybe it's not Roy who will do the advantage taking. I know my daughter. And she has the look."

"The look."

I nodded.

"Was it the look you had when you first met her father?" Tom asked. It was the first personal question he'd asked me since we'd met.

"Actually, no," I replied. "It was the lack of that look that should've warned me."

Tom cocked his head to the side, as if waiting for me to explain; when I didn't, he changed the subject. "Well, a woman shouldn't go through life without having the look at least once. Would you be willing to go out with me tonight and see if I can put that look on your face?"

"I didn't say I never had that look." It felt good to joke with Tom. I realized I hadn't done that with anyone in a very long time. Life had been way too serious.

"Then let me see if I can put that look there again."

After that night, Tom and I started seeing more and more of each other. And it wasn't just at work. We often went to dinner together and just as often had dinner with the kids, and often included Roy, much to my daughter's delight.

I was beginning to feel like we were a family again. In fact, in many ways, we were more of a family than we'd been with Jimmy.

Then one morning when I looked in the mirror, I realized something. The woman staring back at me had the look. I not only looked in love, I felt it, too. It was wonderful. It was the best I'd felt since the day I'd walked in on my husband. No, it had been even longer than that. But Tom made me feel like I hadn't felt about a man or myself in ages.

There was a bounce to my step when I arrived at the hotel earlier than usual that morning. I knew Tom always arrived early, too, and I wanted to talk to him before things got hectic, like they inevitably did later in the day. Besides, what I wanted to say couldn't wait until later. I wanted to tell him, "Thank you for the look."

I laughed as I imagined his face when I told him that. I really

126

doubted it would come as a surprise. Just like I wouldn't be surprised when he told me he felt the same.

Unfortunately, when I walked into his office, the smile on my face quickly faded. Tom was holding Roy in a warm embrace.

It was like walking in on Jimmy all over again. Without another word, I turned around and walked out of the room, just like I'd done when I walked in on Jimmy. As I walked away toward my own office, my anger was going from a simmer to a rapid boil. I slammed the door to my office after I stepped inside, then instead of sitting behind my desk, I paced in front of it.

I could feel the ribbons breaking. Colorful paper tearing away. My monster was reaching between the bars of his cage and about to open the door. At that moment, the door to my office opened. Tom stepped inside and my monster escaped.

"Get out of my office now!" I shouted. "In fact, get out of this hotel. You're fired!"

"Fired! What the hell are you talking about?"

"You! You and Roy!"

"What about Roy and me, Tanya? What exactly are you implying?"

"I'm implying nothing. I'm coming right out and saying it. I want you and your boyfriend out of here. This hotel is no place for that."

"Excuse me!" he shouted, his own words clipped. "First of all, you have no idea what was going on in my office before you barged in. Second, it wasn't any of your business until I told you."

"So when were you going to have the decency to tell me?"

"Third," he continued, as though I hadn't interrupted, "be careful about what you're assuming. You may have a lot of crow to eat."

"I know what I saw."

"Really? And what was that, exactly?"

"You and Roy." My lip quivered as I pictured their embrace. Tears were spilling from my eyes. I couldn't force out the words. My entire body shook. I couldn't stand it any longer and I turned for the door.

Tom reached out and stopped me. "I think you should hear me out."

"Just be out of here before I return. I never want to see you again." With that, I rushed out the door.

"Too bad it looks like you won't get that wish," he said after me.

I walked back to my apartment, hoping by the time I got there, I'd have myself under control. I was thankful that Hunter was in school. I wasn't ready to face him and tell him that he couldn't see Tom again. I knew it was going to hurt him. He was going to want to know why. And it wasn't going to be any easier for me to tell him the truth about his friend than it would've been to tell him about his father.

I was sitting in a daze when the door opened and Melody stepped in. I frowned, realizing Hunter wasn't the only one who was going to

127

be hurt by what I knew. She was already halfway in love with Roy—more than half, if I was right about the signs.

"Mom, we need to talk," she said softly as she came to sit on the floor in front of me.

"Yes, sweetheart, we certainly do," I whispered, reaching out and cupping her cheek with my hand.

She covered my hand with her own and gave me a grim smile. "You can't go through life judging all men by what Daddy did," she said, surprising me. "Especially decent men like Roy and Tom."

I was stunned by what she said, uncertain if she meant what I thought she did. If she did, then she knew, and I hadn't told her. I wondered if Jimmy ever had.

"What do you mean about your father?"

She frowned. "Mom, Dad wrote me a long letter when I graduated. I guess he figured I was finally old enough to understand."

I sighed. "Were you? Because I wasn't, and I was twenty years older than you."

"He wasn't my husband, Mom. He's my dad. He'll always be my dad. I don't like what he did to you, but. . . ." She sighed. "He can't help it, Mom. He tried. I think he really did, at first." She shrugged. "He just couldn't pretend any longer."

Tears filled my eyes, tears of pride for a daughter who had so much love and compassion. Suddenly, I wondered about what else she'd said, about Roy and Tom.

"Honey, I walked in on Roy and Tom this morning. It was just like when I walked in on your dad."

"No, not just like that, Mom. Very different, in fact." She went on to surprise me even more when she explained that Roy hadn't just "happened" to arrive at the hotel for a job the day he'd been interviewed. He'd been there because his search had finally ended. He was about to come face to face with a man he'd searched for over many years: his father.

Tom had never even known he had a son. Never even known the young woman had been pregnant. They were lonely kids. There wasn't any love involved, just a mutual attraction that was over when his ship left port for a six-month tour. By the time Tom returned, she'd married someone else. It wasn't until Roy was a teen that his mother told him about his real father. That was why he'd gone into the Navy, to try to be like the man he didn't know, hoping their paths would cross.

"Mom, Roy didn't tell Tom before today because he decided he wanted time to get to know him better first," Melody continued. "He told him today for a reason. Two reasons, really. Because it's his birthday, and because he wanted to ask Tom to be his best man."

"Best man?"

128

Melody was smiling now. "Yes, Mom. Roy asked me to marry him last night. I said yes. I was going to tell you after work tonight."

"Then they weren't. . . ." I sighed, feeling every bit the fool for what I'd done. "I can't believe I said what I did."

"Mom, what did you say? Roy only told me that Tom was really upset when he came back from your office."

"I fired him. I told him I wanted him out of my hotel by the time I returned." I stood, suddenly in a panic. "I hope he didn't listen to me. I hope he'll forgive me. I hope I find him."

"Stop hoping and start doing," Melody ordered. "Maybe we can have a double wedding."

I turned to look down at her, reaching out and cupping her cheek again. "I'd be honored. But let's take one step at a time."

I returned to the hotel and went straight to the security office. Tom wasn't there, but Roy was. "Where's your father?" I demanded.

"Said something about setting the boss straight about a few things."

I turned to go, then turned back again. "By the way, I apologize for my interruption this morning," I started. "And I look forward to having you for a son-in-law."

"Yes, ma'am. One way or another, I think I'll soon be calling you Mom."

I didn't think much about his words as I hurried to my own office, not surprised to find Tom sitting behind my desk. I stood on the other side, looking down at him.

"Sit down, Tanya," he said softly. "There are a few things I want to say to you."

"I want to say some things first. Please. I really need to say how sorry I am for what I said. I doubt you can forgive me, but. . . ."

"Why do you think you know what I can or can't do, Tanya?"

"What?"

"Why do you think I can't forgive you?"

"Because what I said was unforgivable. I jumped to a terrible conclusion. Well, not terrible under other circumstances, except no one should be hugging on the job. I'm not a bigot. It's just . . . this time, it was too much to bear."

"Why, Tanya, why this time?"

"Because I was on my way to your office to tell you that you succeeded in putting the look on my face. I saw it this morning when I looked in the mirror." I blushed, looking down at the floor. "What I'm trying to say is that. . . ." I looked up at him again. "I love you."

He smiled as he got up from my chair and came around the desk. He pulled me up from my own seat, about to wrap his arms around me. Then he stopped. "Do you think the boss could permit a little hugging on the job under the circumstances?"

"I suppose, since it seems we're going to become in-laws, a bit of hugging in celebration is in order."

"In-laws is only the beginning, honey," Tom replied. "Only the beginning."

And it was only the beginning. Though Melody had suggested we have a double wedding, Tom and I both insisted that she and Roy have their own very special wedding. It was going to be their day.

I had mine two weeks later, after they returned from their honeymoon.

To think I almost lost the best opportunity of my life, the opportunity to become Mrs. Tom Sheridan. I never want to let that happen again. And Tom insists it won't if we have an open, honest relationship—one where we can talk about anything, good or bad. He says he has a theory about my monster. He thinks if I don't keep him locked up so tight, he won't get so out of hand the next time he gets loose. I tend to agree. I do need to talk more about what is bothering me, instead of letting it fester until it's out of control.

However, I know I will never have a reason to be that angry with Tom again. I know in my heart now that I can have complete faith and trust in him. Just like deep down, I knew I couldn't with Jimmy.

I'm happy now. And though I know there will be good times and not-so-good times, our love will sustain us.

THE END

Attention Ladies:
BLUE-COLLAR HUNK AVAILABLE!
Plus, he's great with kids!

"This is my dad, Mr. Mann." My daughter, Lexie, smiled as she introduced me to Britney, her new friend whom I'd been hearing about ever since school had started a couple of weeks ago.

"My mom's classroom is this way." Britney took Lexie's hand and I followed the two girls down the corridor of the elementary school.

The red lights in Lexie's sneakers lit up with each step she took. My throat caught as I watched her shiny hair swaying as she walked. I was glad that Lexie had found a new friend; at least that aspect of our move back to Oceanside was working out better than I'd hoped. As for me, each day was a painful reminder of how much I'd lost, both personally and financially, ever since I'd been laid off from my job at a large software company.

I was at the school on this particular day because Britney wanted Lexie to spend Saturday afternoon at her house. I had no problem with Lexie going over to her friend's house, but I wanted to be sure this was all right with Britney's mother. I also wanted to meet Britney's mother, who was one of the schoolteachers. I was sure that she was a safe person for Lexie to be around, but I always liked to meet the people my daughter spent time with. After all, a six-year-old is hardly the best judge of character. Not that I was always perfect at judging people; I'd certainly misjudged Julia, my ex-wife and Lexie's mother.

An image of Julia with her silky, long, black hair and incredible brown eyes flashed through my mind. We had met at work and I'd thought she was everything I had ever wanted in a woman—until the day when she told me she was pregnant. We had never talked much about children, but I'd always assumed that she liked them.

I was very wrong. In the same breath that she told me she was pregnant, Julia also told me that she'd made an appointment for an abortion. She was working her way up the career ladder and had no time for children, and besides—she felt uncomfortable around them. Thankfully, after days of heated and long discussions, I talked her out of the abortion and convinced her to marry me.

Julia never was a loving or patient mother toward Lexie. Fortunately, I'm not sure that Lexie even knew what she was missing in a mother. But I could see it every day. So when Julia told me that she wanted a divorce and would give me full custody of Lexie, I didn't even argue.

131

For six years, I'd been struggling to build a relationship between Lexie and Julia, and to make my marriage into something fulfilling. Neither effort had been rewarded.

Now, I was back in my hometown, divorced with custody of my daughter, and working part-time at a dead-end job in an electronics superstore. I turned my focus back to the present as the girls slowed their pace.

"Here's Mom's room." Britney held the classroom door open so Lexie and I could enter.

"Mrs. Madigan is really nice," Lexie whispered to me as she walked past me into the classroom. I smiled to myself; Lexie had only told me this a hundred times.

Mrs. Madigan was standing with her back to us, writing on the chalkboard. The first thing I noticed about her was her pretty hair and her slender build. A wide belt wrapped around her tiny waist, and her navy slacks fit snuggly around her bottom—not too tight, but just enough to get any man's attention. She really got my attention when she turned to face us as Britney announced our arrival—

She was Holly Miller!

Madigan must be her married name, I realized.

Holly looked quizzically at us for a moment, and then her lips broke into a big smile. "Truman." She walked toward me and held out her hand. I took her slender hand in mine and gently shook it.

In high school, I'd had a crush on Holly that was bigger than the ocean. We were from different sides of town, which, in Oceanside, was like being from different planets. My father was a fisherman, and my mother was a waitress in one of the town's diners. Holly's dad was the town doctor, and her mother didn't work at all except for coordinating society luncheons. A girl with Holly's background would never be interested in a guy like me from the poor side of town.

I groaned inwardly as I remembered some of the adolescent antics I'd pulled to get Holly to notice me. Even though she'd always dated the popular jocks, I'd continued to dream that someday, she'd see me through different eyes, and then I would be the one carrying her books and walking her to class. After I graduated, I'd always planned that when I saw her again, I'd have an important job and look like a real success. Not like the man I was today—employed at a flunky job, and dressed in my scruffiest clothes. Even though I realized she was married now, I would've liked to present a better image to show her that I'd finally made something of myself.

Lexie and Britney's gazes were both moving back and forth between Holly and me like they were watching a tennis match. "Do you know each other?" Lexie asked.

"We went to school together," I explained. I looked at Holly. "I knew I was going to meet a Mrs. Madigan. But I sure didn't expect her to be you."

She grinned. "I got married."

I quickly put two and two together. "To Dennis Madigan?" Dennis had been our class president. He and Holly had dated during the last part of our senior year. Dennis, of course, was the type of man whom Holly would marry; he was a football player, a member of all the important clubs, and his father was a lawyer.

Holly nodded.

"Daddy doesn't live with us anymore," Britney announced in that frank manner that children unfortunately possess.

Holly's eyes met the question in mine. "We're divorced."

"Mom doesn't live with us, either," Lexie chimed in.

The conversation was getting far too personal for my comfort; I imagined Holly was feeling the same way. "Lexie told me that Britney would like her to come over this Saturday," I said quickly before Lexie or Britney could say anything more about their absentee parents.

Holly nodded. "You can drop Lexie off around one o'clock. She can spend the afternoon, and stay for dinner."

"Sounds like a nice day," I said. I put my hands on Lexie's shoulders and squeezed them gently as she leaned back against me. I smiled down at her, and her gaze met mine and she smiled back up at me.

I got Holly's address and the directions to her house. As I'd expected, she lived in the nicest part of town.

"You left Oceanside right after graduation," Holly commented.

I'd been hoping to avoid talking about my current situation, but it looked like I wasn't going to escape that shame. Before I could put two sentences together, Lexie began answering for me.

"We live here now. Daddy sells computers at Electroworld."

Lexie made my job sound like I owned the company. Nevertheless, I quickly explained to Holly that I'd been laid off from a software company, and that I'd decided it was a good time to move back home. "Dad died a year ago, and I wanted to be closer to Mom," I told her.

A few moments later, we said our good-byes, and then Lexie and I headed for the door. I'm sure it was just my imagination, but the whole way, I felt Holly's eyes on my back. I realized she was probably thinking that I hadn't done much with my life at all.

On Saturday, I dressed with more care than usual. As I thumbed through the shirts in my closet, I told myself that all I had planned for the day was dropping Lexie off at Britney's house, and then going over to my friend Rob's to help him with his new computer. Rob, of course, couldn't care less about what I wore; it was the possibility of seeing Holly that inspired my clothing selection that day. When I'd seen her the other day, I'd been dressed in my old jeans and a faded flannel shirt because I'd been doing yard work at my mom's house. I told myself that I might not even see Holly today. But if I did, I wanted to look my best. I pulled out my best cords and one of my newer knit shirts.

"That's where you work," Lexie said, pointing her finger at Electroworld as we drove past it on our way to Holly's house.

Her voice was filled with a pride that I didn't feel. I glanced at the slate-colored concrete building with its bright neon signs and aisles packed with computer merchandise, and wondered briefly what had happened to my life. The software company where I used to work was located in a brick-and-glass skyscraper. A bronze statue in the middle of a reflecting pool greeted employees and visitors alike as they entered the building. My coworkers and I used to joke about the cubicles we worked in, but looking back, my cubicle seemed like an executive suite. Now, I didn't even have my own desk, let alone a cubicle.

When I left Oceanside after high school graduation, I had one goal: to become a success. I didn't want to wind up like my dad. Oh, he was happy with his life and happy being a fisherman, and he didn't seem to care that he wasn't a success. But I wouldn't live that way—I was going to be a success.

So I got my computer programming degree and immediately landed a job with a recognized software company. I was a good programmer; I had even garnered company awards for some of my designs. But all of my skills couldn't help me when the software company merged with another company and proceeded to lay off staff. I probably could've found a programming job with another company, but that would've meant relocating to another state, and as much as I wanted to follow my career desires, I knew that Lexie's needs had to come first. In Oceanside, Lexie would have the love of both my sister, Beth, and my mother to guide her. I knew that Lexie needed a woman's love in her life, and women to serve as her role models. As Lexie's mother, Julia had never given those things to Lexie.

Moving back to Oceanside was more than painful for me—it marked the end of my dreams of making something of myself and proving that I could escape the small fishing town and be somebody. But Lexie was happy. She was blossoming with the love and attention that her Aunt Beth and grandmother were giving her. Plus, Lexie had a new friend now—Britney.

I pictured Holly again—how she'd looked as she'd turned from the chalkboard and our eyes had met. She'd grown from a cute teenager into a beautiful woman. Her friendly greeting had reminded me of years ago when she would greet everyone with a genuine smile and bright, blue eyes. Her eyes were different now; there was a seriousness about them. Probably from getting older, I thought. Then Lexie asked me a question and I turned my attention to her, where it should be. We were almost at Holly's by then, anyway, so I knew I should be reading house numbers and keeping an eye out for Holly's place.

"I don't know what I would've done without you." Rob stood looking over my shoulder as I displayed one of his accounting programs on the computer screen.

I laughed. "Tell that to my boss. George keeps complaining that I take too long with the customers, and that my software sales are too low."

"George doesn't know the first thing about customer satisfaction," Rob said, shaking his head. Rob and I had had several discussions recently about my job at Electroworld and George's emphasis on selling rather than having satisfied customers.

"Your computer is all set up," I said as I pushed my chair back from the desk and turned to face Rob. I'd helped him shop for a computer on the Internet; I knew that Electroworld was overpriced and wouldn't have a machine reliable enough for Rob's accounting practice.

"Of course it took a computer whiz to load all the software and move the files from the old computer." Rob grinned and shook his head.

"Not really—"

"Do you know how long it would've taken me to do all of this? Hours. And it still wouldn't be done right." Rob opened a bottle of beer, handed it to me, and sat on the edge of the desk. "With your background, it's got to be daily torture for you, working for George."

I nodded and took a swig of beer. "It doesn't pay much, either. He gives shifts with high customer traffic to the staff members who sell the most. Unfortunately, there aren't many computer buyers on Monday mornings, when I usually work."

"You should think about going into business for yourself, consulting for small businesses."

I thought he was joking and started to laugh until I could see that he was dead serious.

"Business people like myself don't have time to install computers, upgrade software, and all that magic stuff that you can do with one hand tied behind your back. I lose production time whenever I get involved with this computer stuff."

"I never looked at it that way," I admitted. "But I don't think there would be enough business in a town this size for me to make a living."

"I'm sure you could draw business from the small towns around here. Heck, you could always do consulting on the side to supplement your income from Electroworld."

My first thought was that if George believed I was doing anything that could put me in competition with him, he'd fire me so fast, I wouldn't know what'd hit me. "I'll think about it," I said finally. But

I knew that I probably wouldn't. "Hey, remember Holly Miller?" I asked suddenly.

Rob grinned and chuckled. "The cute blonde you were gaga over back in high school? How could I forget?"

I told Rob about the surprise I'd had of discovering that Holly was Britney's mother.

"I guess this means you'll be seeing lots of her." Rob gave me a lecherous grin.

I shrugged. "Holly's still way out of my league. At least now, though, I'm wise enough not to make an idiot of myself trying to get her to notice me. I wasn't surprised when she told me that she'd married Dennis Madigan."

"That was no marriage made in heaven," Rob said as he set his empty beer bottle down on the desk. "I've got a friend in the police department, and I guess old Dennis was arrested more than once for hitting Holly."

I straightened up in my chair. Just thinking of anyone striking Holly—or any woman, for that matter—made me angry. And Dennis? He'd always looked like Mr. Perfect to me. "Does he still live here in Oceanside?"

"Nope. After the divorce, he moved up north. From everything I've heard, the guy's bad news."

"Who would've thought he'd turn out to be a wife beater?" I mused.

Rob and I talked some more, and then I got up to leave. I had some errands to run and then I needed to pick up Lexie at Holly's. I figured maybe I'd see Holly this time; when I'd dropped Lexie off earlier, I hadn't. I'd gone up to the door with Lexie, but Britney had answered the doorbell. She'd explained that her mother was on the telephone in the kitchen. Since we'd already made arrangements about the day, I'd left without seeing her.

"Anyway, keep thinking about doing some consulting," Rob advised as he locked his office and we walked out to our respective cars. "I know a couple of businesses that'd be glad to pay for some of your time—and they'd probably give you some work right away."

"Let me think about it," I said again, and then I added, "At this point, I wouldn't even know what to charge."

"That's the easy part." Rob quickly slipped into his accountant's role and quoted an hourly rate that made me think twice. He was right: Consulting could be the perfect deal for me, if it worked.

As I drove away, I thought about what he'd said about Holly. Dennis had hit her! That probably explained some of the seriousness I'd seen in her eyes—she was carrying psychological scars. Maybe I'd see her when I picked up Lexie. Oh, not that I'd mention Dennis; I just wanted to see her again.

Britney and Lexie answered the door together when I rang the doorbell. A garlicky, tomato fragrance whetted my appetite as I stepped into the Miller entry hall. Holly must've made spaghetti for dinner, I thought as my stomach growled. When I got home, I was going to nuke a frozen dinner in the microwave.

Holly stepped into the hallway carrying a spoon in one hand and a dishtowel in the other. "I'm sorry—I thought we'd be done with dinner by now," she said. "But you're welcome to join us."

"We set a place for you at the table," Britney announced.

I grinned. "It smells too good to refuse." A home-cooked dinner was a far better option than a frozen, cardboard-textured meal. Not to mention that I'd get to talk to Holly. Still, I reminded myself that I had to keep my head in line and not try to make a big deal out of getting reacquainted with Holly.

But it was impossible to think straight as I followed Holly down the hallway and into the kitchen. My fingers itched to touch her soft, bouncy hair, and the way her bottom moved in her tight jeans raised my temperature.

"We're having spaghetti," Holly said as we stepped into the kitchen.

A pan of sauce was simmering on the range beside a large pot of bubbly boiling water. Britney and Lexie both headed to the kitchen counter, where they'd been in the midst of chopping vegetables for a salad.

"Anything I can do?" I asked. Everyone had a task but me.

Holly met my gaze and smiled. "Yes. You can select a bottle of wine." She pointed to a wine rack across the room. "Believe me—I need it today."

"We had a flood," Britney said to me, by way of explanation.

"A flood?"

"The washing machine hose sprung a leak," Holly supplied.

"There was water all over." Lexie's eyes were wide as she described how the water from the utility room had seeped into the kitchen.

"Well, everything must be okay now," I said, looking down at the dry floor where Lexie pointed.

"I taped the leak," Holly explained.

To me, that sounded like a temporary fix. "Do you want me to take a look at the hose?"

She hesitated like she didn't want to trouble me, so I didn't wait for an answer. I followed the girls into the utility room. Holly had certainly fixed the hose; she must've used a whole roll of duct tape. But a quick glance told me that there was too much strain on the hose and that her repairs wouldn't last.

I sensed Holly's presence behind me before I heard her voice. "It may not look pretty, but it sure stopped the leak," she said with a chuckle.

I turned my gaze from the hose to her pretty, ocean-deep eyes. She was standing inches from me; her soft perfume of summer flowers was gently teasing my nose, and the warmth of her body made me want to wrap my arms around her so I could feel her body next to mine. Still, I pushed my physical desires aside and made myself focus on the situation at hand.

"It's fixed, all right—but I don't think you're ready to quit your teaching job and go into plumbing."

Holly laughed. She motioned for me to follow her back into the kitchen. "It's time to put the noodles in the water. And where's that wine?"

I perused Holly's well-stocked wine rack and selected a red wine that would go perfectly with our dinner. While I opened the bottle, Lexie and Britney put the salad and garlic bread on the table, and Holly tended to the spaghetti. A feeling of warmth and family filled my bones as we all worked in harmony; I couldn't remember ever feeling like this before. I liked it, all right, but it sure frightened me, too, because it felt so good and I knew it couldn't last.

"I can get a hose and fix your washer for you," I offered when we were all seated around the pretty, pine kitchen table.

"Oh, I don't want to bother you with that," Holly said as she piled steaming spaghetti onto Britney's plate from the pot.

"I'd be glad to do it. And it'll give our girls more time together." Smiles broke out on Lexie and Britney's faces as I explained that I could come over the very next day to make the repair.

"Okay," Holly said, grinning with pleasure. "But only if I can fix you dinner—again!"

"It's a deal," I said, as I picked up my wineglass.

And what a deal, I thought. Now, I'll get to see Holly again.

Alas, back at home later, I came to my senses by the time I'd tucked Lexie in for the night. The warm family feeling, Holly's innate sexuality, and the wine had certainly distorted my thinking; the old torch I carried for Holly had been re-ignited full force, and I realized that now, I was once again thinking of her romantically.

Well, I might've had a chance with her back when I was working for the software company, but now, I realized, all too painfully, that I had nothing to offer a woman like her. After all, why on earth would she be interested in a guy like me—a roughhewn, simple guy with a part-time job at Electroworld? It didn't matter what I had been months ago; what mattered was the person I was now—a complete and total flunky.

Oh, I'd fix her washer tomorrow, but I'd also keep my feelings in check. Nevertheless, Holly had a warm, outgoing personality that made it hard for anyone not to like her. Coupled with her easy sexual attractiveness, I realized it was going to be all too easy for me to get carried away.

"I'm sure glad you brought your toolbox."

Holly leaned over the dryer and handed me another tool. Like most utility rooms, hers was small, and the quarters had gotten even closer after I'd moved the washer out from the wall. I'd vowed to not let my emotions or my physical desires get the better of me that day, but I was finding it impossible to contain my feelings when I was constantly brushing elbows with Holly and I was enveloped in the captivating scent of her perfume. Besides, I was having a good time—Holly was fun to be around.

I looked up from the washer and grinned at her remark. "I don't think your tools would've worked." When I'd arrived, Holly had handed me an old shoebox filled with a motley assortment of screwdrivers, pliers, and hammers.

"Dennis took most of the tools when he moved out," she explained.

I wanted to ask her then about her marriage, but I wasn't sure about how to broach the subject, especially since Rob had told me about Dennis's abusive behavior. Finally, though, I did ask her how long they'd been married.

"Five years. We got married during our junior year of college."

"Does Britney see him very often?"

She shook her head. "Nope. He doesn't have visitation rights."

"Oh," I said, thinking that was odd. I glanced at her face. Her lips were thin suddenly, and her eyes were distant and filled with pain. Instantly, I was angry with myself for pushing the subject, but I hadn't thought that talking about her divorce would be so painful for Holly. Now, though, I realized that she must've been crazy about the guy. And, judging by her expression, I realized that she must still care for him. I'd heard about women who kept going back to their lousy, abusive husbands, even though they were beaten every time.

Holly pushed away from the dryer. "Looks like you're done. I'll go check on the Crock-Pot."

I realized she was using the Crock-Pot as an excuse to end the conversation about Dennis. At least now, though, I knew her feelings about Dennis and her divorce. A few moments later, when I went into the kitchen, Holly was laughing with Lexie and Britney as they cleaned mushrooms for the salad. Behind her eyes, though, I still glimpsed a hint of lingering sadness.

I was so busy thinking about my feelings for Holly and hating my job situation that I wasn't prepared for the conversation that came up at dinner. Knowing kids like I do, I realize I should've been better prepared.

We had just filled our plates with a chicken entrée that looked like a picture out of a cookbook, and smelled like a taste of pure heaven, when Lexie asked, "Can Britney come visit me next Saturday and have dinner?"

Britney's eyes lit up at the idea, and Holly gave me an expectant look.

"Sure," I said.

I hoped I hadn't hesitated too long before giving my answer, but a hundred thoughts had run through my mind at Lexie's request. Thought Number One: I'll be seeing Holly again.

"I'm afraid I'm not much of a cook," I said sheepishly, feeling myself blush, "but we can always order a pizza."

Ear-to-ear smiles appeared on the girls' faces and their eyes danced with impending merriment.

"Holly, you're invited, too," I said.

"Oh, okay—if you're sure it won't be too much trouble?"

I shook my head. "I'm a pro at ordering pizza for a crowd."

The conversation immediately shifted to everyone stating their favorite types of pizzas, and jokes about the pizza toppings we couldn't stand. Everyone, including me, talked and laughed all through dinner. Still, besides worrying about spending more time with Holly next Saturday, I also had to fight those feelings of togetherness and family that warmed my soul every time we all had dinner together.

The next morning I was getting ready to leave for work when Rob called. A friend of his had some computer work that he wanted me to do for him. I started to hedge—until I remembered the hourly rate that Rob had suggested.

"Let me look at my employment agreement with Electroworld and I'll get back to you," I told Rob.

"I called last night, but you must've been at your mom's," Rob continued.

"Actually, we were over at Holly's." I explained then about the leaky hose on her washer and having dinner with her for the second night in a row.

"I told you you'd be seeing lots of her." Rob chucked, and I felt him grinning through the phone.

"It's not what you think, buddy. Besides, she's still hung up on Dennis."

"You're kidding."

I told him about her reaction when we'd talked about him previously.

"Yeah, well, I suppose she could still have feelings for him, but she's been divorced for a couple of years now, right? So, why don't you ask her out—just the two of you, without the kids around—and see what happens?"

"I don't think so, Rob."

"And why not? Because she's way out of your league? I seem to recall that you made some crazy remark to that effect the other day."

140

"I just don't have much to offer her right now—let alone any woman, for that matter," I said, surprised that Rob couldn't see this for himself.

"Truman, you were laid off. Along with thousands of other people this year. It's not like you're a lazy deadbeat."

"I know, I know. I just don't want to get involved with anyone until I'm more financially stable."

"Personally, I think you're more worried about your image. Just remember, though, buddy—money and a job title don't make the man. Dennis may have a good job, but the guy's a jerk."

As I hung up the phone, I knew that, as close as Rob and I were, he would never understand my need to make something of myself. His parents didn't have a lot of money when he was growing up, either, but it didn't seem to bother him. Me—I wasn't ashamed of my parents, but I wanted to have a job where I could be proud of myself and be respected by others.

Now, I rummaged through my desk and found the packet of information that Electroworld had given me when I went to work for them. From what I could tell after studying the content, there was nothing in their literature that said I couldn't work for another company or do computer-related work on my off hours. Doing the consulting work would certainly be more mentally rewarding than my job at Electroworld. Plus, I could really use the money. Thankfully, I'd saved quite a bit with my bonuses and raises from the software company. But every month recently, I'd had to dip into that money, so I knew darn well that it wouldn't last forever. I called Rob back and told him that I'd do the work.

By Saturday, I'd lined up two more consulting jobs through Rob. The first job was going to require quite a bit of time, but the client didn't even flinch when I gave him an estimate. I knew I couldn't depend on always having these jobs, but for the time being, it was great to know that I was using my brain again, and to know that a little extra money would soon be coming my way.

When Holly dropped Britney off, I confirmed with her that she'd be coming for pizza that night. She nodded, and gave me a smile that made my heart pound.

"I'll bring a video for the girls to watch."

A video? Obviously, Holly wasn't planning on having a quick dinner and leaving immediately afterward. Still, I put her comment out of my mind and started cleaning my duplex. The place was several years old, but I kept it in fairly tidy condition, even though it was small and often cluttered with Lexie's Barbies. As I vacuumed the living room, I wondered what Holly's marriage to Dennis had been like; I imagined that they must've gotten along at first, and then Dennis

141

must've gradually revealed his true colors. I shuddered just thinking of Dennis striking Holly; Rob was right: The guy was a jerk. But I was even more disturbed as I recalled the expression on Holly's face when we'd talked about Dennis the week before. The pain in her eyes had told me that she still missed him.

I told myself for the thousandth time to forget her. But the more I was with her, the more difficult it became for me not to think about her. I liked talking and joking with her, and I liked the warm feeling of togetherness I felt being around her. I'd never felt that way with a woman before. Holly was also sexy; her soft hair had brushed my hand the week before when she was handing me tools, and heat had rushed through my veins from head to toe. I longed to run my hands through her hair and hold her face close to mine while I kissed her soft mouth. . . .

I jerked myself away from my lustful thoughts. After all, she was obviously not over Dennis; I wasn't her type; and I didn't have a decent job. Those were three very good reasons for me to keep my distance.

I imagined that dinner that night would be like the two other dinners we had shared—with everyone sitting around the table together, talking and eating. But Holly had other ideas.

"How would you girls like to watch a movie and eat pizza in the living room?" Holly asked as she pulled a Finding Nemo DVD from the plastic sack she was carrying. Of course, Lexie and Britney were thrilled by this idea, so Holly and I helped them fill their plates with Hawaiian pizza and then Holly seated them at the coffee table in front of the television while I started the movie.

"I thought this would give us a chance to talk," Holly said as we walked back into the kitchen together, leaving the girls ensconced. "I feel like every time we're together, we wind up talking about kids' stuff and nothing else."

"Good idea." Although I didn't really want to talk about me, and I doubted that she wanted to talk about Dennis.

We sat down at the dining room table and filled our plates with pizza. Even though I could see the girls on the floor in the living room, I felt like I was alone with Holly, and I was all too aware suddenly of my desire for her, and how much I liked being with her. I kept telling myself that she was strictly off-limits, but my body just wouldn't cooperate with my mind.

Holly started off our dinner conversation by telling me about the people she'd seen that afternoon that I knew. We reminisced and talked about people and events as we ate a pizza topped with everything but anchovies. Occasionally, Lexie or Britney would need something, like another napkin or a refill of Pepsi, and we'd take turns helping them. My lustful feelings were now joined with the warm feeling of togetherness that I felt whenever I was around Holly—each was a dangerous emotion for me to let myself feel, but combined, the mixture was lethal to my resolve to remain detached from her.

"It had to be a real blow to you, getting laid off like you did," Holly was saying. "Every day I read in the newspaper about people in technical fields losing their jobs."

"Yeah, it's a tough job market right now," I said absently.

"What kind of software did you write?"

Her question opened the door for me to tell her all about my special projects and awards. The more I talked, the more I wanted to show her—to prove to her—that I'd been a success—once. A couple of times, I paused in my conversation because I thought I might be boring her, but the keen look in her eyes and her pointed questions told me that she was hanging on to my every word.

"Oh, well," I said, wrapping up, "at least I was a success once in my life." I figured there was no point in trying to gloss over my current situation. She knew darn well that I now worked part-time at Electroworld.

"It all depends on how you define success." Her blue eyes were dark and somber as she spoke. "Our values for success were so wrong when we were growing up; living in the 'right' neighborhood and being friends with the 'popular' kids meant everything to us. And yet, so much of it was a sham. The things that we thought were symbols of success have nothing to do with what really matters in life."

Her words and tone surprised me. I didn't know what to say, so I let her talk.

"So often, we think that working a high-paying job makes a person a success. But I happen to think that it's more important that a person is a good parent, and kind to others."

She was sounding like Rob suddenly, with his statement about how money and job titles don't make the man. As I listened to her, though, I kept thinking that she didn't really know what she was talking about. After all, she didn't know what it was like not to have money to buy the "in" things. She'd never been unpopular because she didn't live in the right neighborhood. She hadn't watched her parents come home every night, exhausted from working too hard at difficult, low-paying jobs.

Then it hit me—she was saying those things to make me feel good about working at Electroworld. She was kindhearted, after all, and she was probably trying to lessen my pain over being laid off. I realized there was no point in arguing with her, so I just let her talk and nodded in agreement. I was actually relieved when Lexie and Britney came to the table because Finding Nemo was over.

"We need to talk about the carnival," Lexie announced.

The Oceanside Carnival was next Friday night, but I didn't know what there was to talk about. Unless the two girls wanted to go together, which was probably where Lexie's statement was headed. I was right, of course: The girls wanted to go together.

By the time Britney and Holly bid us good night, we'd made plans for all of us to go to the carnival together. Honestly, it seemed like I kept getting thrown together with Holly at every turn. I wondered how she felt about seeing me so much; for me, it was becoming almost painful. I knew it was a relationship without a future, and yet, I couldn't seem to put the brakes on my feelings.

The annual carnival was sponsored by Oceanside High School and held in their gym. I hadn't been near the high school since graduation; with the exception of fresh paint, though, it hadn't changed a bit. What had changed was that Holly was at my side at the carnival that night, acting like my date—something that I would've given my right arm for back when I was a student. She stood close to me, and occasionally, she would reach for my arm or hand. I welcomed the physical closeness; I didn't have the strength to ignore it.

The gym was packed that night with everyone from town, which gave me the opportunity to talk to people I hadn't seen since I'd moved back to Oceanside. I enjoyed seeing the familiar faces that I'd known since I was a kid; when I wasn't watching Lexie and Britney playing games, I was talking to people who wanted all the details about my return to Oceanside. I liked talking to the people, but I didn't like having to admit that I was working at Electroworld. Still, several professional types came up to me and said that they'd heard I was doing computer consulting, and that they were interested in hiring me. After I'd scribbled my name and phone number on scraps of paper numerous times, I decided I'd need to get some business cards and treat my sideline like a real business—a genuine going concern. Holly was always at my elbow during these conversations, so after the first time the topic of consulting came up, I explained to her what I was doing.

"What a great idea!" Her voice rang with enthusiasm

I blushed sheepishly. "It's not exactly a sure thing yet." I didn't want her to think I'd be making the kind of money I'd made at the software company.

"Maybe not, Truman, but I can tell that you like the work." Her gaze met mine and I felt, suddenly, as though she could read my soul. "Truman, you should see your face when you talk to people about what you can do to help them. You come alive, Truman. It's what you should be doing, even if there's risk involved."

Her comments didn't come across as platitudes. Her eyes and the tone of her voice were serious and filled with genuine sincerity. But did she really understand that a business venture such as this one had no guarantee of success?

Usually, carnival games bore me, and the crush of people generally makes me wish I were back at home, drinking a beer in front of the television. But that night, I enjoyed talking with everyone, and I didn't even mind that Lexie played too many games that she could never win. All too soon, though, Britney and Lexie were worn out and it was time to leave. Then the four of us piled into my car and I headed for Holly's place. Earlier in the week, the carnival plans had been expanded to include an overnighter for Lexie at Britney's house.

At Holly's, I started to leave as soon as I saw that Holly and the girls were safely in the house, but then Holly asked me to stay. "I'll get the girls settled. Then we can have some wine and unwind from the evening."

While Holly was upstairs settling the girls for the night, I found the bottle of white wine that she had chilling in her refrigerator. She must've planned on me staying for a drink, I mused as I took the bottle from the top shelf of the refrigerator. I pulled the cork and carried the bottle and wineglasses into the living room. I was just filling Holly's glass when she came into the room.

She took the goblet from my outstretched hand, kicked off her shoes, and curled up in a corner of the sofa. I sat at the other end. Still, her sofa was so short that her bare feet were only inches away from my leg, sending warmth into my leg and throughout my body. I fought the urge to put my hand on her foot, though, throughout the evening, I'd picked up vibes that Holly wouldn't refuse my romantic advances. There had been many touches from her hands, combined with warm smiles.

Still, as much as I wanted to reach over and pull her into my arms for a breathtaking kiss, I wasn't about to get hurt just because she was still in love with Dennis—or because she suddenly realized that she didn't want a part-time salesman in her life. So, I decided right then and there to find out, once and for all, about her feelings for Dennis before she and I got thrown into another evening together.

"Last week over pizza, I told you all about myself since I left Oceanside," I began as I met her gaze across the sofa. "Tonight's your turn."

She laughed and rolled her eyes. "Jeez! Where do I start?"

Then, while we drank our wine, she told me about her lifelong desire to be a teacher, and how she'd gone to college to pursue just such a career. She told me about her first year teaching and other experiences, but skirted the subject of her marriage and Dennis. When she paused as though she was done, I reached for her glass and refilled it from the elegant bottle.

"What about Dennis, and your marriage?" I asked. I felt bold asking; yet last week, I'd quietly shared with her the problems in my own failed marriage. I'd even told her about Julia's plans for an abortion.

She shrugged, looking down into her wineglass. "It didn't work out."

I looked deeply into her eyes when she returned her gaze, somewhat shyly, to mine. "I've picked up that you still have feelings for him."

Instantly, her eyes turned dark, and quizzical. She shook her head. "No. Why would you think that?"

I told her then about how she'd looked when we'd discussed Dennis previously, while I was replacing the hose on her washing machine.

She looked thoughtful for a moment. "You're right; I was thinking of him then. But not in a caring way." She studied her fingers as they toyed with the stem of her wineglass. "Remember the other night when I talked about what success really means, and how sometimes, the things that we think show the world that we're successful, are really shams?"

I nodded. How could I forget?

"My marriage to Dennis was one of those shams. Being married to him opened my eyes to what's really important in life. I was dazzled by his popularity, his success in school, and his rich family; I thought those things were important to my happiness. But I found out the hard way that a person can have money, status in the community, and lots of friends, and still be woefully unhappy inside. Dennis . . . he was abusive, you see . . . he hit me."

"I'm sorry, Holly," I told her softly.

She shook her head dismissively, reflecting. "I never should have married him. I was so stupid."

"You weren't stupid. Unfortunately, that often isn't something you realize until you've lived with someone."

She bit her lip and shook her head. "No—I should've known better. He—he hit me a few times—even before we got married. Every time, he always told me that it would never happen again. And I believed him, every single time. But I was so wrong."

I reached over and covered her hand with mine.

"Everything came to a head for me one night when Dennis hit me in front of Britney. He didn't know that she'd come into the room because he had his back to the doorway. That's why Dennis doesn't have visitation rights now; Britney is afraid of him even though he never laid a hand on her. Dennis—he didn't even fight for visitation rights; he just moved out of town and out of our lives."

I leaned closer and pulled her into my arms so that her head rested on my shoulder. She wasn't crying; she was just quiet. I laid my head

146

on top of her silky hair and breathed in the soft fragrance of her shampoo.

After a few minutes, she moved her head, looked up, and met my gaze. "The expression you saw on my face that day when you were fixing the washing machine hose—I was thinking about how stupid I'd been to marry Dennis, and how wrong my values had been. What I really want now, in life, is love, and to be with people who are kind and caring." She took a deep breath, but her eyes never left mine. "I want somebody like you, Truman."

"But—"

"Don't tell me about your job situation. I don't care about it. And I don't care that your dad was a fisherman, or that you didn't grow up in a fancy neighborhood. None of that is important, Truman. What matters is that I think you're a kind man, and a wonderful father. And I like being with you, Truman—in fact, I love being with you."

I pulled her close and touched my lips to hers. Our first kiss was soft and gentle, but the ones that followed were deeper and filled with the fire of love. We kissed and held each other for some time, and then she talked more about her life with Dennis, whom I'd always foolishly thought was Mr. Perfect.

As we talked, I thought about my own values. I'd always thought that success was having an important job; I'd never looked at how a person's character is really the mark of true success. I'd thought that Dad wasn't a success because he didn't sit behind a desk in a big office, or live in a fancy house. Now, though, I was finally realizing, through Holly, that Dad was successful at what truly matters in life: He was a kind and caring man, and an excellent father and husband. Those qualities come from the heart, not from the size of a paycheck or a job title.

That night happened almost a year ago. Since that time, Holly and I got married, and I've turned my small consulting business into a full-time job. Even though my business is a success, though, I now know that what matters most is that I'm a kind and caring man. Being a good husband, father, and stepfather—those are the great successes of my life.

THE END

TARGETED BY A HIT MAN
Cops say my wife's to blame

"I don't know what you want from me, Carly."

"Then you're more stupid than I thought."

Instinctively, I raised my hand to slap her. I'd never struck a woman before. Yet, at that moment, I wanted to smack her as hard as I could for insulting me. I hated her for nearly driving me to do an awful thing.

"That's right. Slug a defenseless woman."

"I'm sorry."

"Sure you are. Like you're sorry for everything else. What's the use of talking? My mother always said it was cheap. Just like you."

"How can you say that?" I asked.

"It's easy. Want to hear it again?"

"Everything I've ever done was for you and Bart."

"Really?"

"You complained I wasn't making enough as a delivery man, so I went into business to make more money. Then you complained that I was working too much—"

"I'm sure you filled those longer hours well."

"What's that supposed to mean?"

"Come off it. Do you really think I'm that stupid?"

I ignored that comment, wondering if she ever really knew about Sally. "They call it work for a reason."

"Well, what does any of it matter anymore?" she said.

"What are you saying to me?"

"I can't live with you any longer, Mike."

"That's it? You're finished. You want to throw all these years down the toilet."

"I guess."

"You guess? Have you given any idea where you'll go and how you'll support yourself and Bart?"

"I don't know. The one thing I do know is that none of this fighting is good for the kid."

"You can't just split. You don't even have a job."

"I'll get one."

"Doing what? Stripping? Turning tricks?"

"You jerk! Is that all you think I can do?" She stormed out of the kitchen.

She moved out a week after that fight. How had we come to this?

We had been such a happy couple once. But all we ever did lately was bicker and argue. Some of the stuff we fought over was ridiculous. I didn't remember changing. When had Carly?

I first met Carly, of all places, in the dentist's office. I was there for a routine cleaning. She didn't seem to be as fortunate. I could see that she was in a great deal of pain as she waited to be seen by the dentist. The dead giveaway was that her pretty face was somewhat swollen, making her look like a chipmunk. I felt sorry for her and wanted to try and take her mind off the pain. She probably thought I was trying to pick her up, but she gave me her telephone number just the same. I truly had every intention of calling her later on in the week, especially to see how she was feeling, but Sally—the girl I'd been dating on and off for some time—showed up on my doorstep and I forgot about the girl from the dentist's office.

Four months later, Sally and I broke up for good. I began to wonder about the missed chance I'd had with the pretty girl I had spoken to at the dentist's office. Unfortunately, I had lost her number. Not knowing her last name or where she lived, it seemed that I was out of luck.

Nearly a year later, my friend Sam dragged me to a club. "Either you're a man or a monk. We're going out tonight," he declared.

I gave in to his arm-twisting tactics. During the drive to the club, he kept telling me, "The guys say it's wall-to-wall hotties at this place."

"And you believe them, Sam?"

"The bouncer at the door is instructed to keep out all dogs."

"That's unconstitutional, discrimination by face."

Sam cracked up. "Save the funny stuff to amuse the chicks."

The place was jumping when we walked in at ten-thirty. We could hear the music all the way in the parking lot at the back. Something humorous occurred to me. Maybe if I got real lucky I'd pop an eardrum and have to go to the doctor. Then perhaps I'd meet a nice girl there. I chuckled.

"What'd I miss?"

I shook my head.

"You're getting strange, man." Sam patted my shoulder.

Inside we met a soft wall of bodies. Nudging our way toward the bar, I noticed that many of the girls were lookers, but I saw a few that probably snuck inside while the bouncer at the door wasn't looking. Sam ordered two beers and we looked around the club.

"So was I lying?" he tried to ask over the drone of the music.

I shook my head, glad I was a good lip reader.

"Look, man, if you see something you like, make your move quickly before someone else snatches her up," Sam advised.

"Okay, Dad."

That's when I saw Carly, the pretty girl from the dentist's office, talking with a guy on the other side of the room. What were the chances of me bumping into her again? But she was already with a guy.

"See something hot?" Sam asked as he looked in the direction I'd been gazing.

"You're not going to believe this, but remember the girl I told you about from the dentist's office?"

"Refresh my memory."

"The one whose number I lost," I filled in.

"Oh, yeah. Don't tell me she's here."

"Talking to a guy across the floor." I pointed in their direction.

"So go over and interrupt."

"I can't do that."

"Why not? You've already met."

"Nah, it wouldn't be right."

"Don't be a jerk. Go say hello."

"She probably hates me for not calling."

"Tell her you lost her number."

"I can't just horn in on that other guy."

"You're afraid she's going to blow you off, aren't you."

"I guess."

"Well you can't lose something you never had."

I began to mull that over in my mind when Sam added, "You're not going over there, are you?"

"I don't know."

"Don't be a loser, man. Why let her slip away again?"

Sam was probably the only guy I'd ever let call me a loser. I loved him like a brother. We'd been friends since grade school, and nothing short of death could ever pull us apart.

"I don't know about you, but I see a chick that needs me," he said. "See you later."

I turned back to Carly. The guy was walking away and yet I still hesitated. I guess I just didn't feel like hearing what a jerk I was for not calling. But, on the other hand, what did I have to lose? After all, Sam was right. You can't lose something you never had in the first place.

I pushed through the crowd before she disappeared into the masses.

"How's your tooth?" I asked as I reached her.

"What?" she looked at me as if I was crazy. As her memory returned she touched her cheek and said, "You're that guy from the dentist's office."

Wearing a sheepish look, I began to tell my white lie. "I lost your number and couldn't call. I thought I'd never see you again—until fate brought us together again tonight."

She smiled. I fell in love with her right then and there.

"Perhaps this time I should tattoo my name and number to your hand," she joked.

"So I get a second chance?"

"Only because it's fate. You lose my number this time, you're a dead man," she said, trying to keep a straight face.

By the end of the evening, I knew that she was the one girl put on this planet for me, the one person who I was destined to spend the rest of my life with. We began to date and got married a year later.

Like most couples starting out, we found a small apartment close to both of our jobs. I delivered office supplies for a large chain, and she worked as a bank teller. Of course we wanted to be able to afford our own home one day and start a family. We felt we were just as entitled as the next couple to our own slice of the American dream.

It would've been nice if I'd been born into a rich family, but I wasn't. Besides, my parents died when I was a kid and my grandmother raised me until her death. So everything I got I'd worked for—not that I was complaining. Hard work never scared me.

We hardly saw much of Carly's family. That was her choice, though. I could hardly blame her. She had an older brother who left home at seventeen to join the Navy. No one in the family had heard from him since. As far as her mother and father went, they hardly spoke to one another even though they lived under the same roof. So it wasn't much of a surprise when Carly's mother got a divorce and moved. I did raise my eyebrows, though, when she moved in with another woman.

Our first few years together were the happiest of my life. Everything suddenly had meaning. I couldn't wait to get home to be with Carly. She became the ultimate housewife. Not only could she cook superb dishes, but she turned up the heat in bed as well. I was truly a happy guy who thought I had it all.

One of our most special nights together was my twenty-fifth birthday. We'd been married nearly two years. I walked into the apartment and was greeted by a candlelit table and delightful cooking aromas wafting from the kitchen. She could've stopped right there, but it turned out that she was merely warming up.

I remember telling her how great everything looked. "When did you have the time to do all this?" I asked.

"I stayed home from work and have been preparing this meal most of the day."

To show my appreciation, I took her in my arms and kissed her.

"Slow down, big boy. Have some dinner first."

She'd made a special chicken dish. The name escapes me, but it was delicious. Carly was an excellent cook, which my waistline reflected. After sharing a bottle of wine, I was feeling no pain. She bought me a new watch, and as I put in on she hit me with the real present—I was going to be a father. Having a kid certainly completed our happiness. Only it also helped contribute to our money problems and subsequent quarreling.

After Bart was born, we needed a bigger place. If we still had two incomes coming in this would've been no problem, but with Carly home taking care of our son, things were tight. Bart quickly became the center of our lives. Carly only wanted the best for Bart. Who could fault her for that? Unfortunately, it led to a humdinger of an argument. I'd been socking away as much money as I could so we could afford to move. Carly had tapped into those savings for some stuff for Bart. When I gave her flack for doing so, she flew into a rage. I'd never seen her like that. It was a side of her that I never knew existed.

"Look at the swing I got for Bart," she began.

I saw the price and asked, "How'd you pay for this, Carly?"

"I wrote a check."

"You know we can't afford it. Besides, it's not the one we picked out."

"It's better."

"No, it isn't. It's only nicer looking. And so is the price."

"So what? Bart deserves it."

"I want my son to have the best just as much as you," I explained. "But you've got to bring this swing back."

"I won't."

"You've got to. We can't afford it."

"You're just a cheapskate!"

"You know that's not true."

"All you do is hoard your money."

"I'm saving it for us, so we can move to a bigger place."

"That's what you say."

"You sound like you're unhappy."

"That's because I am. When was the last time I bought myself a new dress?" she shouted.

"When was the last time you worked?" I shot back. "I only make so much, Carly."

"I don't think you're telling me the truth. I think you're just a cheapskate."

I went to reach for her, I guess to comfort her, but she viciously spat, "Don't touch me! Get away from me!"

Who was this woman standing there shrieking at me? Why did we suddenly have to keep up with the neighbors? It had never bothered her before. She always knew how much I made. Figuring I'd never win this crazy argument, I grabbed my jacket and left the apartment. Besides, I thought it best that I get out of the house and clear my head before I said something I'd be sorry for. By the time I returned, Carly was apologetic. I could tell she'd been crying. The bottom line was that she promised to return the swing and exchange it for the more reasonably priced one.

Things seemed to settle down after that argument. We'd disagree from time to time, but nothing major. I figured Carly was content, because she didn't talk about going back to work. With some overtime whenever I could get it, we were able to move to a larger apartment.

Around this time, Sam joined a gym and suggested I come with him and try it out. I was toting around an extra fifteen pounds and decided something should be done about it, so I joined the gym as well. It turned out to be a terrific idea and I felt better because of it.

Carly soon began to drop subtle hints that she wasn't too happy about me coming home for dinner later. I chose to ignore them and continued to stop at the gym after work. One night as I walked through the door, she asked quite nastily, "Where were you, Mike?"

"Where I go every day—the gym."

"Well, dinner's burnt."

"Like you didn't know what time I'd be coming home. What did you do, put the flame up too high?" I said, hanging up my jacket and walking into the kitchen to grab a beer.

"I can't believe you don't care about me slaving over the stove."

"A wife is supposed to do that. Besides, you're home all day."

"Well, a husband should be home on time," she shrieked, picking up one of the pots and throwing it at me. It missed my head by inches and hit the wall behind me.

"What's wrong with you?"

"You're never here," she screamed.

"So where am I at this moment?"

It turned out that Carly was upset by a great deal more than my stopping off at the gym. Basically, we never truly resolved her dissatisfaction with our meager lifestyle. She wanted to be able to spend more money on luxuries and go away on exotic vacations. She conveniently forgot that if she wanted to own a home one day, there was no way we could afford to be extravagant on my salary alone. She'd have to go back to work, but she wouldn't leave Bart with just anybody. And baby-sitters didn't come cheaply.

A solution fell into my lap unexpectedly. The owner of the gym wanted to retire. His wife had just died from a sudden heart attack and he wanted to move closer to his only daughter. I asked him what kind of money he was looking for. It wasn't a great deal, but still more than I could ever swing alone. With a partner, it was doable. The hours of operation were long, so I needed someone to help me run the place, anyway.

By this time, Sam had gotten married to a real sweet girl named

Natalie. I knew he didn't want to be a car mechanic forever, so I asked him if he was interested in buying the gym with me. He thought about it for a few seconds and then broke into a huge grin. "You and me, together. What do you think?"

"So, you'll go in with me?"

"You bet," he said, slapping me on the back.

"But shouldn't you talk it over first with Natalie?"

"Nah. She lets me make all the financial decisions."

Of course our combined savings still weren't enough and we had to take loans out to complete the deal, but with a little luck and a lot of hard work, we'd be able to pay them back in no time.

The only problem was that the hours would be long for a while until we began to turn a profit and could afford more help. I knew Carly wouldn't be happy about that. But eventually we'd have more money, so how could she really complain? I really wanted to make her happy and give her whatever her heart desired. I'd concluded that this was the way to do it.

A few months later I did something really stupid. Of all the people who decided to get in shape and join the gym, in came my old girlfriend, Sally. She left me for a guy old enough to be her father because he had lots of money. When I saw her that day, she told me how upset she'd been without me and how finding me at the gym, of all places, was fate. I should've known better and kept my hands to myself. However, she showed up at a point when my relationship with Carly was shaky and we were arguing constantly. Sally gave me an ultra-soft shoulder to cry on. I only saw her a few times before I applied the brakes. Instead of playing with Sally, I realized I should have been trying to straighten things out with Carly.

My relationship with my wife went up and down like a yo-yo. Things would be fine and smooth for a while until something sucked the wind out of our sails. Then nothing I did made Carly happy. We'd sit down and talk and things would be smooth again, but like a boxing match, a bell would go off and we'd end up sniping at each other. I loved Carly, but I really couldn't continue living that way. Yet I was willing to work at it, while she was the one who walked out on our marriage.

Carly took Bart and went down to her mother's. At first it was for a vacation, but the weeks turned into months. I missed Bart most of all. He was going to be four and needed his dad. Besides, I really didn't want him living with that crazy, mixed-up bunch. I decided that if Carly didn't return home soon, I'd divorce her and start custody proceedings.

A few weeks after I'd made my decision to give her an ultimatum, Carly called and asked for money. She read off a list of things that Bart needed.

"I'm not sending you any money. Come home."

"You're going to deny your son?"

"Not at all. Bring him home and he'll get everything he needs."

She began to scream at me. I warned her that I would hang up if she didn't speak to me like a human being. That quieted her down.

"How's Bart?" I asked.

"Fine. He likes it down here."

"Can I talk to him?"

"He's outside playing."

"Tell him I love him."

"Sure."

I wondered what she was telling Bart about us.

"I miss my son. I'm sure he misses his dad. It's time to come home," I said.

"You know why I can't do that."

"I don't know that at all."

"Because things aren't right between us."

"We can't fix them if you're down there."

"Things are better for Bart and me down here."

"Not if you need money."

"I'm happier down here."

Happier? Then it slowly began to dawn on me—she was seeing somebody down there. I should have known.

"So are you going to send some money?" she asked.

"No."

"Don't make things tough for us."

"Things are tough all over. I miss my family."

"If you don't send the money, what will I do?"

"Get a job."

"I gotta be around for Bart." She started to cry.

"Let your mother or her girlfriend watch Bart."

"They have their own lives."

"Come home, then," I said and hung up. She was giving me a headache.

I got in touch with a lawyer and filed for divorce. I wanted my son back, and there was nothing I wouldn't do to accomplish that. My lawyer said I had a good chance of winning a custody battle. Things were different today. The family court judges didn't automatically give the children to their mothers anymore.

The following months seemed to be an ordeal for me. I'd work all day and come home to an empty place. In my mind I could hear Bart's sweet giggling and see him running. I missed him terribly. I even found myself missing Carly.

Sam and Natalie would constantly hound me to come to dinner.

Unfortunately, seeing how happy they were together only seemed to make me more miserable. They had a beautiful baby girl now who would grow up one day to be as pretty as her mother. I was glad for Sam. He was a good friend and a genuinely nice guy who deserved his slice of happiness. Perhaps that's why I couldn't understand why somebody would want to kill him.

It was a Monday morning and Sam was scheduled to open the gym. He never even got the door opened. Somebody was waiting in the bushes near the entrance and blew him away with a shotgun. A member coming to work out found him there and called the cops. It wasn't long before they came looking for me.

The first thing I thought when the two cops knocked on my door was that something had happened to Carly and Bart. I never thought the reason they were there concerned Sam. Who would want Sam dead? It made no sense.

The cops introduced themselves as Detectives Jay Roach and Luke Dobson. They were dressed in suits like the detectives on TV cop shows. Roach was younger and taller. He looked like he knew his way around the inside of a gym. Dobson was shorter and sported extra bulk. He was also an older guy.

"We'd like to ask you a few questions, Mr. Grosso," Dobson said.

"Sure, come in. I was getting ready to head out to the gym my friend and I own."

"That's who we're here about, Mr. Grosso," Dobson said.

"Sam? Did something happen to Sam?" I could feel my throat tightening.

"Somebody was waiting in the bushes and shot him this morning," Roach added.

"Is he okay?"

"No. He's dead," Dobson said.

"This is crazy! Who would want to hurt Sam? Everybody loved Sam, detectives. He was a real good guy. He never even cheated on his wife."

"Well, somebody didn't think too highly of him," Dobson replied.

"Was it a mugging?"

"Nothing was taken. His wallet and jewelry were still on him when the police showed up," Roach said.

I had gotten up and was pacing. My mind was racing, trying to understand what had happened and why. I could feel the makings of a headache building as my temples throbbed in unison with my heart. It was at this point that I realized that Detective Roach was studying me. Surely he didn't think that I would hurt my best friend?

"Mr. Grosso, something just occurred to me. Your partner was built a lot like you, right?"

"Yeah."

"You both have the same coloring and build. Sam got it in the back. What if the killer mistook him for you? Do you think that might be a possibility?"

I looked at Roach. "I can't think of anyone who'd want me dead, either."

"Well, from past cases, it's usually somebody close to home, a relative of some sort."

My mind began to whirl with activity as I saw where he was heading with his questioning.

"Are you married, Mr. Grosso?" Dobson asked.

Technically, I was still married. I nodded my answer.

"Where's your wife?" asked Roach.

"In South Carolina."

"Vacation? Visiting relatives?" Roach probed further.

"She's living with her mother. We're getting a divorce."

"Would she be better off with you out of the picture?" Dobson asked.

"She wouldn't kill me," I assured the detectives.

"You didn't answer the question," Dobson reminded me. "Would she profit by your death?"

The last conversation that Carly and I had concerned money. She would get everything if I were dead. But to think she'd even contemplate that boggled my mind. "I guess, but I doubt she'd resort to something as drastic as that."

Roach said, "People are known to do terrible things for less rational reasons."

"She may not have pulled the trigger herself, but she could have hired someone else to do it for her," Dobson explained. "It's becoming more common these days."

"That would explain how Sam was mistaken for you," Roach added.

"We don't know that," I replied.

"But you said he didn't have any enemies." Roach looked up from his notepad. "And you're the one with the troubled marriage."

I couldn't believe that Carly would want to hurt me. I was Bart's father.

From that point on the detectives' investigation focused on Carly as the primary suspect. They wanted to know her whereabouts, how long she'd been living in South Carolina, and anything else I could recall. I tried to tell them as little as possible about our marriage, though they could read between the lines. Nobody ever divorced because they were crazy about each other.

I got a call from Carly right after news of Sam's death hit the airways. She was coming home with Bart to pay her respects.

"I can tell you're devastated about Sam. I should be there for you," she explained.

If ever I needed her, it was then. I was glad she was coming back. To me, this proved that she had nothing to do with Sam's death.

"What airline are you taking?" I asked.

She gave me her flight information. I was like a kid, bubbling over with excitement. I couldn't wait to hug my little boy. I found myself counting the hours until their arrival.

I got to the airport early after having bought Bart something nice to play with. My first sight of them as they approached would be forever tucked away in my memory bank. Bart had gotten so big. I hardly recognized him. He looked like a little man. He ran into my arms and I hugged him. He had noticed the package. "Is that for me?"

"You bet, sport," I said, handing it to him, my eyes on Carly.

She melted into my arms as if we'd turned back time. Even though it was a period of mourning, it was still a wonderful time for me. I had my family back again, which was priceless. It was amazing how quickly kids changed. I got Bart a small bicycle and taught him how to ride. He was a natural. And I liked being a father again.

Carly was warm and loving, definitely not the manner in which a woman who wanted me dead would act. This was the woman I had fallen in love with six years ago. With the investigation of Sam's murder still going on, I had no idea how long the good times would last, so I lived one day at a time. Not too long after our reconciliation, Carly discovered she was pregnant. I was thrilled. She seemed genuinely happy as well. Then the other shoe dropped when I least expected it.

Detectives Roach and Dobson, who'd first spoken to me months ago, showed up at our door. I figured that they had news about who murdered Sam. They did.

Aghast, I watched as they read Carly her rights and handcuffed her. They were charging her for the murder of Sam. They had the proof that she had hired a hit man to kill me, only he botched the job.

"This is all a terrible mistake," Carly cried out. "Mike, tell them."

"She's right. This is crazy. She could never hurt me."

"That's why she hired a hit man," Roach said, as they led her out.

"Please be careful, she's pregnant," I told the detectives.

"Who's the father?" Roach asked.

The D.A. got in touch with me. According to him, the State had enough for a conviction. They were positive that Carly hired a man to kill me to put an end to our divorce and save her from losing Bart. Unfortunately, the man had mistaken Sam for me.

Though I was shown the evidence, I couldn't believe that Carly was the cold, calculating woman they portrayed her to be. If she was guilty, why did she come back? They didn't know her the way I did. Even so, I had to hear the truth from her.

I went to see Carly in jail. I had to find out more about this alleged hit man. My senses had been stripped raw and my feelings needed to be sorted out. If I were going to be any good to Bart, I needed some answers so I could straighten myself out.

"I know what they're saying, but I could never hurt you, Mike. You believe me, don't you?" Her eyes were wild.

I nodded. "But I need to hear the truth from you."

"I'll tell you whatever you want to know," she assured me.

"How did you meet this guy?"

"My mother introduced us."

"Where'd she know him from?"

"A friend of a friend."

"Some friend."

"He seemed nice, so I went out with him couple of time. I had no idea he was a hit man."

"You did more than go out with him," I challenged her.

"I was lonely. I missed you."

"If you missed me, why didn't you come home?"

"I was tired of the fighting."

"So who hired this guy to kill me?"

"I don't know."

"Your mother?"

"She lives on a fixed income. She couldn't hire a cleaning lady if she wanted to?"

"Did you and this guy ever talk about us?" I asked.

"Maybe. I don't recall."

"Did you love him?"

"I thought I did, but you're the only guy for me. You know that, don't you, Mike?"

I smiled. She smiled back.

By the time I arrived back home, I decided that I would stand by Carly and be there for her, and for Bart, who needed his mother.

Call me crazy. Call me a fool. No matter what I've been through or what the D.A. says, I still care for Carly and believe her when she says she had nothing to do with that guy coming to kill me. The only thing Carly's guilty of is having an affair with him. And after Sally, how could I point a finger at her?

The media had already tried Carly and her lover in the press and found them guilty. Sex and money were their motives. I expected nothing less from those reporters, after all it was a business and they were in it to sell newspapers. Of course it hurt to read such trash, but that's what it was, garbage and nothing more. No matter what they or anyone else said about Carly, I wanted to believe that she was innocent. I couldn't fathom that the same woman who had given me Bart could want me dead. Especially not now, before the gym was turning a profit.

The D.A. nearly blew his stack when I told him that I wouldn't testify against Carly. He told me that I was certifiable. He didn't know my wife the way I did. Sure we'd argue, but we always seemed to be able to make up. No matter what he said, I wouldn't change my mind. I wasn't going to be the instrument that helped put her behind bars. No, it would take a great deal more than just talk to convince me that she'd hired a hit man.

The D.A. claims that the hit man, and not me, fathered the child Carly was pregnant with. Maybe I'll never know the truth about that. I guess it really doesn't matter since I believe that I'm the baby's dad. Besides, the timing is in my favor. Carly gave birth nine months to the day she returned home.

What does matter is what the jury believes, because ultimately Carly's fate lies in their hands. And no matter what, I'll be there for my wife.

THE END

DID MY SON
MAKE A BOMB?

My life was pretty happy. Although I was divorced, I had a boyfriend, Travis. And my little son, Chad, was the light of my life. My ex, Marshall, and I were civil to each other, and that's the best you can hope for after a divorce.

Chad had adjusted nicely to the divorce and was pretty good kid, or so I thought. That was until I heard the explosion and everything in my world changed. . . .

I was in the kitchen making cookies for my son's birthday party when the phone rang. From the tone of my boyfriend's voice, I immediately knew who it was.

"Yeah, she's here," Travis said. His sarcastic shortness seemed rude even to me, and I was used to his brisk military personality. He held the phone to my ear as I scraped cookie dough from my fingers. I fed Travis little bits of cookie dough, and he sensuously licked my fingers as I began to talk to my ex-husband on the phone.

"Hello?" I answered, tilting my head to cradle the receiver firmly between my head and shoulder. Travis let go and left the kitchen with a roll of his eyes and a sarcastic smile.

"Carrie? Hey, it's Marshall," he said.

I had to smile at the way the way he always identified himself on the phone, as if after fifteen years of marriage I wouldn't recognize his voice.

"Yeah, Marshall. What's up?"

"Whatcha doing?"

I didn't mean to be snippy, but I didn't have time to chitchat. "Making cookies for Chad's party. What do you need?" I regretted the harshness of my tone, but he responded as if he didn't even notice.

"Chad e-mailed me his birthday list, and I wanted to ask you about some of the stuff."

I snapped at him again. "Look, he is your son. I don't care. Buy him whatever you want. I'm not doing your shopping for you."

There was a slight pause before he continued calmly without any anger.

"Carrie, you don't have to be hateful. I just wanted to go over the list. I don't want to get him something you don't approve of. We used to be kind of picky about what we let him play with."

In spite of myself, I softened to his gentle voice. "Look, I'm sorry.

Your right." I put the bowl of cookie dough in the fridge to chill. "I'm just kind of in a hurry. Chad wants me to make those special cookies that he loves for his party tomorrow, and I'm—"

"The ones we use to make every Christmas Eve?" he interrupted.

"Yeah," I said shrugging the memory away "And Travis has tickets to a ball game tonight."

"Really? That sounds like fun. Chad should love that. I'm glad the two of them are getting along." Marshall sounded genuinely pleased.

I didn't continue my sentence that would have ended with me saying I wanted to get the kitchen clean before the baby-sitter got here. I didn't want another lecture from my ex-husband about how my boyfriend treated our son.

The truth was I wished Travis would pay more attention to Chad. I would gladly stay home and let the two of them go to the game without me.

Travis wasn't used to kids. He had joined the marines right out of high school and had no brothers or sisters. Travis treated Chad as if he were just a little eleven-year-old private. Anxious to change the subject and end the call I continued.

"Yeah, anyway . . . the birthday list?"

"Oh, right. Um . . . it starts with a note. Dad, here is my wish list. I have not listed them in any specific order. Isn't that cute?"

The impatience swelled in me "Marshall, get on with it please."

"Okay. Sorry. Chemistry set, telescope, BB gun, wrestling video collection, computer games, walkie-talkie, and a book about Desert Storm. That last one threw me."

"Travis was in Desert Storm. He talks about it with Chad sometimes." Not that Marshall deserved an explanation, but I was touched that my son wanted something that would help him connect with the man I loved. And I secretly hoped that Marshall would pick up on that.

"Nothing scary I hope!"

The snippy tone crept back into my voice "No, Nothing like that . . . it's just--"

He interrupted as if he was my therapist and my hour was almost over. "It's just Chad wants so much for Travis to like him."

"Marshall you don't know--"

"Oh, I know. Carrie how could you get serious with a guy that doesn't like our kid?"

"Enough! Marshall. Enough."

There was slight pause from his end. "Your right I'm sorry. So, What do you think about the chemistry set?"

"What? Oh um. Too young for one." I answered, relived that he had dropped the Travis issue so easily.

He continued with a casual tone. "Well I don't approve of the wrestling videos or BB gun. Do you know which computer games?"

The ease of his conversation annoyed me. "No, I don't even know which ones he has. I can go check for you." I tried to sound friendly.

"Naw, don't bother. I'll get the telescope and the walkie-talkies. Do you need extra money this month? What with the party and all."

I fought the bristle that began to run down my spine by reminding myself he was being sincere. "No, I am doing fine."

"Okay, let me know if you need anything. Bye."

"Marshall?"

"Yeah?"

There was a pause as I wrenched up the word I wanted. "Thanks."

"Sure."

I held the receiver for several seconds before hanging it back. There were moments that I had to stop and mentally list the reasons I had divorced Marshall. I was struggling to come up with three when Travis came behind me, wrapping his muscular arms around my waist, and resting his chin on my shoulder. He may have been the same age as Marshall but, boy, did his hard Marine's body make him seem years younger and so much sexier."

"What did wimp boy want?"

"Don't call him that. Chad might hear you." But, Travis still raised his eyebrows at my defense of Marshall.

"He wanted to go over Chad's birthday list."

"Hey! You think I should get him something? You know, just a video or game?" Travis sounded almost boyish

I maneuvered around in his arms to face him as a smile of approval crept across my face. I rose up onto my toes and kissed the tip of his nose. "Yeah, I think that would be great."

The excitement in Travis's voice grew. He seemed anxious and insecure. A side of him I had never seen. It was cute. "Well, what should I get him? What does he like?"

"Sweetie, why don't you try asking him? In fact . . . why don't the two of you go to the game tonight? I really have a lot to do for the party, still."

"You mean alone? Just me and him?" His eyebrows furrowed as he thought about it for a second or two. "Yeah. Okay. Why not? I can do that."

Chad was thrilled when Travis called him to come downstairs and asked him if he wanted to catch the game with him.

I watched the two of them crawl into Travis's pickup truck and drive off. A sigh of contentment escaped from deep within my chest as I kicked off my shoes and pulled my sweater over my head, letting it drop to the floor without a thought. A vague sense of freedom began to creep over me. I was alone in the house, something that didn't happen often, and I felt like a naughty child. I went to my bedroom and took Travis's duffel bag from the chair and carefully unzipped it.

The smell of laundry soap tickled my nose as I carefully went through the bag. I didn't know what I expected to find. I didn't even know why I was searching his things. Maybe it was curiosity, maybe I just wanted to be closer to him, and somehow, I thought this would do it. All I found was a change of clothes, shaving things, and a western paperback. I still had a sense of satisfaction and contentment having his masculine things in my bedroom.

It had always been like that with me. I didn't feel whole if I didn't have a boyfriend. I was nine when I realized the security a boyfriend could give. Some girls were being mean to me on the playground, and Ian Soltare came over and rescued me by asking me to be on his kickball team. Suddenly, I was accepted because Ian Soltare liked me, and I learned having the right boyfriend was power.

Marshall was powerful. I had been a dental assistant when Marshall came in for a root canal. He was dressed in expensive shorts and a golf shirt with a prestigious club logo. Rich boy play clothes, I called outfits like his. He smiled a crooked grin as I checked him in at the desk, and I smiled back. One date led to two, then three, and then a year later marriage.

He didn't make my heart beat wildly. I didn't feel great passion when he took me in his arms, but he made me feel safe and secure. He bought me expensive jewelry and a beautiful home. People called me to serve on committees, and my picture was on the society page. Life was nice. Marshall loved me with all his heart, and I was proud to be his wife.

When Chad was born our life became even more picture perfect. But, that is all that it was . . . a picture. I was unhappy. I didn't know why. I had everything I wanted or should have wanted. Yet, I still felt incomplete.

Marshall tried to understand. He suggested that I go back to school. He took Chad on camping trips and to movies, so I would have time alone. But the more I was alone, the more I realized I didn't know myself at all.

So I left. I spent six months "finding myself." Actually I spent six months finding Henry and having a two-week affair, then moving onto Nick, then Jack, and then Fred.

Then I met Travis while I was out two-stepping at a country bar with my friend Barb. I felt like a breathless teenager when he asked me to dance. His muscular legs strained against the fabric of his jeans, and his tanned arms bulged under the rolled up sleeves of his white shirt. I was amazed at how graceful this beast of a man was as he led me around the dance floor.

We went outside to escape the smoke and noise. He dropped the gate on his pickup truck, and we sat looking at the stars and talking. He clasped his hands behind his neck and lay back in the pickup's bed. My feet hung over the edge of the truck, and I swung them back and fourth like a nervous little girl.

"Hey, I can't see you way up there. Come here. I'll be good. Promise."

I stretched out on my side and lay next to him. The moonlight was bright and cast a hazy glow over his sharp features.

He rolled over on his side and pulled me close, cradling my head in his large warm hands. He kissed me fully on the lips, coaxing them open for a deeper more passionate kiss. I arched against him, and he rolled over pulling me on top of him. I had never felt such raw passion. My insides were on fire as if a hundred fireworks were exploding inside me. I threw my head back as he nuzzled my neck with playful nips and licks.

With a breathless sigh I sat up. "I'm sorry . . . I can't . . . we should really stop . . . somebody might see us. . . ." He sat up next to me and burned my neck with more kisses. "We are in a parking lot! I can't."

"No problem. We'll go to my place," Travis said.

"No, I've got to get home; I told the baby-sitter I wouldn't be late."

"You have kids?"

"One . . . just one . . . a boy." I hated the slight defensive almost apologetic tone in my voice. But, I didn't want to scare this one off.

"Fine we'll go to your place," he said as wrapped his arms around me and continued to kiss my neck and nibble my ear.

He followed me to my house and waited at the curb until the baby-sitter left, and I made sure that Chad was asleep. I flashed the porch light, and I met him at the back door.

This became the ritual we would follow for two months. Travis would come pick me up for a date. After he would bring me home, he would wait for the porch light before coming back into the house . . . to my bed where he would spend hours making love to me. My body had never responded to a man's touch the way that it did to Travis's. After Chad seemed used to seeing Travis and I dating I began letting Travis stay the night.

As I sat on my bed going through Travis's duffel bag I considered cleaning out one of my dresser drawers for him to use.

I glanced at the clock and realized that I had a good three hours left before Travis and Chad would be home from the game. I could clean out a drawer, put away a load of clothes, finish the cookies, and still have time for a hot bubble bath. I had just bought a cute little nightie that I couldn't wait to wear for Travis that night.

I cleaned out my bottom dresser drawer but decided I had better let Travis put his own clothes away. When I took Chad's laundry to his room. I was just tempted to throw it on the floor with the rest of his junk. I could not believe how messy his room was. The floor was littered with little pieces of wire, screws, paper, springs, and what looked like parts of a robot. I kicked a path through the mess and made my way to his dresser. I remember thinking that I really needed to be more strict with the room cleaning because it smelled like rotten eggs.

Chad's computer screen saver had little cartoon fish skeletons bouncing up and down. I wished I knew how to use the thing. Marshall was always saying what Chad e-mailed him about, and I wanted to be able to snoop and read what was going on in my kid's life.

I guess it was the same logic that drove my mother to read my diaries, which made me sit at the computer and try to open Chad's files. Looking back, I know that I could have prevented the tragic events that followed if I had only been more aware of Chad's hobbies and life.

I had used a computer at work for booking appointments, but when it came down to it, I really didn't know a thing about them and gave up after fifteen minutes. I kicked and raked the junk on the floor into a pile with the side of my foot and made a mental note to have him clean up his room before the party the next day.

I padded down the hall to take a soothingly long bath. I had saved some sweet eucalyptus bath salts for just such a chance.

The years of living with Marshall had spoiled me with some of the finer things in life and expensive bath salts were one of the things I was having a hard time letting go of. At seven fifty an ounce, the salt I was using now had become a luxury instead of the daily indulgence it once was. I had learned at a spa I had gone to that bath salts helped the bath water stay hotter longer.

I smiled at the memory of me sitting in classes on aromatherapy and how to take the proper hot baths. Had that really been me? If Jan and Victoria or any of the women who were supposed to be my friends back then would see me in my cowgirl jeans two-stepping with Travis and drinking out of a brown long neck bottle, they wouldn't recognize me.

Sometimes, I didn't even recognize myself. I mean Marshall had given me everything I had always said I wanted, and yet, I wasn't happy. I sank further down in the tub letting the hot water flow over me covering me to my neck. I was happy now, wasn't I? Of course I was. I loved Travis. The sex was amazing. Something didn't seem right, though. A vague gnawing sense of uneasiness seemed to always be present in the pit of my stomach.

Even while I was relaxing in my sweet bath, my mind raced. I tried to picture Travis, Chad, and me as a family doing family things, but images of my life with Marshall kept intruding in my daydreams. I even tried closing my eyes tighter as if that would squeeze the thoughts of the past away.

Then I heard Chad's voice shouting, "Hey, We're home!" I hastily threw on my bathrobe and headed down the stairs.

"Did you two have a good time?"

"Oh, Mom we had a blast. Travis's old girlfriend was one of the cheerleaders, and she had the girls sign a poster for me. And we got to meet some of the players. It was so cool!" He babbled excitedly as I fixed an icy glare on Travis. He met my look with confusion and smiled a crooked little half smile.

"That's great I'm glad you had a good time, honey." I ruffled my hand through his hair and smiled at him before I continued. "You really need to go upstairs and clean your room."

"Aw, okay." He ran past me up the stairs stopping to add, "Thanks Travis."

Travis was trying to figure out what had set me into Ice Princess mode as he cautiously watched me cross into the living room and drop into the recliner.

"Carrie, what's wrong? Are you mad that I didn't take you to the game? You're the one who wanted me to take the kid—"

I cut him off with a cold stare. "An ex-girlfriend? You went to see an ex-girlfriend with my kid? I don't know if I am more hurt or mad."

"Carrie, Tawny is a cheerleader. I thought Chad would get a kick out of being made a fuss over by a cheerleader, and he did. I bet that's all he talks about at the party tomorrow."

It wasn't logical but I wouldn't let go of my anger over it. Travis was still on good terms with an ex-girlfriend who was a cheerleader. He could go over and have a friendly conversation with a woman who could stand in front a thousand people wearing spandex and sell posters of herself. It rattled me.

I suddenly didn't feel like wearing my cute new nightie as I sulked off to the bedroom and put on an old T-shirt. Several hours later I felt the bed give with Travis's weight, and he snuggled close to me. "Mmmm, you smell good."

I pretended to sleep through his advances until he sighed and rolled onto his back. All night long I had nightmares of Travis being in the arms of a beautiful cheerleader, laughing at some secret joke.

Travis was so good-looking; he deserved a beautiful woman who would jog with him in the morning. Maybe I should go with him to the gym when he asked me. Maybe I could keep him from leaving me for someone better. I tossed and turned with each as each new terror of losing Travis flashed in my mind.

I felt Travis leave the bed and heard a groan as he gave a stretch. I knew it had to be five in the morning, and he was going out for his morning jog. Obviously, he didn't lose any sleep over my coldness.

I awoke to a playful slap on the butt. "Hey, Lazy, it's ten-thirty. Are you planning on getting up? The party is in two hours."

I must have finally dozed off and now sat up in a panic. Chad's party! I hadn't even finished the cookies he wanted or wrapped his presents.

"Oh my god. How could you have let me sleep in like that?"

"Calm down, honey. You seemed to really need the sleep. You tossed and turned all night." He kissed my forehead. "I'll go pick up the cake and the snacks."

He grabbed my keys off the dresser and sprinted away. I ran my hands through my hair and mentally mapped out my plan of action.

By the time the doorbell rang with the first guest, the house was decorated with balloons and streamers, and the cookies were cooling on the kitchen counter. I was still in my old T-shirt, and Travis hadn't made it back with the cake.

"Chad, unless you want your friends to see me like this, I have got to go change."

Chad rolled his eyes. "Mom, I know how to answer the door! Go change."

I heard the house fill with the laughter of ten-year-olds as I stepped into take a quick shower. I knew the kids could care less what my hair and makeup looked like, but I wanted to look cute for Travis. I felt badly about the way I had treated him the night before. If I kept pulling little jealous fits like that I would lose him. And that would serve me right. I was once again thinking of my new nightie when I saw Travis's silhouette pass across the frosted shower glass.

He stuck his head in the door. "Cake is here, pizza is ordered, and the boys are playing in the backyard." He smiled sheepishly. "You still pissed at me?"

"Naw, how could I stay mad at the hero who saved the party?" I paused and added, "I'm sorry. I was being stupid."

"Darn right you were. Don't you know you are the only woman for me?"

He leaned in and kissed me, the shower mist spraying his head. I grabbed the collar of his shirt and pulled him halfway into the shower devouring his mouth with mine. He stepped into the shower fully clothed. He kissed me as I tore at his shirt and pants, throwing them over the shower door until they were in a soaking heap on the bathroom floor.

He pinned both of my hands to the wall of the shower in one strong hand and covered my neck with kisses as his other hand stroked my body until I was wild with desire. As we were making passionate love with the water beating down on us a loud explosion and screaming stopped us cold.

Travis grabbed a towel and wrapped it around his waist as he raced from the bathroom. I was on his heels taking the stairs two at a time.

Travis reached the backyard before me and parted the circle of boys some of who were crying "Call 911! Chad is hurt!" He shouted to me.

I didn't want to stop and call. I wanted to get to my son. As I dialed, I realized I didn't even know what was wrong. I grabbed one of the boys that had begun to run into the house hysterically.

"Lenny, what happened?"

The 911 operator was firing questions at me. All I could do was tell her send an ambulance and scream at Lenny for answers.

I hung up and ran to the backyard. Chad was stretched lifeless on the ground. "Bring a blanket and towels!" Travis shouted. Once again, I didn't want to stop and follow instructions. I just wanted to get to my baby. The backyard was beginning to fill with neighbors. I still didn't know what happened but I heard crying boys whimper out words and sentence fragments: "bomb," "explode," "blown off."

Some of the boys were bleeding. Neighbors were screaming. It was utter chaos. The squeal of sirens was coming closer, and I still had no answers about what had happened. The police car was the first to arrive and an officer began to organize the pandemonium. The first thing he did was clear the backyard of everyone not directly involved while his partner rounded up all of the boys and took them into the kitchen--all of the boys except Chad.

I stood in the backyard in my shabby bathrobe unable to go to him . . . afraid of what I would see. I felt an arm go around my shoulder and looked over to see the face of a police officer. He led me back into the house.

"We need to start calling these kids' parents, so if you could help us."

I took the invitation list off the refrigerator and handed it to him. A third uniformed face appeared in the kitchen.

"What happened? Please somebody tell me what happened." I begged of anyone who was there.

"Near as we can tell ma'am, your son ignited a homemade bomb in the backyard injuring himself and six friends. The ambulances are here. We are having all the boys' parents meet us at the hospital. You and your boyfriend need to get dressed and follow us to the hospital. The ambulances have already left. Is there anyone else you like us to call?"

"Yes, my husband . . . I mean my ex-husband. His number is on the fridge. Thank-you."

Travis and I quickly threw on whatever clothes were the closest. We never spoke. He didn't offer any comfort.

"What was the kid thinking pulling something like that?" He walked out of the room leaving me on the floor trying to tie my shoes as my hands trembled uncontrollably. From the hallway, he shouted at me to hurry up. I gave up on my shoes and fled the room after him.

At the hospital I had to wade through news cameras and reporters to get to the emergency room. I felt a firm grip on my arm pulling me; making my already fast-paced steps speed to a run tearing my hand from Travis's grip. I noticed then that it was Marshall. Tears were streaming down his face, and his jaw was set with an anger that I had never seen before.

He pushed open a door and practically flung me into a dimly lit room. I found a vinyl chair in the shadows and crawled into it.

"How the could you let this happen? Where were you while my son was making bombs?" I stared at him dumbly.

"Well!" His voice boomed till it was almost unrecognizable as human. "Is this what you Marine boyfriend teaches my son? Woman, what kind of mother are you?"

I tried but couldn't find any words. All I could do was sputter and cough as tears choked me. I still didn't know any details. I didn't even know if Chad was alive or dead. Marshall was looking down at me huddled in the chair, and I saw a softness come over him.

"Oh, Carrie." He sank to the floor and pulled me into his lap rocking me like a frightened child. I swallowed and managed to squeak out a few words

"Please, tell me. No one has told me anything."

"Chad is in surgery. He will live." His words were almost whispered. He brushed my tear damp hair from my face and tied my shoes. "They don't know if they will be able to save his hand"

I dissolved into fresh sobs as Marshall pulled me closer. "Shhh. The other boys had only minor cuts and scrapes."

Travis opened the door sending a wedge of light across us as we huddled on the floor. Marshall gently pushed me from his lap and stood toe to toe with him. His fists were clenched, and I knew he was reigning in his anger. It was obvious he wanted to blame Travis for the entire incident. But that was unfair. Wasn't it? He stepped around Marshall and extended his hand toward me. I reached up for it, and he pulled me to my feet. He flicked the light switch.

"The press was screaming for details. So I went ahead and made a statement for you," Travis said with his quick military efficiency.

"Thank-you." I waited for him to open his arms to me or pull me close. But he didn't so I stood there shivering wanting more than anything to collapse and sob. It was Marshall who led me back to the sofa and placed his coat over me like a blanket.

"Your hair is wet," Marshall said as he brushed it back from my face.

Fresh sobs sprung from my eyes. "Oh Marshall, I was in the shower. I was in the shower while my baby was blowing himself up!" I rolled over and pulled my body into a tight ball as the tears and crying shook me uncontrollably. I was vaguely aware of Marshall and Travis. They were talking in a calm, businesslike manner.

"So, what did you tell the press?" Marshall asked.

"I told them it was just boys being boys." Travis replied with a shrug.

"Since when does 'boys being boys' involve explosive devices?" Marshall asked in a tight self-restraining way he used when trying not to lose his temper.

"Oh, come on. Didn't you ever play with fireworks when you were a kid?"

"Fireworks? Yes, I played with fireworks. Is that what you think this was?"

"Sure, kids like to see things go boom. He made the fuse too short on this one is all."

I sat up stunned. " 'This one'? What do you mean, 'this one'? Marshall, what does he mean 'this one'?"

"Calm down Carrie," Travis said sounding more annoyed than comforting. "He told me about it on the way home from the game. He found a website on the computer that showed him how to make bombs, so he thought it would be fun."

Marshall lunged at him. "How can you be so matter of fact about a ten-year-old making explosive devices?" He turned before actually hitting Travis. "Don't you see Carrie? He was doing it to impress G.I. Jerk here. My kid is making bombs so that his mommy's boyfriend will like him."

I sobbed uncontrollably. "Marshall that's not fair." He stared at me with such anger and hurt that I think he would have smacked me if the doctor hadn't come in at that moment.

"Mr. and Mrs. Walton?" he asked looking at me then, Marshall and Travis. It seemed as though he were trying to decide who was in charge. Marshall stepped forward.

"I'm his father. This is his mother and her . . . friend."

"Well, it looks like Chad is going to keep his hand. The first aid that Travis did before the ambulance arrived made the difference there. The police will want to question him when wakes up. Then he should be able to go home in a day or two. If you follow me I'll take you to him."

The police questioned Chad, and we had to appear in juvenile court. The judge ruled that there was no criminal intent and no charges were filed. Chad went to court ordered counseling where I learned that he had wanted to impress his friends and didn't think anything bad would happen. I also learned that I hadn't been paying nearly enough attention to him. I should have been more worried about the boy in my life and less worried about the man in my life.

Marshall petitioned for an amended custody agreement and Chad went to live with his father.

I stayed with Travis another six months. I think more out of spite toward Marshall than love for Travis. I came up with that during a counseling session and broke up with him the next day. I see Chad on the weekends, and Marshall has been very supportive.

I'm working on figuring out who I am without defining myself as someone's girlfriend or wife or mother. It was hard, and at first, I was incredibly lonely. But, every day is easier, and I'm beginning to know and like Carrie.

THE END

ONE NIGHT STAN
He Become My Wingman

"Getting a date isn't that difficult," Stan said over coffee one Saturday afternoon, after we'd played a little one-on-one basketball and he'd beat me by three points. We'd stopped afterward in a diner near the highway about halfway between our two homes. "Not nearly as hard as it was when I was younger."

"Why's that?"

"I've reached the magic age," he explained.

He'd been divorced nearly a year and, after figuring out how to do his own laundry and clean his own house, he'd jumped back into the dating pool. "I just turned fifty and I'm now in the age group where available women outnumber available men. The older I get, the better my odds get."

I sipped my too-hot coffee and made a face.

"And I've aged well. I look better now than I did when I was in my twenties."

I had to give him that much. Stan didn't look his age. He still had all of his hair, all of his teeth, and, even though he'd gained weight over the years, he'd become stocky rather than fat. Most men our age had already crested the hill and were rapidly rolling down the other side. I know I had.

Stan leaned across the table and lowered his voice. "And I'm getting plenty of action, too. You won't believe how things have changed. When I was younger, the women I dated were looking for 'Mr. Right,' now many of them are happy with 'Mr. Right for Tonight.'"

"Be careful," I said. "You're going to catch something."

"I am careful." He leaned back and signaled for the waitress, an attractive honey blonde in her early forties. When she stepped up to the table, he asked me, "You want pie with your coffee?"

I shook my head.

Stan turned to the waitress and said, "A slice of coconut cream, Wanda."

"Anything else?"

Without hesitation, Stan said, "Your phone number."

Wanda smiled. "I'll think about it."

After the waitress walked away, I said, "You struck out."

Stan shrugged. "We'll see."

Wanda brought Stan's pie a moment later, and she topped off both of our coffees.

Worried that our conversation might turn to my dating drought if it continued the direction it was going, I changed the topic. While Stan ate his pie, we discussed the local university football team's ongoing residency at the bottom of the conference standings.

When we finished, Wanda slipped the bill under the corner of Stan's plate. After she walked away Stan glanced at the bill, and then flipped it around so I could read it. Wanda had written her name and phone number on the tear-off receipt at the bottom.

"Simple as that," Stan said.

"You going to call her?"

"Of course." He tore off the receipt and tucked it into his shirt pocket.

My house was quiet when I returned home later that afternoon, just as it was every time I returned home, and I had yet to grow accustomed to the silence.

One morning, after twenty-seven years of marriage, Marsha had rolled over and said she no longer wished to be married. By the end of that week she had moved out, and within a month movers had taken everything she felt belonged to her. Eight weeks later our divorce was finalized, and I had been numb ever since.

That's why Stan's breezy attitude about dating again at our age, and the ease with which he had gotten our waitress' phone number, floored me.

In the two years following my divorce I hadn't had a single date. The closest I had come was lunch with Terri, an attractive brunette from payroll who had invited me to join her for lunch one afternoon at the Thai restaurant near work when all the other tables appeared to be filled.

We'd had a pleasant conversation—mostly about work, but about movies as well—and on the walk back to the office Terri had said we could have lunch together anytime. As I sat in my empty house I realized that she'd been flirting with me.

I spent the rest of the night wondering how long that invitation would be open.

Monday morning I sat in my cubicle and stared at my phone for twenty minutes, drying my sweating palms on my pants every five minutes before I worked up the courage to pick up the phone.

I dialed Terri's extension and waited until she picked up after the third ring. "Terri? This is Brian over in customer service," I said, rushing through what I wanted to say without stopping to breathe. "We had lunch a couple of months ago at the Thai restaurant and I, um, you said, um, are you free for lunch today?"

"Sure, Brian," she said without hesitation. "Eleven-thirty work for you?"

"Sure, um, we could walk over together."

"That would be great," she said. "Meet you in the lobby at eleven-thirty?"

"Sure. Yeah. Of course."

The next couple of hours crawled by and, even though I hurried downstairs, Terri was already waiting in the lobby when I arrived. Terri is two years younger than me, but, like Stan, doesn't look her age. She keeps her dark hair fashionably short and dresses conservatively, but her style of dress does nothing to mask the genuinely female figure beneath the clothes.

"Thai food okay with you?" I asked.

Terri smiled. "Oh, Brian, you remembered!"

"Remembered what?"

She threaded her arm through mine as we walked toward the door. "You remembered where we went on our first date."

Terri's brain was clearly operating a few steps ahead of mine and I hurried to keep up. "Of course I remembered. How could I possibly forget?"

We walked to the end of the block and around the corner. We'd beat the lunch rush and found an empty booth near the door. After we ordered, Terri stared into my eyes and asked, "Why did you wait so long to ask me to lunch?"

"I—" I swallowed hard.

"I thought I was pretty clear that day. I was, wasn't I?"

I must have looked like a deer caught in the high beams because she explained.

"I thought I made it clear that I was interested in you," she said. "When you never called, I thought maybe I'd misjudged things. So, why did you wait so long?"

I explained that I hadn't been on a date in more than three decades. "It's been a long time since I asked a woman out. I wasn't sure what to expect."

"And you couldn't tell that I was interested in you?"

"I just thought you were being nice."

Our food arrived, but Terri picked up the conversation after the waitress walked away. "So, what changed?"

I told her about my conversation with Stan. I didn't tell her everything, of course, just that he'd been particularly successful at getting dates following his divorce.

"And you figured if Stan could do it, you could, too?"

"Not exactly," I told her. "I figured if Stan could do it so often, maybe I could do it once."

Terri reached across the table and patted the back of my hand. "And I'm your first. That makes me feel special."

I wasn't sure if she'd intended the sexual innuendo, but I felt my cheeks warm and I'm certain that I blushed.

She laughed, and then said, "You really are new to this!"

Officially, we only had an hour for lunch, but we ran a little long. I learned that Terri's divorce had been finalized only a few months before mine, and that being suddenly single hadn't stymied her the way it had me.

"So you've dated a lot?"

"Not really," she said. "Enough not to be afraid of it, not so much that I'm jaded."

No matter how many dates she'd had since her divorce, it was still more than I'd had, and I was feeling my way through the conversation. I was more nervous than the previous time we'd had lunch together, because this time it was intentional. It wasn't two coworkers sharing a table because all the others were filled; it was a man and a woman dining together on purpose—it was a date.

Terri must have sensed my nervousness. She changed the subject, and soon we were talking about favorite TV shows and movies we'd seen recently, pets we'd had as a kid, and that guy from the mailroom who wore a nose ring and black nail polish.

I was first to notice how quickly the time had slipped away from us, and only because Terri reached across the table again and took my hand. I glanced down, saw my watch, and told her we needed to get back.

"You think the place can't run without us?"

"I think it'll run just fine without us," I told her. "I just don't want them to realize it."

I paid the tab and we headed back.

We were only a few steps from the entrance of the building where we worked when Terri stopped. I must have traveled three more steps before I realized she wasn't beside me. I had to turn around and walk back to her.

When I reached her, she looked up into my eyes, and asked, "Did you enjoy lunch?"

"Sure," I said. I had no idea where our conversation was headed.

"Do you want to see me again?"

"Yes."

"Then why haven't you asked me?"

I was flummoxed. "I—"

"I'll make it easy for you," Terri said. "I have two tickets to the Civic Theatre's opening night performance of "Annie" on Wednesday. The show starts at seven-thirty. You want to pick me up at seven?"

"Sure."

She pulled a business card from her purse and wrote her home

176

address and cell phone number on the back. Then she handed it to me. "You won't forget, will you?"

I promised her that I wouldn't forget.

That night I told Stan about my lunch with Terri.

"Sounds like you picked a firecracker," he said.

"I suppose so," I told him. I had the cordless phone trapped between my ear and my shoulder while I tried to grill myself a cheese sandwich. "She made it very clear that she was interested in me. She even invited me out Wednesday night."

"So you're playing it slow?"

"How's that?"

"Waiting until Wednesday to see her again," Stan explained. "If she's that interested in you, you should have asked her to dinner tonight."

"Really?"

"You have to strike while the iron's hot," Stan said.

"So what about you?" I asked. I flipped my sandwich over. "You have any irons in the fire?"

"I have a date later this evening," Stan said. "I'm leaving here in fifteen minutes."

"So how long have you known this woman?"

"We met at the coffee shop this morning, and we hit it off real well. Turns out she likes Italian food, so I'm taking her to The Pasta Bowl."

"You'd better be careful," I told Stan as I slid my sandwich out of the frying pan and onto a plate. "You don't seem to know these women very well. You never know what could happen."

"Don't worry," Stan assured me. "I always carry protection."

I arrived at Terri's front door promptly at seven Wednesday evening. She opened the door wearing a sexy little number that revealed nothing, but hinted at everything. I told her how beautiful she looked and she thanked me.

"You look pretty sharp yourself," she said. "New suit?"

"Yes, actually," I told her. "How'd you know?"

"Let me get some scissors." She left me standing in the foyer, returned a moment later with a tiny pair of scissors, and reached behind my head. A moment later she showed me the tag that I hadn't cut from my jacket collar before slipping it on.

"That's so embarrassing," I said.

"I think it's charming that you would buy a new suit for our first evening out." She planted a quick kiss on my cheek, and then placed the scissors and tag on a small table next to the front door and grabbed her clutch. "Shall we go?"

The Civic Theatre is less than two miles from Terri's house, and we arrived with time to spare. She was well known to the theatre staff and we chatted with several other patrons as we made our way to our seats. Then the lights went down, and we spent the next couple of hours watching local actors and actresses mangle the musical.

The Civic Theatre held a reception backstage following the opening night performance—a reception for performers, staff, and sponsors. I quickly realized Terri was a sponsor, and she explained her involvement with the theatre during a lull in one of the many brief conversations we had with other people at the reception.

"I majored in theater, but I was never able to do anything with my degree after college. Marriage killed that dream," she said. "After my divorce, I thought maybe I could do something to foster someone else's dream, so now I donate a little money to the Civic Theatre."

Before she could say any more, the theatre's executive director joined us, and the two women discussed the rest of that season's schedule.

The reception was still going strong, especially because the parents had whisked all of the underage performers home, when Terri suggested we take our leave.

"After all," she said with a wink, "we have to work tomorrow."

A few minutes later I parked in front of Terri's house, and she waited patiently until I rounded the car and opened her door. As we walked to her porch, she slipped her hand—her warm, soft hand—in mine.

Once we reached her porch, she released my hand long enough to open her clutch, find her keys, and unlock her front door. Then she turned to me and took my hand again. "I had a wonderful evening."

"So did I," I told her.

"We should do this again."

"Of course."

"Soon."

"Certainly."

Terri looked up into my eyes. "Are we going to stand here all night or are you going to kiss me?"

Decades had passed since the last time I had kissed a woman other than my now ex-wife, and I hesitated, unsure of how to proceed.

"Don't be shy," she whispered. "I'm not fragile. I won't break."

I leaned forward, Terri stretched up, and our lips met. I quickly realized that I had no reason to doubt myself. As our kiss stretched out, she melted against me, and I felt my heart flutter. I felt alive in a way that I had not felt in too many years.

When our kiss finally ended, I looked into Terri's eyes and realized she had similar thoughts rushing through her mind. That's when I wished her a good evening, promised that we would see each other again soon—and not just at work—and stepped away. I left Terri standing on her porch, fully aware that she might have asked me inside if I'd given her a chance.

But I was no One Night Stan. I was looking for a relationship and had no desire to use a woman just to satisfy some fleeting physical desire.

I drove home with a smile on my face.

"You didn't seal the deal?"

Stan and I were back at the diner after our Saturday afternoon one-on-one basketball game—he beat me by two points—and I'd just told him about my first date with Terri.

"Our relationship isn't like that," I protested.

"What relationship?"

"The relationship I hope to have," I explained.

Stan snorted his derision.

I continued, "If I ever wake up next to a woman, I'll want to remember her name, not resort to calling her 'honey,' and I'll want to offer her breakfast, not cab fare."

"You expect a lot for a guy who isn't getting any."

"And you expect so little."

"So, Mr. Sensitive," Stan said, "I'm going to a new bar tonight and I need a wingman. You up for it?"

"No thanks," I said. "I'm seeing Terri tonight."

Stan winked. "Good luck, tiger."

I took Terri to an early evening movie and then to dinner. Over filet mignon, baked potatoes, and asparagus, we discussed the movie we'd just seen, a comedy that had a lower laugh-per-minute ratio than an insurance salesman's life insurance pitch. Before long we were discussing the career of an actress in the movie, a character actor near Terri's age that you see in everything but who never plays the lead.

"So what about you?" I asked. "You ever think of returning to acting?"

"Once or twice," she said. "But it's too late to start a career. That's all behind me."

"Does it have to be a career?" I asked. "You think all those people we saw in "Annie" expect to make a career of acting?"

"Only if they're delusional," she said with a laugh. "The best actor on stage that night was the guy who does the late-night used car commercials."

"But they were having fun, weren't they?" I continued. "And because it was obvious they were having fun, we had fun watching them, didn't we?"

"I suppose."

I'm not sure I convinced Terri to try out for a part in the Civic Theatre's next production, but we certainly enjoyed discussing the possibility.

Before we realized how much time had passed, we had finished dinner, dessert, and our second cups of after-dinner coffee. I didn't want the evening to end, but the waiter was giving us the evil eye, so I suggested that we go. I settled the bill and walked Terri to my car.

After I slid into the driver's seat, Terri asked, "Don't you live near here?"

"Eight blocks over," I said.

She placed one hand on my thigh. "Why don't you show me your place?"

I started the car and drove home. My place isn't much—a little two-bedroom brick ranch in an older neighborhood—and the tour didn't take long.

We entered through the kitchen, walked through the dining room and living room, and stopped for a moment at the second bedroom while Terri admired my three acoustic and two electric guitars—all that remained of my own childhood dream of being a rock 'n' roll star.

"And this is the bedroom," I said a moment later, wishing I had made the bed that morning.

"So it is." Terri turned to me and began unbuttoning her blouse. "Perhaps now I can show you something."

The phone rang at three in the morning and I had to reach over Terri to answer it.

"Can you pick me up?" Stan asked.

"Where are you?"

He told me.

"What are you doing way the heck out there?"

"I'll tell you when you get here," he said. "And bring me some pants and shoes. I'm freezing my ass off."

Terri listened to my side of the conversation and, when I finally disconnected the line, asked, "Who was that?"

"Stan," I said. "He needs my help." I pulled on the clothes I'd worn earlier that evening. "Should I take you home, or –?"

Terri smiled up at me from the bed. "I'll keep the bed warm," she said as she patted the empty space beside her. "Hurry back."

Thirty-five minutes later I found Stan standing beside the road in the middle of nowhere, wearing nothing but a long-sleeve shirt that he had fashioned into an apron to cover his lower anatomy. I pulled up next to him and lowered my window.

"So, what happened?" I asked.

"Crazy broad took my car."

"How come you're naked?"

"My clothes were in the car."

I looked questioningly at him.

"We were in the front seat," he explained as he pulled on the

180

clothes I'd brought. "We were going to get in the back where there's more room. I left the keys in the ignition. As soon as I got out of the car, she slammed the door and hit the automatic lock. Then she started the car and drove away. I'm just lucky my cell phone fell out before she closed the door, or I would have had to walk back to town like this."

I drove Stan to the police station and sat with him until he had a chance to talk to a detective.

He reported that a woman he'd picked up in a bar two hours earlier had stolen his car at gunpoint. He hadn't said anything to me about the woman having a gun. Maybe he'd forgotten to or maybe he was making himself sound less emasculated to the officer taking the report.

"You've never seen her before?"

Stan shook his head.

"And what did you think was going to happen?"

"We were going back to her place," Stan told the detective, "but she said she couldn't wait and so we pulled over. That's when she pulled the gun on me and made me get out of the car." He didn't mention that she'd left him practically naked on the side of the road and that he was wearing clothes I'd brought him.

"You obviously had a cell phone," the officer said. "Why didn't you call 911?"

"I—I didn't think of it," he said. "Not right away. I was embarrassed to admit that a woman had taken advantage of me."

I didn't return home until sunrise. Terri was still asleep, so I quietly disrobed and slipped into bed beside her. She rolled over and flopped one arm across my chest. She must have sensed my presence because she opened one eye and asked, "Everything okay?"

"Stan's fine."

"You're a good friend."

"Better than you can even imagine."

Terri kissed my chin, closed her eyes again, and returned to slumberland. A few minutes later I followed her there.

When I finally awoke, I discovered that Terri had been up for almost three hours. She'd made coffee and had spent her time reading a collection of mystery short stories she'd found on the bookshelf in my living room.

I offered Terri breakfast, but my offer was too late. She already had a quiche warming in the oven. I set the dining room table for two and soon I was drinking coffee, eating sausage-and-mushroom quiche, and telling Terri what happened to Stan.

"When I'd told Stan to be careful," I said as a wrap-up to the story, "I'd been worried about him catching a disease. I never even considered the possibility that some woman would steal his car, and I suppose he was lucky he didn't get shot—if the woman actually had a gun."

"Sounds like it couldn't have happened to a more deserving man," she said.

Three months later Terri auditioned for a role in one of the Civic Theatre's productions and landed a small speaking part. She only has two lines, but she's really excited about returning to the stage when the play opens next week.

I met a couple of musicians—a guitarist and a harmonica-playing singer—while attending Terri's rehearsals at the Civic Theatre, and we've gotten together a few times for jam sessions, playing classic rock in my second bedroom.

And One Night Stan? The police never located his car, and he hasn't gone on a date since that night.

Maybe he can be my wingman next Friday when Terri makes her debut on the Civic Theatre stage.

THE END

LOST IN HIS EMBRACE…

A week after moving into our new home, I sat in front of the fireplace with my husband and baby and thought that things were going to work out. I was truly content. My daughter was crawling and attempting to pull herself upright. I knew she'd be walking in no time. I had a job that let me keep Eleni with me when I worked, and Rance— my husband—had been promoted to crew supervisor.

We were a far cry from where we'd started. Rance and I had gone to school together, but we'd never traveled in the same circles. After graduation, I went to work in a sports bar, and he took a job with a company that installed air conditioning units.

Rance was engaged to a girl named Liliana, and I was deeply in love with Zachary McGuire.

We were a far cry from where we'd started. Rance and I had gone to school together, but we'd never traveled in the same circles. After graduation, I went to work in a sports bar, and he took a job with a company that installed air conditioning units.

Rance was engaged to a girl named Liliana, and I was deeply in love with Zachary McGuire.

Zachary and I met at the restaurant. I'd waited on his table. He stayed through three ballgames so he could talk to me when I wasn't busy. I accepted his offer to go out the next night. Our attraction to each other was immediate. Falling in love with him was the easiest thing I'd ever done.

After dating for three years, I wanted to get married and start a family. Each time I brought up marriage, Zachary changed the subject. The more I pressed, the more irritated Zachary became.

"Brenna, I've told you that I'm not ready for marriage. It might be years before I am. What we have is great."

My pro-marriage arguments never got me anywhere. Zachary began to withdraw from me. Eventually, he dumped me in the most painful way possible.

I was working when he brought another woman into the bar and sat at a table in my section. They held hands, talked intimately, and sent the message loud and clear that Zachary had someone else.

I called him when I finished my shift. "You have some nerve bringing another woman into the bar when I'm working."

"Brenna, I've tried for months to tell you that you were pushing me too hard for marriage. I'm not ready to commit to one woman. I won't be seeing you, anymore. I'm sorry, but we're just not right for each other; we want different things," he told me.

There was so much to say that I couldn't get out a single word, so I slammed down the phone. Zachary had taken three years of my life with no intention of a permanent commitment. Now, he was dumping me with a lame excuse.

Zachary didn't take my calls, and he didn't come to the bar anymore. Eventually, I accepted the fact that we were over. If I was going to have a life, I would have to move on—but there was no one I wanted other than him.

Then Rance came back into my life. Rance Payton had been the class clown, always ready with a joke. I'd enjoyed his sense of humor, even though we weren't close. I was glad to see Rance the day he came to the bar with some friends. They sat at my table, laughing and joking with me as I served them. When the others left, Rance hung around. We talked about old times, people we knew, and what we'd been doing since graduation.

"I heard you were engaged," I told him.

"It didn't work out. She said I didn't have enough ambition, and she told me to either take some classes and go to work for her father or the wedding was off. I didn't want to work for her father, so the wedding was off. What have you been up to?"

"This," I said, gesturing to indicate waiting tables. "I was seeing someone, but we broke up."

"You know what that makes us, don't you?" he asked, teasingly. "Rebounders. I, for one, believe that rebounders should stick together. It keeps them out of trouble. So how about you and I rebound together? That way, we can keep an eye on each other."

I smiled. "Just what do rebounders do?"

"Oh, go out to a movie, hang out. Stuff like that. It lets you be with somebody so you won't get involved with anyone else too fast. And it lets your ex know you're not wasting your life pining away for him."

"Sounds like a very good arrangement," I said. We shook hands and laughed.

It was summer, and we spent lots of time at the river, water skiing, swimming, and going to outdoor parties. Our relationship was casual and fun. Sometimes, we'd share a kiss. Rance often put his arm around me in the movies, but sex wasn't part of our bargain.

All of that changed one starlit night. We were at a party, and we both had had too much to drink. Somehow, we ended up on a blanket in the bed of his truck, looking up at the sky. A kiss led to a touch, and the touching led to more until we were taking off each other's clothes. Sex was inevitable. Afterward, we both felt awkward.

"I'm sorry, Brenna," Rance said. "I didn't mean for that to happen."

"Was it so terrible?" I asked, wanting to lighten the moment.

"Not at all, but I don't think either of us are ready for an intimate relationship."

"You're wrong. I'm finally getting over Zachary—thanks to you."

"If that's how you really feel, I'm okay to taking our relationship to the next level," he said. "I care about you a lot, Brenna. You've become my best buddy."

"Friends make great lovers, I've heard."

That is how Rance Payton and I became lovers. I think we talked ourselves into believing we were really in love, though marriage never entered my mind, or his. Sometimes, I sensed that he missed Liliana, and much too often, my thoughts would turn to Zachary, and I'd wonder what he was doing.

Rance and I could have enjoyed each other without things getting too deep, had it not been for an engagement announcement in the Sunday paper. I was reading the paper before getting ready to go to brunch with Rance when I saw the announcement. Zachary was engaged to be married to the woman he'd brought to the bar just before we broke up.

Tears filled my eyes, I couldn't catch my breath, an ache stabbed my heart, and soon I began sobbing—unable to stop. How could he marry that woman? As far as I knew, they had only dated for a few months. I'd spent three years with Zachary.

I was too depressed even to think about going out with Rance, so I called him and told him I had a headache, and I wanted to sleep it off. He accepted my explanation and told me to call if I needed anything.

After the call, I took a sleeping pill, and cried myself to sleep. When I awakened, I began to think of ways to get back at Zachary. I wanted to show him he didn't mean a thing to me; that I was completely over him. And I didn't want to hear sympathetic remarks from friends who knew how much Zachary's marriage would hurt me.

My warped solution was to get married. That would really show Zachary. Rance was the logical choice. Somehow, I'd get him on the subject and feel him out. And as soon as we were married, I'd get pregnant.

On my next date with Rance, I slipped marriage into the conversation. "I wonder if I'll ever be ready for marriage. How about you?"

"Marriage fell off the radar after I broke up with Liliana. I can barely support myself—much less a wife. I'm thinking about enrolling in technical school and going at night."

If Rance went to school, he'd have less time for me. I had to change his mind, and I had to do it fast. As shameful as it is to admit, I fell back on the method women have used for centuries to get a reluctant man to the altar: I set out to get pregnant.

First, I convinced Rance I was on The Pill and that he didn't need to use condoms anymore. We were monogamous, so there was no fear of getting an STD. A month later, my home pregnancy test registered positive. Now, I had to tell Rance.

Before the baby was just an idea; now it was a reality. He could walk away, tell me to get an abortion, or just stop seeing me. I'd created a risky gamble. On our next date, I told Rance we needed to talk.

Wasting no time, I blurted out: "I'm pregnant with your baby."

His expression changed and color left his face. For a long time, we sat in silence. "Please say something," I pleaded.

"I don't know what to say. You're on The Pill. Maybe the test is wrong."

"I'm going to see a doctor as soon as possible."

"Good. Brenna, I need to get some air and do some thinking. I'd like to go to the doctor with you when you go. So if you can, make it for early in the week. I can get a half day off work."

"It isn't necessary for you to go with me," I said.

"I'd never let you go through something like that alone." He stood and took his keys from his pocket. "Call me with the date and time. I'll check on you, tomorrow."

When he walked down the stairs to the parking lot, I wondered if I'd ever see him again. What had I been thinking? Getting pregnant just so I could throw it in Zachary's face was the dumbest and cruelest thing I'd ever done.

And there was someone else to consider. The tiny life growing inside of me deserved a better person than I was for a mother. If Rance never saw me again, what would I do with the baby? I hadn't thought that far ahead when I planned my revenge against the man I was still in love with. As stupid as it was, I couldn't get my mind off Zachary.

Rance did call. "It takes two people to make a baby, Brenna," he said. "I'm as responsible as you are. Whatever happens, I'll take care of you and the baby."

He didn't mention marriage, though. A pregnancy without being married would make me the target of gossip. Zachary and his fiancée would probably get a good laugh out of my predicament.

My doctor's appointment the next week confirmed that the test was correct. I was going to have a baby. Rance sat with the doctor and me as my prenatal care was outlined, and I was given instructions about doctor's visits and nutrition. Rance asked more questions than I did, and he took notes.

The next night, I wasn't scheduled to work. Rance and I made plans to have dinner at my apartment. He brought over a pizza, and we talked.

"Brenna, we have some heavy decisions to make," he said. "Honestly, I'm not ready for marriage. I'd like to have a better paying job and some money saved. And we haven't known each other very long when you get right down to it."

"What are you trying to say, Rance?" I held my breath and hoped.

"I think we should get married. We're good friends and we enjoy each other's company. But most of all, we have a child coming, and the baby deserves two parents and a stable home."

"This isn't the way I wanted it, either," I lied, "but I'm willing to do what's best for the baby."

"Can you get some time off on Friday? We can go to the courthouse and get married."

It wasn't my dream proposal, and it certainly wasn't my dream wedding. "Why so fast? We could still have a church wedding. I'm not that far along."

"They cost money—even for the smallest wedding. We're going to need every cent we can scrape together to cover our expenses. Babies aren't cheap."

"The baby's not due for months."

"Time passes fast. I'll have to go to night school, or I'll never get a promotion. I can't blow my tuition money for a wedding."

"If we go to the courthouse, everyone will know we had to get married," I protested.

"Who cares? We're doing this for the baby."

He was right, and I should have appreciated the way he stood up and took responsibility. Had I dared to put Zachary in such a position, I'd be sitting in the waiting room at an abortion clinic or planning a stay in an unwed mothers' home. Zachary wouldn't have married me because I was pregnant.

Rance arranged for our parents to be present at our wedding, and he presented me with a beautiful bouquet. Afterward, there was a party at his father's house. Family members and friends had been invited. Rance even planned a short honeymoon for us at a spa, where I was pampered with facials and massages.

"I can't thank you enough for this," I told him. "I'd expected a quick ceremony and maybe a pizza afterward."

"I like doing things for you, but I have to confess something. The party and honeymoon were Dad's idea. He's thrilled about the baby, and happy to have you in the family."

Rance's dad had been wonderful to me. His reaction was nothing like I'd imagined. He didn't blame me for disrupting Rance's life. On the other hand, my family was not as generous. They blamed Rance for the pregnancy. My father was especially vocal.

"Tell Mr. Rance Payton that from now on, you are his responsibility,

Brenna," Dad said. "I won't help you with your rent or your car payments. If he can get you pregnant, he can take over your bills. I hope he's prepared to work two jobs. That's what it will take to keep you in cosmetics."

"Rance and I will be fine. I'm going to work until my sixth month, and by then, we should have enough saved to carry us through until the baby is born."

"How nice for you; I'll make sure to forward your bills first thing tomorrow."

Dad had helped me since I moved into my own apartment. He'd paid my rent and utilities, as well as my car payments. Rance was stunned when my bills began coming in.

"Brenna, we don't make enough money combined to pay the rent on this place and to cover the cost of your car. How did you afford it, before?"

"My parents helped, but now that I'm married, they believe you should be responsible for me."

"I wish I'd known before."

"Why? Would you have run out on me? Did you marry me because you thought I had money?"

And that began our first huge argument. Though I knew Rance was right, I wouldn't admit it. We fought for days over the mountain of bills. I tossed around the word, "divorce," a dozen times.

In the end, it was Dean—Rance's father—who bailed us out. We couldn't afford my apartment, so Dean converted the downstairs of his house for us. He put in an efficiency kitchen, made a living room and a bedroom for us, as well as a bathroom and a private entrance. He even put a door at the top of the stairs that locked on both sides to give us privacy.

I hated it. This was not the life I'd imagined. Even though Dean paid off my credit cards, there still wasn't enough money to cover my luxury car, so Rance insisted I sell it and get a less expensive car. Dean found a used economy car that was in great shape, and that was what I drove.

Living under Rance's parents' noses was miserable for me. They didn't interfere unless asked, but I never felt like it was my home.

"We're going to get our own place when the baby comes," Rance promised. "Honey, I've got to finish technical school so I can get a promotion. Once that happens, my income will practically double and we'll be able to afford a house."

Each day, I asked myself what I'd gotten into. Months passed. My belly grew. I had cut my hours because I was too tired to work a full shift. On a day when I looked my absolute worst, Zachary came in.

Zachary smiled when he saw me. "Long time, Brenna. How are you?"

I gazed down at my swollen stomach. "Pregnant," I said.

"When is the baby due?"

"Four months. My husband wonders if I'm having twins because I've gotten so big."

"I think you look beautiful," Zachary said. "I'd love to talk to you. Can you take a break?"

Everything I wanted to throw in his face slipped from my mind. My heart beat fast, and the rush I felt when I looked at him consumed me. Revenge and anger were gone. I took a break; Zachary and I went to a table in the back to talk.

"I saw your engagement announcement in the paper," I said. "When is the big day?"

He lowered his eyelids, and his thick lashes made shadows under his eyes. "I broke off the engagement. It was a big mistake from the start, only I didn't realize it until it was too late."

"Too late?"

"Too late for us. You were married when I came to my senses. It didn't take you long to get over me."

"Getting over you was the most painful thing I've ever had to do, Zachary. You shattered my heart. I could barely function. After seeing your engagement announcement I wanted to die."

"But you didn't die," he said. "You moved on. And now, you're going to have a baby. Brenna, I can't talk about this, anymore. It hurts too much. Guess I'm getting what I deserve. We blew a good thing, sweetheart. I only hope he loves you as much as I do."

Zachary stood and walked out of the restaurant, leaving me in a daze. I'd gotten my revenge, so why did I feel so lousy?

After that day, I began making excuses not to have sex with Rance. I resented him in my bed, and was angry with myself for being such a child. If I had only waited a few months, Zachary and I would have been back together. My life was a disaster of my own making.

Then Eleni was born. Rance and I fell in love with her the instant we saw her. It was Eleni who brought Rance and me together again. She was a combination of both of us, with my brown hair and dimples, and his hazel eyes with the comical, expressive brows. She also had his wide smile.

Things changed with her birth. Rance wanted me to be with her, instead of working in the restaurant. A couple who had an elderly grandmother needed a daytime sitter to take care of her. They hired me, and agreed to let me bring Eleni to work with me.

Eleni was a joy, and the way she smiled when Rance walked into the room, could light up six city blocks. She was a daddy's girl from the start. I know she loved me, too, but he had her little heart in his pocket. Her love for him made me love him, too. We were a family, and though we were still living with Rance's parents, our nest egg for a home of our own was growing.

Rance graduated from technical school. The next week, he was promoted, and he was given a bonus for signing a three-year contract with the company. His bonus gave us enough money for the down payment on a house, and to buy new furniture.

We chose a subdivision made up of couples close to our age. The day we moved in, Eleni crawled around the house—exploring it. She giggled as she climbed over the smaller boxes, sensing her toys inside.

On a cold November night, we made our first fire in the fireplace and celebrated with a bottle of champagne. That night, I was happy. Zachary never crossed my mind. Rance was a wonderful husband, and Eleni owned my once broken heart.

"Did you ever think we'd be this happy?" I asked Rance.

"Are you happy, Brenna? I've often wondered if you regretted marrying me."

"I'm happy, Rance. And I have no regrets. I love you, and I love Eleni. It's as though our life is just beginning, and our future is going to be fabulous."

He put his arms around me and kissed me. We toasted our future. Eleni, who had been sitting in her musical swing, had gone to sleep. I changed her and put her to bed. Rance and I went to our own bedroom and made love. It was a sweet time. A perfect time.

Working for Mrs. Avery was an easy job. Eleni loved her, and she loved Eleni in return. If I had to take time off for Eleni's check-ups, the family always made arrangements. If Eleni was sick and I couldn't go to work, they understood and never docked my pay.

The only drawback was that Mrs. Avery was from a generation where old wives' tales were the gospel when it came to childcare. One day, she pointed out that Eleni was especially gassy.

"Her little tummy is as hard as a brick," Mrs. Avery said. "Are you feeding her prunes? You should be. If she doesn't like them, mix them into her milk with some cereal, and she'll soon be regular again."

I agreed to get prunes for Eleni. A few days later, the baby began whimpering and became touchy when I picked her up.

"Brenna, I think you should take Eleni to the doctor," Mrs. Avery said. "If the prunes didn't work, it could be something more serious."

I agreed, and made an appointment. The appointment led to the worst day of my life. Eleni's liver and spleen were swollen, so the doctor sent me to a specialist. I called Rance, and I told him what was going on. He left work early and met me at the specialist's office.

Tests were run, blood drawn, and dozens of questions were asked. Eventually, we were sent home and told that we'd be contacted with the test results in a few days. It was dark when we started the long drive home. Eleni was fretful and tired.

We reached home. Rance carried Eleni inside while I got the diaper bag. The phone was ringing. It was a cordless, and I couldn't remember where I'd had it last. Rance punched the speaker button and said, "Hello."

"Mr. Payton, this is Dr. Campbell's office. Your daughter's test results are back. Her white count is extremely high, and we found leukemia cells in her blood. We want to admit her to the hospital as soon as possible."

I watched Rance's face go white, and I felt a dizzy, overwhelming feeling come over me. How could this be happening to us?

Sure, children got cancer, but not children like Eleni.

She was so healthy, so bright, and always smiling. Soon, I was shaking and sobbing. Rance held me—not to comfort me—but to use me for support because he was also trembling and weeping.

Eleni began to cry because we were crying. Rance grabbed her from her car seat and held her as though trying to take the cancer from her little body into his own. I put my arms around them, and we all cried together.

"Brenna, pack her bag," Rance said. "I'll call our folks. We have to pull ourselves together and get Eleni to the hospital."

For the next week, I learned more about cancer than a new intern. Rance was by my side the entire time. We hardly slept, and neither of us left Eleni alone for more than a minute. She was isolated, and we were the only ones allowed in her room.

Eleni was diagnosed with acute lymphoblastic leukemia, or ALL. ALL is the most common type of the disease, and—thank God—the most curable. Even so, Eleni had a long fight ahead of her. She would need chemo, and she would spend most of the next year in the hospital. There would be days at home, but even then, she would have to be isolated because her immune system was being destroyed in order to fight the cancer.

Rance had to go back to work. Even with insurance, the bills were staggering. His father stepped up, and he offered to supplement my loss of income. My family sent teddy bears to Eleni, but as far as offering any real help, Dad—who had never gotten over my being pregnant before marriage—said that Rance's family was his responsibility.

The pressure was intense. When we only wanted to think of Eleni and her recovery, we had to face facts that life went on. Bills became due. Her medication cost into the thousands of dollars each month—of which, we paid twenty percent. I checked on government assistance, and I was told that our income was too high to qualify.

How could our income be too high? It took almost everything

Rance earned to cover the expenses of Eleni's illness. We sold my car, and even then—the money was gone in two months, and we were back where we'd been.

Worry over Eleni was all consuming. The only one taking it well was the baby herself. She still beamed her wide smile each time Rance walked into the room, and she was cheerful with the nurses and doctors.

I, on the other hand, was sullen and depressed. The isolation was getting to me. Though I talked to friends on the phone, other than that, I only came into contact with the medical staff and Rance.

During one of Eleni's times at home, I was watching television while she slept. Rance was at work. The phone rang, and to my shock, it was Zachary.

"Brenna, I heard about your baby, and I just had to call to see if you were okay," he said. "I found your number in the phone book. I hope I'm not overstepping by calling."

He wasn't. In fact, it was so good to hear his voice, I felt like laughing. Zachary belonged to a time in my life when there was no cancer to fear, or huge bills to worry about.

"I'm glad you called," I said. "How have you been?"

"I'd rather talk about how you've been," he said.

"Zachary, all I talk about is sickness. Everyone who calls me wants to discuss Eleni's illness. Please, talk to me about something else. Make me laugh, or at least help me get my mind off my problems."

"There's nothing I'd rather do," he said, and he began to tell me funny stories about some people we'd known when we were dating. I wanted to ask him if he was seeing anyone, but that wasn't any of my business.

Our conversation lasted over an hour. He asked if he could call again. I told him he could, and I suggested the best time for him to call me. That time was when Rance wasn't at home.

I always perked up when the phone rang—hoping it was Zachary. When another voice was on the other end, I fell back into depression.

Rance didn't notice anything different, and I didn't want him to. His every thought was on Eleni and how to get her through her illness. He was considerate of me, too, and offered to stay with the baby so I could have some time to myself.

"Call one of your girlfriends and go to a movie, Brenna."

"Can we afford it?"

"We will afford it. You've been cooped up with the baby since we learned she was sick. You need to get your mind off it for a while."

The prospect of going anywhere, felt like Christmas Eve when I was six—all anticipation and excitement. When Zachary called the next day, I told him about my upcoming night out. "I don't know who to call, though. All my friends ever talk about is Eleni's condition."

"How about me? I consider myself your friend, and I promise, we won't talk about Eleni's illness. Let's have dinner."

"I don't know. If someone sees us and Rance finds out, it would kill him."

"We'll go somewhere that he won't find out. Brenna, at least give it some thought. It's not like you're cheating on Rance. We'll only be two friends enjoying a meal together."

The next day, all I thought about was seeing Zachary again. And like he'd said, we were just friends. There was no reason for Rance to be jealous. I loved my husband, didn't I? So dinner with Zachary wouldn't be like cheating.

A desperate woman could convince herself of anything. Zachary and I weren't friends. He was the ghost of happy times. When I looked at him, I didn't see a constant reminder that my daughter had cancer. Looking at Rance, I was always reminded of the hell of Eleni's illness. Seeing Rance was seeing Eleni go through spinal taps, losing her pretty brown hair, having needles stuck into her tiny arms.

Zachary and I met for dinner. The conversation was so warm and familiar that for a while, I forgot that I was no longer the girl who'd been so hopelessly in love with him. As the evening drew to an end, I was sad. I liked the way Zachary made me feel.

The next day he called, right on time. "When can I see you again?" he asked.

"I don't know. Eleni has to go back to the hospital next week. Maybe I could grab a sandwich with you when she's sleeping."

And so it began. After lunch, Zachary walked me to Eleni's room. She was just waking. I picked her up, and I held her next to the window so Zachary could see her. He winked and gave me a smile. Ten minutes later, he called.

"She's beautiful—just like her mother. I wish she were ours. I was a fool to let you slip out of my life, Brenna. You're the only woman I've ever truly loved."

"Zachary, it's a little too late."

"It's never too late. Tell me the truth; do you love Rance the way you loved me?"

I couldn't speak. To admit what I was feeling at that moment was to betray a man who had always been good to me. Rance was the person who had shared the darkest moment of my life, the father who cared so much for his daughter that he would have given his own life to make hers better. Yet, the truth was, I did still love Zachary.

"I love Rance. He's a good man."

"But do you love him like you loved me?"

The memory of hot passionate nights spent making love washed through my mind. In a husky voice, I answered, "I've never loved anyone the way I loved you. Maybe I still love you, but it isn't right."

It took two more secret meetings for Zachary to convince me that there was nothing wrong with our love. In his bed, all of my problems washed away. I was sexy, wild, free, and young. There wasn't a cancer-stricken child, a troubled husband, or a stack of bills to deal with. Then reality would slap me like cold water.

"Zachary, we can't keep this up. Rance will find out. My God, I have a baby who has cancer. What kind of mother would leave her sick child to romp around in bed with her ex-lover?"

"A mother who has her own life, and knows her own heart. What message will you send Eleni if you're not courageous enough to admit your true feelings? She won't always be sick. You said her treatment is going better than expected."

"Yes, but she's a long way from being well. There are several months more of treatment, and I have to be there for her."

"Of course you do, but you don't have to be there for Rance. He's a grown man, and if you have any respect for him, you'll tell him about us before he finds out some other way. I'm not giving you up, again."

I believed Zachary, and made up my mind to tell Rance that I wanted a divorce. Somewhere in my addled brain was the idea that if I were married to Zachary, all of my problems would vanish. Eleni would get well. Zachary and I would be married and live in a big, beautiful home. Where Rance fit in, I didn't know. There was no room for him in my imagined fairytale life.

After Eleni's chemo, when we were once again at home, I picked a fight with Rance. He'd gone out with some friends after work to celebrate their bonuses. His crew had been chosen as the most productive in the company. When he came home, I could smell beer on his breath.

"Looks like you've been having a good time," I said. "I hope the beer was free, because we've got bills due, and Eleni's prescriptions need refilling."

"I spent twenty dollars," he said. "It's the first money I've spent on myself since the baby got sick. Why are you acting this way?"

"Your daughter has cancer, I'm unable to work, I have no car, I can't even buy a tube of lipstick, and you just blew twenty dollars?"

"Brenna, you've spent money. We budgeted for you to have a night out every two weeks."

"And you see people every day. It's not fair."

"I see people at work. Honest to God, I'd rather be here with Eleni than on the job, but one of us has to make a living."

"You make it sound like I sit around on my butt watching soaps all day. Every minute is taken up making sure Eleni has what she needs."

"What do you want from me, Brenna? I'm sorry I spent the money."

"You were out drinking. How dare you go out to a bar and drink while your baby is home fighting for her life? Rance, you make me sick. I will never be able to trust you again. I wish to hell you'd just leave. In fact, I want a divorce!"

"Honey, you don't want a divorce. You're just wound up and stressed out. If it upsets you this much, I won't go out with the boys again."

I had talked myself into believing I had a justifiable reason to divorce Rance. "I mean it. I don't want to be married to you, anymore. Leave. Get out of here."

"I'm not leaving you and Eleni without transportation."

"Where was our transportation, tonight? What if she'd gotten sick?"

"I have a cellular phone for emergencies, and I'd have been here in ten minutes."

"Yes, drunk—and of no possible use to either of us. Get the hell out, or I'm taking Eleni and going to my parents' house."

"Brenna, Eleni can't go over there, and you know it. Do you really want me to leave?"

I nodded. Rance went to the phone and called his father, and then he packed a suitcase. Dean came about twenty minutes later. He stayed in the car and honked for Rance. When Rance walked past me, I turned my back on him.

"The car keys are on the dresser. I'll borrow Dad's truck until I can get a car. Brenna, I'll leave you, but I will not leave Eleni. You can't force me out of her life."

When I told Zachary that Rance had moved out, he was thrilled. "It's going to work this time, Brenna. Don't worry about a thing."

"What should I do, now?"

"Get to an attorney and file for divorce. Make sure you get a decent settlement. Rance owes you. He rushed you into marriage when you were on the rebound."

Hearing Zachary say it convinced me that things had happened just the way he said. Selective memory kicked in, and I began to think of Rance as a man who had taken advantage of me.

My attorney advised me that Rance would have visitation rights to Eleni.

Rance was furious that I'd jumped so fast at finding a lawyer. He thought I was in a bad mood and everything would work out. I put up an iron wall against his attempts to make me reconsider. Zachary's was the only voice I wanted to listen to.

One thing that never occurred to me was how the divorce would affect Eleni. Each day, when it was time for Rance to come home, she began watching the door with a smile on her face. When it didn't open, her little face would scrunch up and her baby lips would quiver. Day after day, that happened. When my attorney called and said Rance's lawyer had petitioned for visitation, and that he would be allowed to spend the weekend with the baby every other weekend, I was glad.

Also, anytime she was in the hospital, Rance was allowed to be there. On his weekend visits, I could stay with a friend, or my family, but Rance would have Eleni to himself. I hated it, but Zachary loved the idea. We had long weekends together, but as wonderful as they were, I couldn't get Eleni off my mind.

When I returned, and Rance set out to leave, Eleni cried as though her heart were breaking. Rance also had tears in his eyes. I felt guilty at those times for putting my happiness above everyone else's. But I couldn't live a life pretending to love a man whom I didn't love.

Soon the divorce papers were ready. I talked to Zachary about our future. "I want us to live together," I said. "Of course, it means living in my house because of Eleni. Zachary, why don't you buy the house from Rance? We can sell it later."

"Don't you think your ex-husband would get upset having me living with you and his daughter?"

"Who cares once you and I are married?"

He was quiet; too quiet. Finally, he said, "Wait until the divorce papers are signed, and we'll discuss our options."

I didn't like the sound of that, but I decided not to press the subject. Of course, he loved me, and wanted to marry me. I'd put Rance, Eleni, and our families through hell to be with Zachary. If he didn't love me, it would have all been for nothing.

After the papers were signed, my life changed completely. Eleni was happy only when she was around Rance. Though we'd gotten permission for Zachary to visit, he seldom came over. He was happier spending our occasional weekends at his apartment.

"She's so sick," he explained once. "If I gave her a cold or something, I'd never forgive myself."

"I'll be so glad when we get married and you move in here," I said one evening. "I know that once you and Eleni are with each other more, you'll grow closer."

"Hon, we can't rush things. Think of Eleni. How would it look? In the meantime, we can enjoy where we are now."

Where we were was in bed most of the time. He'd come over after Eleni was in bed, have a couple of drinks, and then it was time for sex. Afterward, he'd dress and leave. The calls became less frequent, too.

Someone has to knock a person like me over the head before I'll see the light. I'd been in a dreamy darkness since the day Zachary first called. The person who turned on the light switch in my brain was

Dean. He asked to come over and said he was bringing someone with him. Dean suggested I put Eleni down for a nap.

"Brenna, there's someone you should talk to before you get screwed over big time by Zachary. This has nothing to do with Rance. My concern is Eleni."

The person he brought over was Dee Roswell. I knew her at once. She was the woman Zachary had been engaged to before. I thought Dean had gone over the edge. Of course, this woman wouldn't have a good word for Zachary. She was his ex-fiancée.

"Brenna, just listen to what Dee has to say." Dean went out to the back patio and left me alone with Dee.

"I don't know what you have to tell me about Zachary that I don't already know," I said. "After all, I've known him a lot longer than you have."

"Dean hunted me down because he wanted to know why Zachary and I hadn't gotten married," she said. "All of this is Dean's idea. After I told him, he badgered me into telling you."

"Just say what you came to say," I spat.

"I'll make it short. Zachary and I broke up because he wanted to. I wasn't a challenge, anymore. When I was unattainable, he couldn't get enough of me. After he won me, and we became engaged, things changed. He changed. But he didn't do it all at once. He waited until two weeks before our wedding, after my parents had shelled out almost fifty grand to tell me he wasn't ready for a lifetime commitment."

"What do you mean by unattainable?"

"I was engaged to a friend of his. We met at a party, and after that, Zachary began calling me. He said he'd fallen for me the minute he saw me, and that it killed him when he found out I was engaged to Joe. Brenna, Zachary had to win me. He's a player, and that's his game. He said he'd never been deeply in love before. His thing with you was puppy love. It was when he met me that he learned what the real thing was. I think Zachary likes being able to take a woman away from another man. It's his form of dueling or jousting. He's too big a coward to go fist to fist."

"It's not like that with us," I said.

"That's what I thought—once. Now, I'm married to Joe, who forgave me my stupidity, and I'm happy. Brenna, from what I hear, Rance is a good man, and a loving father. Zachary will never be a good father. He wants all of a woman's attention. Just remember that."

Dee and Dean left. I sat in my rocker, and I thought about everything Dee had told me. She was wrong. I'd call Zachary right that minute and he would reassure me. I knew ours was real love, and it would last the test of time.

"Brenna, you caught me on the way out," Zachary said.

"We can talk when you get here, then."

"I'm sorry if you got the wrong impression, but I'm not coming over tonight. There's a poker tournament at the club."

The coldness in his voice was like before—just before he dumped me. "We have to talk. It's urgent."

"I don't have time for this, now."

"Either I'm going to call Rance and ask him to stay with Eleni, and meet you at the club, or you're coming over here so we can talk."

"I'll see you in an hour," he said and hung up. He arrived two hours late. When he came in, he was in a lousy mood. "What's this urgency?"

"Zachary, I'd like to set a wedding date. We can get married next weekend. Eleni will be with Rance."

"My God, Brenna, talk about rushing things. A wedding takes planning."

"Not ours. We can't go on a honeymoon because of Eleni. A big wedding takes time and money. You might have the money, but I don't have the time."

"Then let's wait until Eleni is well. Afterward, we can discuss the wedding. She can be our flower girl."

"So you are going to marry me?"

"Eventually, yes, I will marry you, but not while the child is sick. Your life is too restrictive. In my line of work, I have to have the freedom to entertain, and to be with people. A few more months won't hurt. In fact, if you want to set a date, I'm ready."

I relaxed and smiled. He did want to marry me, and we were going to set a date. I got the calendar from the kitchen. "Eleni's treatments end in May. I've always wanted to be a June bride."

"You mean this June? Honey, that doesn't give us time. A year from this June was what I was thinking."

Then I knew. He wasn't thinking about marriage—-just a way to get out of it. Dee was right. I was an unattainable married woman, and I had a sick baby. To win me was a conquest, and Zachary had put everything into his quest. Now that I could be his fully, I wasn't a challenge, anymore. And he wanted a new challenge.

"Get out of my house! Don't ever come back or call me, again! You've ruined my life, caused me to break the hearts of everyone who ever truly cared about me, and you made a fool of me for the last time. I met Dee, tonight. She told me about you, and I said she was wrong—but she wasn't wrong. I was."

"I'll gladly leave. I've had about enough of your demands. You haven't changed a bit. Love, for you, can't be simple. You have to have a ring on your finger and a guy wrapped around it. Maybe you'll get lucky and find another chump like Rance Payton!"

Zachary left. Only this time, my heart didn't break. There was no room in it for feeling sorry for myself. I had too much guilt because of the things I'd done to the people who really loved me.

The next day, I contacted the attorneys and told them that I wanted to restructure Rance's visitation. He could see Eleni anytime he wanted to. I'd stay out of their way when he visited.

Rance called that night to thank me. The first week, he came twice, then later every afternoon. He'd hold Eleni, feed her dinner, play with her, and he'd give her a bath before putting her to bed.

The goodness of that man was evident in everything he did. If I needed money, he gave it to me without a word said. When my car wasn't working, he left me his and took mine to be fixed. I had grown up a lot once I stopped living a fairytale and started to appreciate the real men in this world—like the guy who works hard for his family and is decent and loving.

Rance changed in my eyes. I'd loved him as a friend, but never with the passion I'd felt for Zachary. Things were different, now. I wanted him, and not just to take care of me. He was the best thing that had ever happened to me, and I wanted him in my life permanently.

But how do you go to a man whose heart you've broken and ask him to take you back? As it turned out, that was all I had to do. I bared my soul to Rance, admitted how wrong I'd been, and I promised him that if he'd give us another chance, I would be the best wife ever.

"I love you so much," I told him. "It took me this long to realize it, but I do."

He never brought up Zachary's name. Instead, he offered to remarry me unconditionally. I expected the Paytons to call me every name in the book, but they accepted me back into the family as though I'd only been away on a long vacation.

Eleni finished her treatments, and the doctors said she is free of cancer. Of course, we'll have to monitor her closely, but she's the bright happy baby she was before our nightmare began.

To celebrate her recovery, Rance and I renewed the vows we'd taken for the second time at the courthouse. This time, we did it in church. Eleni was my maid-of-honor.

I still work to mend the hearts that my carelessness broke. Eleni is happy just to have Rance come through the door each afternoon, and he's happy to be home, but it isn't enough. I still have a lot to prove, and I thank God for creating a man like Rance Payton, who will allow me to prove that I can be the wife he deserves!

THE END

www.ingramcontent.com/pod-product-compliance
Lightning Source LLC
Chambersburg PA
CBHW051507170626
46811CB00002B/690